The Hidden Dimensions

of

Cathy Campbell

FRAN BRADY

DEDICATION

I dedicate this book to my wonderful grandson Jayden who is my pride and joy

ACKNOWLEDGMENTS

Thanks to my family and friends who have encouraged my writing

CONTENTS

Table of Contents

CHAPTER ONE - THE MEETING 1
CHAPTER TWO – PANTHEISM 10
CHAPTER THREE - THE MOUNTAIN TRAIL 17
CHAPTER FOUR – DISAGREEMENT 25
CHAPTER FIVE - THE OPAL RING...34
CHAPTER SIX - THE HOMECOMING 39
CHAPTER SEVEN - THE TROUSSEAU 45
CHAPTER EIGHT - THE WEDDING 50
CHAPTER NINE – BEGINNINGS 56
CHAPTER TEN - COMPASSION 61
CHAPTER ELEVEN - HAPPY ENDING 69
CHAPTER TWELVE - FEELING LOST..76
CHAPTER THIRTEEN - FINDING COMMON GROUND 82
CHAPTER FOURTEEN - BABY BOYS 87
CHAPTER FIFTEEN - THE DALE 90
CHAPTER SIXTEEN – BERYL...95
CHAPTER SEVENTEEN - THE ABBOT 102
CHAPTER EIGHTEEN - THE FLEDGLINGS.....................................107
CHAPTER NINETEEN - DONEGAL 114
CHAPTER TWENTY - MIDGES 121
CHAPTER TWENTY-ONE - REFLECTIONS......................................126
CHAPTER TWENTY-TWO - BEN NEVIS 131
CHAPTER TWENTY-THREE - MORAG..138
CHAPTER TWENTY-FOUR - MARILYN 143
CHAPTER TWENTY-FIVE - MISSING DIMENSION 149
CHAPTER TWENTY-SIX - ERRIGAL...154
CHAPTER TWENTY-SEVEN - THE REUNIONS................................161
CHAPTER TWENTY-EIGHT - STEWIE 167
CHAPTER TWENTY-NINE - BENNY 173

CHAPTER THIRTY - THE VIEW 177
CHAPTER THIRTY-ONE - INTO THE WESTERN SUN 182
CHAPTER THIRTY-TWO - THE PREVAILING CULTURE 186
CHAPTER THIRTY-THREE - MILESTONES....................................192
CHAPTER THIRTY-FOUR - APPARITION IN A CHURCHYARD 200
CHAPTER THIRTY-FIVE - REVELATIONS 205
CHAPTER THIRTY-SIX - BACK IN THE HIGHLANDS 210
CHAPTER THIRTY-SEVEN - DANCING NYMPH 216
CHAPTER THIRTY-EIGHT - ACTIVISM 224
CHAPTER THIRTY-NINE – EVOLUTION 230
CHAPTER FORTY - SECRETS 237
CHAPTER FORTY-ONE - THE GROVE 242
CHAPTER FORTY-TWO – SAMHAIN 250
CHAPTER FORTY-THREE - THE MONOLOGUE 258
CHAPTER FORTY-FOUR - CHAPEL IN GROVE 265
CHAPTER FORTY-FIVE – DISENCHANTMENT 271
CHAPTER FORTY-SIX – TOGETHERNESS 279

Chapter One - The Meeting

"Well Cathy Campbell, this a great surprise."

"It sure is, Mark. Had you someone singing in the Festival?"

"My mother was."

"My sister-in-law was too."

"We're near your home ground here, Cathy. Are you still living in the Dale?"

"I'm in Glasgow. I came over this morning for the festival."

Cathy has not seen Mark Wright since he left boarding school. He has not lost any of his charm or good looks. He was the Adonis of the school, the one all the girls admired.

"Are you still single?" he enquires.

"I am. Only recently came out of a relationship."

Her own words jolt her into the sad reality. Her loss is still raw.

"I'm sorry to hear that, Cathy. We're probably among the last of the singles from our class in Saint Matthew's."

"I know we're heading towards thirty but we're not exactly ancient," Cathy says defensively.

"There's been a lot of matching and hatching going on. I was at five weddings in the last twelve months and a few christenings."

"I was at one wedding last year on the summer solstice at a stone circle in Orkney, and one on the spring equinox this year in Galloway Forest."

"That sounds very pagan. I couldn't imagine Daisy Armstrong or Stephen Prior getting married at a stone circle or in a forest."

"Did Daisy and Stephen get married?" Cathy's voice is raised in surprise.

"They both got married last year, but not to each other."

Cathy knows she is outside that circle. She was never invited to the wedding of a former classmate. She could imagine how Mark with all his charm would be welcome at any social occasion.

"Stephen was lovely," Cathy recalls. She remembers him, helpful and kindly, yet shy and insecure.

"Did you fancy him?" Mark teases. "He was a ginger like you."

"I thought he put so much into doing his best at everything. Did he meet someone nice?"

"He's safe in the arms of Patience, a lovely vicar."

"I'm glad to hear that."

"She's really special. They're a great couple. They've just had a baby daughter."

"Did you fancy her too?" Cathy asks light-heartedly. Without giving him time to reply she asks the next question.

"Who did Daisy marry?"

"Cecil Brown. He was in Saint Matthew's, three years ahead of us."

"I remember him. He was great at cricket."

"He was a dab hand at cricket alright," Mark agrees.

"Daisy always came first at the cooking in Home Ec. No matter how hard the rest of us tried Daisy added that touch of excellence," Cathy recalls. "Just once I shared the accolade with her."

"Now she's a Home Ec. teacher in Hightown Grammar School," Mark confirms.

"She was focussed from the start."

"What are your all-consuming interests, Cathy?"

"Walking and climbing are my hobbies. My all-consuming interests are campaigning, protesting and such things."

"Protesting, like chaining yourself to railings."

"From time to time these tactics have to be resorted to."

"Were you ever arrested?"

"Often, they can pick me out with my heap of red hair."

"Who'd imagine studious little Cathy Campbell chained to some railing, or in a prison cell?"

Studious little Cathy Campbell, she feels the description makes her sound diminutive and docile and, maybe in Mark's flamboyant circle, dull.

"People can transform, although I don't think you've changed, Mark."

"No, I'm handsome as ever," he jokes. "But transforming's good too. Caterpillars become butterflies."

"And docile school girls can transmute into activists," Cathy adds.

"Docile," Marks considers the word. "No. That word wouldn't describe you."

"Thank goodness for that."

"Diligent would be a better description, and amenable."

"Not amenable. We might stray back to docile again."

"There can be nothing wrong with diligence."

"What are we like? You'd think we were back in Miss Harrison's English class," Cathy chuckles.

A good-humoured banter develops between them. They are at ease in the moment while the singers and the audience spill out from the hall, with members of the audience continuing to adjudicate the singers in their own way.

"We might've time for a coffee before my parents are ready," Mark suggests. "Oh no, we haven't, sorry."

His parents, Marilyn and Benny Wright, arrive on the scene, Marilyn dressed in her choir uniform and bubbling with pride that her choir was awarded first place. Her dark brown hair is neatly cut, and the shade of her red lipstick and her nail varnish match her choir scarf.

"Are you ready to go home, Mark? It's getting late."

"Are you around for long, Cathy?" Mark asks as his mother hastens him along.

"I'm here for two weeks. I just got here today to hear Jennifer. They got third."

"That was the Dale choir. They were very sweet," Marilyn affirms.

"We could try to have a get together before you go back, if you like," Mark suggests.

"That'd be good."

"If you give me your phone number I'll call you in the next day or two."

Mark hurriedly writes the number on the back of his choral festival ticket and places it in the inside pocket of his dark grey suit. Cathy makes her way into the hotel to meet her brother Colin, his wife Jennifer and her parents Andy and Beryl.

"How did you to get chatting to that young woman?" Marilyn enquires.

"She was in my class at St. Matthew's."

"Oh, was she? I never heard you mention a Cathy. Pity we'd to rush."

"I wasn't rushing. I thought we'd have time for coffee."

"You should've introduced her properly. Your father and I would've gone into the hotel and waited," his mother laments. "Never mind you've her phone number. Make sure and call her."

Cathy joins her parents and Colin and Jennifer in the crowded hotel lobby where Beryl has saved a chair by placing her emerald green cashmere coat over it.

"We saw you talking to a handsome young man," her mother speaks expectantly. "That's Mark Wright, from my class. I haven't seen him since he left St Matthew's. Off course, I haven't seen my other classmates either."

"Mark Wright, I never heard you mention him." Beryl looks puzzled.

"All the other girls in the class probably mentioned him," Cathy quips. "He was like an Adonis then."

"It's nice to see you meeting a handsome Protestant man from your school," Beryl encourages.

Saint Matthew's, a mixed Church of Ireland boarding school, facilitated easy friendships among boys and girls. Marriages followed later like night follows day. Cathy was the only student in her class from south of the bay and she went to University in Edinburgh and work in Glasgow. A natural cycle of friendship and marriage had not happened for her.

"Had Mark someone singing?" Jennifer asks.

"His mother's in the Mountview choir."

"They were excellent," Jennifer says enthusiastically. "I knew they were favourites."

"We can't be anything but proud of the Dale Singers. I'm glad I got to hear you."

"And who knows there could be the start of a romance," Beryl speaks hopefully.

"We were just chatting, mother. He asked me for my phone number. He'd to rush. His mother was in a hurry."

"He asked you for your phone number. That sounds good."

"He could forget to phone," Cathy says in a matter of fact tone.

The phone rings in her parents' house bright and early the following morning. It is Mark.

"Haven't much experience at campaigning and such things, but what about a climb tomorrow."

"I'd love to go climbing."

"We could meet at the golf club beside the bay for coffee at ten. What do you think?"

Golf clubs are outside Cathy's area of interest but coffee in charming company could hardly challenge anyone.

"Did you bring a climbing pole, Mark?" Cathy asks as they arrive at the start of their mountain walk.

"We'll hardly need a climbing pole." Mark speaks with some trepidation wondering what this climb entails.

"No worries, Mark, I've two." She adjusts the height of one of the climbing poles and they head in the direction of the highest peak in the Dale.

The footsteps of Cathy Campbell and Mark Wright fall into rhythm as they climb high above the Dale and see the sheep scattered around the fields and the hillsides. It is a tough climb and the backs of Mark's legs are aching by the time they descend the steep incline at the end of the walk. A rivulet gurgles alongside them. He wishes he had some of the energy of this small stream, or of the rooks whose industrious sounds from their nearby nests fill the air.

"You're a golfer, Mark. I wouldn't have thought a climb would faze you," Cathy jokes.

"I used different muscles today."

They revisit the golf club by the bay on their way home. They sit opposite one another in a window alcove where Cathy savours stuffed mushrooms and surveys unfamiliar territory. Trophies and silver cups glisten in glass cabinets. A friendly middle-aged gentleman, with a kindly smile, moves swiftly as he serves each table. This kindly smile alters her perception of golf clubs and gives her a feeling of warmth towards such establishments.

A few days later Cathy and Mark chose a forest walk, in what could be described as a tree lover's delight. Cathy identifies the trees by their Latin names as they walk along. Giant redwoods, Monterey pines, Himalayan Cedars, are among the exotic trees in the park while the most common trees are native trees like beech, ash, birch and oak.

"You're an expert in trees," Mark encourages.

"Trees are very much part of my job."

"I'm impressed. My mother would be impressed too. She's very involved in the Best Kept Villages contest. Trees and plants are among her passions."

"I've great time for the volunteers who work for Best Kept Villages and for Tidy Towns."

"My mother's involved for as long as I can remember," Mark says admiringly.

"They should be called peacetime patriots," Cathy muses.

"Peacetime patriots, I like the ring of that."

"I think volunteers who keep their areas beautiful should be recognised."

Taking the River Trail they walk past rustic bridges and stepping stones and come to a small old hermitage. Standing in the stone hermitage, overlooking cascading water, they marvel at their chance meeting, and how the choral festival brought them together. High pitched sounds of goldcrests and coal tits serenade them. Carpets of bluebell bow beneath newly greened trees. They walk on again holding hands, cross a bridge a mile or so on and walk back on the other side of the river. They leave the more adventurous Mountain Trail for another day.

"How are you getting along with Cathy," Mark's mother enquires.

"Great. Thanks for giving me all the free time."

Marilyn acknowledges his appreciation with a smile.

"We'd a great walk in the forest park. She's sure knows her trees, a landscape designer."

"That's sounds interesting. Now don't let her slip through your fingers."

"I think Cathy likes my style. I might've found Mrs. Wright."

"Don't be over confident either."

"She'd an idea you'd agree with. She said the volunteers of Best Kept Villages should be considered peacetime patriots."

"I'm impressed with such recognition. Now hear what I say. She's probably one of the last of the single girls from your class in Saint Matthew's."

"Saint Matthew's is a school, not a marriage bureau," Mark teases.

"Will we see you soon again?" Beryl enquires as Cathy is about to leave.

"I might get back in a month, or maybe less."

"That sounds good. Romance must be blossoming."

"We'll see how it goes."

"Don't mess it up now," her mother instructs.

"We're only seeing one another for two weeks. I'm not contemplating marriage or anything like that."

"Don't rule it out. It's the best hope for you coming back home."

"Mam, we'll take things a step at a time. I'm not sure if I'd want to leave Scotland."

"I'd love to have you back in Ireland. I never imagined you gone for good." Beryl pulls at Cathy's heartstrings. "I know you'd be north of the bay but it'd great to have you so near."

"Scotland's not that far away."

"No, I think I'd be great to have you back. And if anything happens to me or your father it'd be good for Colin to have you back. You're his only sibling."

"He has Jennifer and Edwin. And you and dad have him next door. You're not in the lonely hearts' club."

"Why are you so insistent that you won't be coming home?"

"It never crossed my mind that I would. I'm sorry."

"Meeting Mark Wright might change that," Beryl persists.

Chapter Two – Pantheism

Cathy is returning to Scotland after a completely different holiday at home. Up until now her holidays revolved around family and farm. She rarely left the Dale. This holiday took her out of the Dale on several of her outings to meet Mark. Beryl's car was always at her disposal.

"You can have my car anytime you need it. I can use the jeep if I need it."

The blue Mazda hugged the bay in both directions for the duration of the holidays. Reflecting back Cathy wonders if they are rushing head-over-heels into a romance. She wonders if she is giving him a wrong signal by keeping up with his romantic pace. It is just a holiday romance, she reassures herself, some fun-filled time with the Adonis of her school, who could have had the pick of all the girls in Saint Matthew's. It is difficult to resist his charms, she concedes. He is easy company and has a captivating smile that lights up his blue-grey eyes.

She boards the ship and places the book she bought at the portside shop on the small round table before her. Relaxing back on the padded seat she reflects again on the happenings of the past fortnight. She missed the interaction with the sheep and the fields that were so much part of her. Instead she has been on several dates with the handsome Mark Wright.

Her mother was never so interested in her love life before. She did, on a few occasions, allude to the heirloom wedding-dress worn so far by three generations of women. Cathy had explained to her mother that if she did get married it might be in Scotland and that she would choose a less conventional form of wedding.

The revelation, on both fronts, cast a cloud of disappointment over her mother. Weddings or romances were never mentioned lately.

Then Beryl got very enthusiastic when Cathy met a man from her old school. Mark is very enthusiastic too. She wonders if he feels there is an urgency to catch up with all their classmates whose lives are spiced with weddings and christenings.

Regular visits to the Dale ensue. A few days of annual leave, or time in lieu of overtime, can be added to a weekend. On one of these visits Cathy and Mark go for a challenging climb to the summit of a mountain north of the bay.

"This'll just be a saunter for you. Be mindful of the novices and don't leave me behind," Mark teases.

"The climb will be worth the effort. I did it a few times years ago," Cathy enthuses. "This is the eve of Lughnasadh. We'll go forth in the spirit of Lugh."

"Who's Lugh?" Mark asks.

"He was a Celtic god.

"You're so pagan, Cathy Campbell."

"Are you thinking the good Protestant values of St. Matthew's were wasted on me?"

"Maybe they were wasted on me too," Mark concedes. "Just I don't publicly aspire to anything else."

"I don't either. You keep saying I'm pagan. Maybe I am."

A forest gently leads them into their trek. Waterfalls gurgle and tumble. Slippery stones demand care and caution. Looking up they see the vastness of the mountain peaks that stretch out around them under a lightly-clouded indigo sky.

"This is the life for me," Cathy exclaims as they survey the beauty from a viewing point on the way up. She swirls about with delight, her arms stretched skywards. The mountain slopes are resplendent in deep pink heather. Moving on again towards their goal they see a wall snaking up the slope towards the summit. They climb in relative silence for a short while until they fall into a harmonious rhythm.

"This is a sacred mountain," Cathy proclaims.

"Why would you call it a sacred mountain?"

"It has historic burial cairns on its pinnacle."

"Oh."

"All mountains are sacred," Cathy continues. "And skies and rivers and woodlands too and the whole universe.

"I believe you."

"I don't think you believe me at all."

"I suppose I don't really. A mountain is a mountain to me," Mark admits.

They admire the panoramic views of the mountains, the coastline and the town below. "You're standing on the top of the highest mountain peak in the province. I know it's a dwarf compared to the great Munro's in Scotland."

"It's perfect for me today, Mark. Look at the marvellous views. I think I see Scotland from here."

"I might even climb Nevis with you one day," Mark enthuses, even though he found this lesser ascent difficult.

Cathy climbs on to the top of the stone wall and holds her palms as high as she can, as if propping up the vast indigo sky. She turns slowly, absorbing the view, looking east and south and west and north and finally back to the east again.

The breeze whips her ginger curls in all directions.

"What are you doing?"

"Worshipping the mountains," Cathy enthuses.

Mark watches intrigued as the reverential circling continues.

"Mountains can be compared to personal summits or hilltops on life's journey." Her words are filtered through the strengthening wind. Mark gets the gist of what she is saying. After a pause of a few minutes he calls up to her.

"I can think of a personal summit. Would you consider getting married to me?"

She decodes the content of his question as the words swirl on the wind towards her.

"Married, Mark? I wasn't expecting a life change like that today. I think we should get to know each other better."

"We do know each other, Cathy?"

"We enjoy our outings. Marriage would need more understanding and deeper knowing."

Her circling has ceased.

"I suppose I didn't expect to witness a ritual of Pantheism. But I hope you won't reject the idea outright." Mark's plaintive voice competes with the wind.

Cathy climbs down from the stone wall. They start their descent in a long period of silence which Cathy eventually breaks.

"I didn't want to spoil what we had, Mark. It wasn't meant as a rejection." She tries to reason with Mark, while the strong wind whips the words from her lips.

"It felt like a rejection to me."

"You don't understand. I'm not ready for a step like that, yet anyhow."

The relentless wind almost throws them together and then chucks them apart again.

"Mark, I understand you're upset with me. But climbing down a slope like this needs full attention, especially with this wind. You can sulk when you get down safely."

He feels miffed. That is how his mother, Marilyn, or his grandmother, Rosetta, might have spoken to him when he was a small boy.

Their descent is tough. The strong wind blows against them and some of the stones are slippery. In school Mark was the most admired young man. Perhaps he could not handle such perceived rejection. By the time they reach the forest at the bottom of the mountain the wind has eased, and Mark has mellowed. He puts his arm around her.

"Maybe I was rushing things. I was just afraid I'd lose you. I'll ask you again though. And I promise I won't sulk."

"That's a relief. I mean a relief that you won't sulk."

"I thought we were getting along well together. I felt flattered that you make the long trips over."

"We're getting along very well, Mark, no doubt about that. But marriage is a lifelong commitment. And because we'll be closely linked with your family and the business there's more to be considered."

"You're not marrying my family," Mark insists. "At least I sort of know now where your doubts lie."

This is the first time she saw him in anything other than a confident mood. He looks vulnerable and disappointed and perhaps because of that more loveable. She puts her arm around his waist. Then they steady themselves again and walk in single file on the narrow track through the rest of the forest."

She mentions his proposal, and her doubts, to her mother. Beryl is gravely disappointed. She was keen on the idea of an engagement and full of praise for Mark even though she only met him once.

"I can't believe you turned down a proposal of marriage from that nice young man."

"Maybe I gave him the wrong signal."

"What do you mean?"

"I enjoy his company and our outings together. But I'm not ready for a commitment like that."

"It's not as if you're a teenager."

"Maybe I'm not ready to make a commitment to Mark."

"That's silly, Cathy."

"I'd have to be sure I was in love with him and that I'd fit into the new situation."

"It's only in these last generations that love became an important part of a choice. Before that other people made the choice and if love happened it was a bonus?"

"Was that how it was for you?"

"Kind of, I suppose. I was introduced to your father as an ideal match and we grew to love one another."

"Oh."

"And my mother and father never met till a few weeks before they got married in 1922."

"I'd hoped for something more magical than that."

"Magical? Will you get a bit of sense? Imagine you let a chance like that slip through your fingers."

"Don't worry. He said he'd ask me again."

"Well don't be playing hard to get or he might give up. Will you meet him tomorrow? It's your last day before you go back."

"No. I want to spend the day here."

"Here? Why would spend the day here."

"I miss having time here when I'm running around all the time."

"I don't know what to say to you."

"You don't have to say anything to me. I told Mark that I wasn't ready to get married. And I'm not. There's nothing that you can say that'd change how I feel."

"Feelings, Cathy, I ask you. It's best just to leave feelings out of the picture and use your head. You enjoy his company what more do you want?"

Chapter Three - The Mountain Trail

Cathy's visits back to the Dale continue. Being in the easy company of Mark added spice to her visits. Because of her petulance, which ended her last romance, there was a void in her life in Glasgow. It was this void that prompted her to come to the Dale for two weeks at the time of the choral festival. Normally she would come over for a long weekend for a family event. Those two weeks afforded time for a romance to start. A serious romance was the last thing on Cathy's mind when she first accepted Mark's invitation to go climbing.

He is so different from her last boyfriend. Cathy wonders would she always compare them, if in fact the relationship proceeded further. Mark is charming and generous and handsome. In Beryl's eyes Mark meets all the criteria for an ideal husband for her only daughter. She thinks her father would prefer her other boyfriend, rugged and land-loving and kindly. She chased him away over a transgression that she often surmised since might be as innocent as he proclaimed. She had hoped he might chase her again and coax her back. It had not happened.

"Let's meet in the forest park tomorrow," Marks suggests over the phone one Friday evening just after she arrived home.

"It should be beautiful there with the autumn colours. By the time I'm back again they'll be gone," Cathy agrees.

Standing beside a giant redwood tree, they gaze up in awe and admire its great height. They each hug a side of the trunk, each marveling at its enormous girth. They have returned, on this crisp November day, to the forest park where Cathy's knowledge of trees enthralled Mark less than six months ago.

Most of the leaves have been swiped from the deciduous trees. An autumnal carpet of russet and red and yellow and orange is unfurled all around. As they swing about the trunk of the giant tree and meet face to face Mark spills out a marriage proposal again.

"This tree looks significant enough to witness a special event," he says hopefully.

"I'd say it has witnessed many great moments in its long existence," Cathy agrees.

"Remember my proposal on the top of the mountain when you rejected me."

"How could I forget it when you gave me the cool treatment all the way down?"

"That's why I chose a ground level landmark this time. Cathy Campbell will you marry me?"

"I will," she mumbles pensively.

"You will. You will. Is that a yes? You've accepted my proposal."

Cathy does not refute her acceptance.

"That's great. That's a lucky tree." He pats its rugged bark again. "What's it called?"

"A giant redwood or giant sequoia, or you could call it by its formal name Sequoiadendron giganteum."

"The middle name sounds perfect, just enough solemnity for the occasion," Mark decides.

He is curious to know what changed her mind and led her to acceptance, at least a passive acceptance, but he decides not to ask. Nor did she tell him about Beryl's encouragement or admonishing, or that she herself compared, and contrasted, him to someone else for the past weeks. She felt fonder of him when she saw his less self-assured side after his earlier proposal and her earlier doubts.

"Let's do the Mountain Trail today to celebrate reaching a new hilltop in life," Mark suggests. "And you can worship another mountain."

"Worshipping sacred mountains is a serious and solemn ritual, Mark."

They begin the trail across a crunchy carpet of beech mast and fallen leaves. It is less than six months since they met at the choral festival. This part of the forest was covered with bluebells then.

"This trail sounds daunting," Mark states as he opens the information leaflet.

"You're not going to back out of it before we start," Cathy teases. "We'll have to test our endurance."

They adjust their walking poles and get on their way. There is no room for dalliance on a November day. Night could fall too soon.

"This pamphlet is almost urging people not to venture out on the trail at all," Mark remarks. "Steps, boulders, gullies and fences are all to be expected. And the way to the top will have severe gradients."

"Let's get going. We're young and strong," Cathy says with conviction.

With that the two thirty-year-olds, planning to embark on a new life, set out on their trek past boulders and gullies and all the other expected obstacles.

Their climb, which takes them over the highest point in the forest park and back, is just about accomplished before the early twilight. Cathy does not allude to the fact that their timing was on the risky side. They had left no room for a mishap.

"We're getting better at this climbing, Cathy. You were always good. I think I'm improving."

Mark appears pleased with his day. His proposal of marriage has been accepted. And he has accomplished a successful climb.

"You're certainly getting better. You persisted to the end despite all the warnings on the leaflet."

"We'll do this one again. It'll be our mountain. It'll have good memories for us."

"I guess we won't be climbing our other mountain again so," Cathy teases.

"A cloud of disappointment fell over it. It's lifted now."

"We'll do it again. It was a great climb and a magnificent view," Cathy enthuses.

"You didn't do any mountain worship today," Mark refers to the practice again.

"I wanted to get you back safely. We hadn't much time to spare."

They are sitting on an old bridge for a rest, just before the final part of the walk, when Mark makes a request which brings doubt floating into Cathy's mind again.

"You won't mention anything about campaigning or mountain worship to my mother."

"Do you mean I shouldn't mention them?"

"I don't think civil disobedience or Pantheism would sit well with her."

"This is a bit of a shock."

"A shock, Cathy, what do you mean? I thought it was a reasonable request."

"I'm wondering do you want to marry me as I am or when I'm tailored to fit some image of the perfect Mrs. Wright."

"I do want us to get married, Cathy. It's just we might be coming in with the heavy stuff if we let my mother, or my grandmother, know all your interests. It might be a shock for them."

"You said I wasn't marrying your family."

"I know. But we'll be very connected. Grandma Rosetta's almost ninety. We should let her die happy."

"Do you think your mother, and your grandmother, only want a nice Protestant woman for you? Or is that your image of the woman you should marry?"

"You are a Protestant woman," Mark encourages.

"Just a nominal one, I must confess."

"I knew you weren't an orthodox follower when you were worshipping mountains. We can cross that bridge when we come to it."

"I think we've come to it now, Mark, and I don't mean this bridge we're sitting on."

"There's no point in giving my mother reason not to accept you totally, especially as you'll be living next door."

"We can talk about it all we like, Mark, but my concern is that you want a different woman than the one you asked to marry you."

"I'm sure I want to be with you, Cathy. I just wouldn't want trouble if my mother didn't approve of what you do."

"What I do is part of who I am."

"Some things you do really impress my mother, like your knowledge and interest in trees, and climbing."

"You're trying to re-fashion me, to fit in."

"Just for the sake of harmony," Mark contends.

"I'd rather risk the disharmony," Cathy persists.

"M aybe you could risk it later when Mam and Grandma Rosetta have seen the good side of you."

"That's so judgmental, Mark."

Cathy thinks back to the elegant Marilyn whose choir was awarded first place at the choral festival. She has some reservations now as to whether she could live up to expectations, without compromising her way of life and her views.

For the next few days, before her return to Glasgow, Mark constantly showers her with affirmations. Not in a subtle way. Rather his assurances are tinged with urgency and excess.

"You're fudging an intrinsic part of me," Cathy insists.

"I know we'll make a great couple. I just fear that civil disobedience would cause raised eyebrows."

"We're not that demure. We can withstand raised eyebrows."

"I don't want to risk it, Cathy. I want things to run smoothly for us. And there's no need for campaigning around Mountview. Everything's safe enough there."

"That's so parochial, Mark. We've to think further than our own corner."

"You can't save the world, love."

Cathy tries to unravel his reasoning and for the time being anyhow, he charms his way out of a thorny situation. However, as she starts preparing to travel back to Glasgow she begins to admonish herself for accepting his proposal so easily while they swung round a giant redwood like two carefree teenagers.

"It's great you and Mark are engaged. I'm so pleased you'll be coming back."

"I'm not so sure about it." Cathy is stuffing the final few pieces of luggage into her rucksack and trying to close the zip.

"You did accept his proposal, didn't you?"

"I did. It's not written in stone though."

"What do you mean? An engagement is an engagement."

"Unless it's broken," Cathy reminds her mother. "Engagements are sometimes broken and this one's in a very fragile state."

"Already, sure you've only got engaged. Tell me what's supposed to have happened."

"It'd take too long. I'd miss the train. I'll give you an up-to-date report some other time. Bye mam."

"Why can't you just simplify life?"

"I thought it was going all right. He muddied it up. Then I thought I'd forgiven him. But I've to think about it a bit further."

"Don't think about it," Beryl says sternly.

Cathy runs towards her father's tractor when she hears it coming into the farmyard. She calls goodbye over the rumbling sound of the engine. Then she runs back to Colin's car and they disappear out through the gate at the end of the driveway.

"I despair of her," Beryl complains to Andy when he comes in for lunch.

"Why?"

"She's only just engaged, and now she's not sure if wants to be engaged. She said Mark muddied things up."

"Maybe he did," Andy answers simply.

"Can they not just get along together? It's not as if they're teenagers. They're thirty years of age." Beryl scolds out loud as she goes to and from the kitchen setting the table and arranging the food in the centre.

"I might turn on the news. Ronald Reagan and Mikhail Gorbachev are having talks about the arms race. We can hear if a different cold war will be settled."

"Do you not mind about our daughter missing her chances?"

"We'll let it be for now and see what happens."

Nightly phone calls jingle in the hall of the house where Cathy lives in Glasgow. She answers the phone promptly to save the residents from upstairs having to run down in vain. Sometimes it's Beryl admonishing her for wanting to let Mark slip through her fingers. More often it is Mark trying to convince her of his ardour, never of his willingness to reveal the true Cathy Campbell.

And so the story proceeds with Beryl's admonishments, Mark's cajoling, and for some unknown reason Cathy's acquiescence, as if her mind has drifted into winter hibernation.

Chapter Four – Disagreement

"We should start making plans for our wedding," Mark suggests as they look out through the window of a cosy café at threatening snow clouds. It is a cold January afternoon and Cathy is due to return to her job in Glasgow in a couple days. A bewildered look appears on her face. She makes no immediate response to Mark's suggestion.

"Things are usually busy with fundraising events in springtime and again in August and September but we've a free period in second half of June or all of July," Mark continues.

"July's very soon," Cathy finally responds.

"We'd be engaged eight months then. And it'd save you all the travelling from Scotland. You'll be the new Mrs. Wright."

"The travelling's grand. Maybe wait till November when we're a year engaged," Cathy suggests.

"The shop would be getting busy for Christmas then. A summer wedding would be better, Cathy. I think July would be good."

Cathy hesitates in her reply.

"You don't look very happy, love."

"Weddings scare me."

"They're not that bad. I was at a good few. They were good fun."

"You saw most of our classmates up the aisle," Cathy teases.

"I know you'd rather something outdoor and bohemian. I don't think that would work here. And I don't think Beryl'd like it either. What do you think?"

"Mam would want the whole razzmatazz," Cathy agrees. "She can't wait to see me in the ancestral wedding dress."

"Neither can I," Mark encourages.

Wedding plans soon seal her fate. Ripples of the news spread through the antennae of Mark's wide circle of associates. The reaction, especially amongst the past pupils of their old academy, is one of astonishment that the charming and affable Mark Wright is ceding his freedom to any woman, especially to Cathy Campbell who never stood out from the crowd.

"I don't think Cathy's the one for Mark," Daisy Armstrong speaks with concern to her husband, Cecil.

"Mark had his pick of the finest girls, including you, and let them slip through his fingers."

Daisy blushes at this remark. The blush softens her strong cheek bones, which are framed by neatly styled blonde hair.

"I'm glad he let you slip through his fingers though," Cecil assures her.

"I wouldn't want him to be feeling desperate just because so many of us got married around the same time."

"You couldn't say someone'd have to be desperate to marry Cathy Campbell," Cecil contends.

"She wasn't part of the circle. She scurried away south of the bay for the whole school holidays."

"That's where she lived." Cecil keeps defending her. "It wasn't easy travelling between north and south."

North of the border Cathy's classmates mixed socially. After the holidays she would hear them talking about romances and break-ups and favourite dances. She had started in St Matthew's in 1967 before the Troubles began. All changed in her second year and the free-flowing passage up towards St. Matthew's was hindered.

"And she studied so hard she didn't take much part in social activities," Daisy remembers.

"You can't fault her on diligence."

"Do you know what I was sorry about? She never got first in the Home Ec. kitchen."

"You probably did," Cecil teases.

"I did and there were times when I thought Cathy's work was excellent. Once we got a joint first and I was mad that Miss Wilson didn't give her an outright first," Daisy recalls. "After all I'd got first several times."

"By the sounds of it she'll make a diligent wife for Mark," Cecil reckons.

"No doubt about that," Daisy agrees.

"I'd say they've made up their minds no matter what anyone thinks about them as a couple."

"I'm not convinced. Things changed for Mark before. And he isn't seeing Cathy that long. I suppose having a mother-in-law and a grandmother-in-law to please is a challenge," Daisy persists.

"Is that what happened to you?"

"I've to admit I haven't the personality that'd fit in as Mrs. Wright, the third."

Mark's advice about non-disclosure of her campaigning activities continues to trouble Cathy. It is as if a part of her is censored, erased from the picture, a hidden dimension. She wonders if Cupid's arrows hit Mark before and were diverted because of conditions placed upon any earlier prospective Mrs. Wright.

"I'm sorry to have to say this, Mark. From time to time I've doubts about our future."

They are having coffee in the golf club at the bay on their way to do a climb when Cathy makes this confession. At that very moment the amiable gentleman, who served them, smiles in their direction and asks if everything is alright for them. This knocks them out of kilter for a few seconds.

"What kind of doubts?" Mark looks troubled.

"I feel restrictions have been imposed upon me."

"Imposed? That sounds a bit strong, love."

"Hiding my whole worldview from your mother troubles me a lot."

"I thought you'd forgotten about that, love."

"You probably hoped I had."

His assumption flummoxes her even more than his first suggestion that she should not reveal her interests to his mother. That was when they were sitting on the bridge in the forest on the day of his proposal. It was an intimidating start.

"It disappoints me that you don't think my misgivings are significant." Cathy appears aggrieved. Mark searches for words.

"I was thinking of the best way to ensure harmony. A hippy or a rebel in Mountview would be like an alien species."

"Alien species, what do you mean, Mark?"

"Maybe the words came out wrong. I'm sorry."

"It's just as well the words came out wrong now and not in a year's time. I think we'll have to go back to the drawing-board."

"Is it that bad?" Mark asks in a bewildered voice.

"You've asked the wrong kind of woman to marry you, Mark. I think we'll have to forego our climb and figure out if we've a future together," Cathy speaks sadly.

The Blue Mazda comes to a jerky halt in front of the kitchen window. Beryl's preparing lunch.

"You're home early. Did you not climb the mountain?"

"No. We didn't climb today."

"It's not like you to miss a good mountain climb," Beryl continues probingly.

"No, I'm usually unwavering in that matter." Cathy answers all her mother's questions briefly and uneasily.

"You're not wearing your ring."

"No."

"What happened?"

"We'd a disagreement."

"I can't believe it, Cathy. How could you have a fight with that nice man? How could you mess things up with everything looking so good for you?"

Cathy is now sitting with her elbows on the table holding up her head on her hands. No words of response are coming out.

"Have you nothing more to say for yourself."

"That's the problem. Mark doesn't want me to say who I really am. He has some idea of what the ideal Mrs. Wright should be."

"There was never anything lacking in the Campbell's of the Dale." Beryl is now becoming defensive on Cathy's part.

"He's not casting any aspersions on the Campbell's. Our pedigree's not in question."

"Well I'm glad to hear that. And what's the problem?"

"It's more my belief systems and interests."

"Beliefs, they're best kept private. People were better off when they didn't talk about beliefs and politics."

29

"I think I was better off when I kept my romancing in Scotland and just came home to see you and dad and Colin and Jennifer."

"Ah no, Cathy, it'd be lovely to have you back. I hated the idea of you living away forever."

"You can be anything you want to be when you're outside the radar," Cathy concludes.

"I think it'll work out with Mark. Just pass no heed on beliefs and things like that. You'll have a good secure life and a handsome man."

Cathy realises she is not getting any sympathy or understanding from Beryl who came from a culture of finding the best husband possible and relinquishing such nebulous things as love or beliefs.

"Won't you get in touch with Mark before you leave," Beryl implores.

"He was the one hurt me," Cathy insists.

"You'll just keep playing cat and mouse games till you break up altogether."

"I might get in touch the next time I'm home. Right now, I want to have an early night. I've an early start in the morning."

The phone rings just after Cathy has gone to bed.

"This is Mark. I wonder if I could speak to Cathy."

"Lovely to speak to you, Mark," Beryl answers him with enthusiasm. "Cathy's just gone to bed. She's leaving early in the morning. But I'll call her."

"No, don't disturb her. I'm going to Belfast in the morning for a meeting. I can go down and pick up Cathy and bring her to the boat."

"That's very thoughtful, Mark."

"Mark's coming down to bring you to the boat in the morning." Beryl partly opens Cathy's bedroom and calls in to her.

"We'd a disagreement. It isn't resolved."

"You can resolve it on the journey. I know it'll work out. Goodnight Cathy."

The shiny dark green Volvo disturbs the pebbles and draws to a halt near the hall door. Mark steps out and before he has a chance to hit the antique door knocker Beryl is out to greet him.

"You're here bright and early, Mark," Beryl exudes. "You might've time for a coffee."

"Thank you very much, Mrs. Campbell."

Beryl brings him into the front room, the parlour as it is called, and seats him among some of the antique heirlooms of the Campbell family.

"I'll pop up and see how Cathy's getting on with her packing."

"Mark's in the parlour, Cathy."

"I heard you sweet-talking him."

"You're wearing a tracksuit. Why don't you put on something more presentable for the journey?" her mother whispers.

"I'm going on a ship. I want to feel comfortable. This is a new tracksuit, well new to me. I bought it in a charity shop a couple weeks ago."

Cathy notices her own reflection in the mirror and feels satisfied that the turquoise blue colour suits her ginger hair.

"I think the colour's good," she continues.

"A tracksuit's a tracksuit. Mark's dressed so smartly."

"He's going to a meeting."

"You'll have to go a bit more up-market in your dress when you're married to a business man."

"If I get married you mean."

"Well hurry down to him and don't leave him alone," Beryl urges.

"Won't I be keeping him company all the way to Belfast?"

"I'm losing patience with you, Cathy. Will you make the coffee and I'll chat to him?"

"Perfect, mam."

Beryl makes haste back to the parlour where she endeavours to compensate for her daughter's tardiness.

The tray arrives.

"Mugs," Beryl thinks to herself as Cathy lays the tray on the rosewood table in front of them and casually flicks a few coasters, depicting Scottish scenes, around the table. There is not a sign of silverware or Wedgewood china, except among the heirlooms in the rosewood cabinets.

Cathy notices her mother's disapproving looks.

"Your standards have dropped since you went to Scotland."

"That was twelve years ago, forty percent of my whole life," her daughter quickly calculates.

"I was very disappointed with your attitude towards Mark this morning. You just threw him a mug. You'd think we hadn't a decent cup in the house. That's not how we treat guests."

Beryl's monologue pours down the phone in the hall just after Cathy arrives back in her Glasgow flat.

"He'll be alright, mam, if that's the worst thing ever happens to him."

"I can't understand why you're so hard to please. You've met an ideal man and you want to complicate matters with beliefs and feelings."

Chapter Five - The Opal Ring

Eventually Mark's charm and cordial nature coupled with Beryl's persistence ensure that the romance gets back on track.

Wedding plans are proceeding in the Dale. Beryl has booked the church for the last Saturday in July. Then Cathy happens to meet her old sweetheart. He sees the engagement ring with the opal stone sparkling. She sees the sparkle in his eyes dim.

"I see you've found someone new," he says sadly.

"I have," Cathy replies. Her eyes become laden with sadness.

"Who's the lucky person?"

"His name's Mark. He's a shopkeeper's son, and a shopkeeper to be. That's the plan anyhow."

"Where'll you be living?"

"In the shadow of the Mourne Mountains," Cathy replies.

"I'd hoped you'd be living in the shadow of one of our Scottish Munro's."

"The world has funny twists and turns. We'd good times together. I'll treasure them." Cathy speaks solemnly.

"I might nae see you again."

"No. But I'll remember you always.

She tries not to let tears fall in front of him. They both turn away sadly. As one, they both turn back and see each other once again. The space between them very slowly widens. It is as if there is a strong magnet preventing their progression in opposite directions. She glances back a third time and sees him sitting disconsolate on the steps of a house, his head resting in his hands and his long dark brown curls covering his cheeks. She runs back towards him. Before he can get to his feet she sits down beside him.

"I'm glad for you, Cathy. Yer folk'll have you back. They might need you when they're old."

"That's a kind thought. My mother says it's what she always wanted. She's not old though."

"But you'll be there for her."

They sit together on the granite steps. The cold seeps through their clothes. Flat dwellers from the house make their way around them.

"And Mhairi and Hamish, how are they?" Cathy enquires.

"We're lucky to have da. He'd a bad heart attack, had to have surgery."

"I'm so very sorry to hear that."

"It happened a few days after we parted. I nae got a chance to go the places we went." He lays his hand on the back of her cold hand.

She feels so sad she was not there for him.

"I'm so sorry," she repeats over and over and the blood drains from her face at the thought of the good-natured Hamish so gravely ill and his kindly family worried.

"I phoned a few times, but you were nae there."

No, I was not there, Cathy thinks, I was hightailing around some forest or mountain with Mark.

"I'm so sorry I wasn't there when you needed me."

"You'll be there for your folk, once you've a fondness for Mark."

"I was in boarding school with him. I bumped into him again by accident at the choral festival when Jennifer was singing."

His hand is still on top of her hand which has regained some heat.

A young girl, pushing a pram, comes to the steps. They raise themselves from the cold steps and help her.

Then they embrace in a fond farewell and he whispers "if ye change yer mind ye know what to do, my Jo." They turn towards their respective homes. They look back once and wave feebly. Cathy sobs all the way back to her flat. She opens the door into the chilly hall where her sweetheart's phone calls often rang in vain. She can just imagine someone running down the stairs and throwing a disinterested 'she's not here' into the line.

Collapsing on to the old settee she cries more. It is the spring equinox 1986. Earlier she was trying to stay aware of the equinox. Now this equinox is etched in her regretful mind. The glitter seems to have faded from the opal ring. She feels she is living a lie continuing with her wedding for the sake of not letting down her mother, or more importantly Mark, at this late stage. The months race on. She has not enough time to work things out, to sit back and take stock of her future life.

Her old flame's words swirl around in her head, "if ye change yer mind ye know what to do, my Jo." She wishes she had met him sooner, before it was too late to turn back. Mark is a very good man. But she does not feel the same sparks of love for him.

Frozen with sadness she is unable to travel home to the Dale on her next planned visit.

"I'm just wiped out," she explains to Mark. He understands, suggesting that all the travel and her work could be taking its toll.

Beryl is less understanding.

"Wiped out at thirty years of age, that's ridiculous. You'll need more resilience than that when you're a businessman's wife."

A businessman's wife, the words spin around in her head as if it is a new concept. She is sitting on the floor in the cold hall, winding a strand of her ginger hair around the finger that is wearing Mark's opal ring. She is trying not to sound irritated. Her mother's monologue continues.

"We've a wedding to organise here," her mother states sternly.

"It's bad enough getting married without having to go through a wedding," Cathy gushes out impatiently.

"I'll pretend I never heard those words," her mother retorts.

"Okay."

"What's wrong with a wedding anyhow?"

"It's too fussy."

"You're our only daughter. A wedding's very important to us. Why are you being so selfish?"

"I'm just being truthful."

"I've been making a lace veil to match the dress." Her mother scolds on.

"I never wanted anything like that," Cathy insists. "It just all kept rolling on, at speed."

Cathy thinks to herself that in four months another matching, as Mark would call it, will be solemnised, hers and Mark's.

"Weddings are elaborate affairs nowadays," Beryl emphasises.

"I'd rather get married in the woods," Cathy sighs.

"That's ridiculous talk. Have you forgotten you're getting married in the church? It's all arranged. And that's there's a reception booked at the Bayview Hotel."

Silence descends for a few seconds.

"I've to go," Cathy says. "There's someone sitting on the stairs waiting to use the phone."

"I'll call back."

"No. It's okay, mam."

She unfolds herself from her lotus posture on the floor and drags herself back into her flat.

"Is Cathy alright?" Andy enquires.

"She doesn't like the fuss of a wedding. Our only daughter doesn't want to give us the chance of a wedding."

"A wedding's just a day for us. It's a lifetime for her."

Beryl does not reveal the full extent of the story. She does not say that Cathy claims it is bad enough getting married without having to go through a wedding.

She sips her tea and nibbles at the home-made almond slices she bought at the Country Market. She re-dials Cathy's number. The phone rings out again in the chilly hall. It is unusually cold for a March evening and there is nothing about to warm up Cathy's spirits.

"I hope you show Mark a bit of consideration next time you grace him with your presence. A bit more enthusiasm about the wedding preparations wouldn't go astray. Do you hear me?"

"Yes. I hear you, mam."

"What's got into you?"

"It's just ever since I spoke to Mark at the choral festival your mantra has been to marry him."

"Only for me you'd have let him slip through your fingers. And he's a fine man, and a handsome man, and a charming man, and he'll give you a good future."

"I know he's all of those things. It's just you won't leave me alone and let me think it out."

"I've to keep reminding you. You've a fine engagement ring on your left hand."

"Okay. Goodnight, mam." Cathy places the phone firmly in its nest.

Chapter Six - The Homecoming

"Only for my scolding she'd have turned her back on him," Beryl boasts to Andy as she continues her intricate stitching on the champagne-pink lace veil.

"I don't know if it's good to interfere," Andy responds worriedly.

"She doesn't know what's best for her. Successful young men don't come ten a penny. She'll thank me for it."

"I'm not sure."

"They're among the last single people from their class. Where would she find someone so eligible?"

"She mightn't have met him at all if they hadn't gone to the choral festival," Andy tries to reason. "It was an accident she met him."

"It was a happy accident."

"I'd rather she'd more space to work things out for herself."

"I know it'll work, if only she'd settle her mind and marry him," Beryl says emphatically.

The stitching goes on. Her knitting activities for the Country Market are placed on hold while this labour of love progresses. The veil incorporates in its design some of the special features of the area, including the dolmen and the standing stones and a backdrop of a mountain. Cathy always loved mountains and although life meandered onto a different path ten months ago when she met Mark she is apparently still destined to live beneath the shadow of one. Still a mountain on a wedding veil holds no enchantment for the bride-to-be just now.

The champagne-pink wedding dress was worn by Cathy's great-grandmother Alice in 1895. It was worn by her grandmother Jane in 1922. That was the bride who only met her husband a few weeks before their wedding day. She probably slipped into the heirloom dress and headed to the altar with a minimum of excitement or preparation. It was worn for a third time by Beryl in 1951 and now it is here for Cathy in 1986. The fitted high-necked dress is non-compromising in its shape.

The last time Cathy was home Beryl insisted that she would fit it on and she almost got wedged into it. Although she is slim her waist is not narrow enough. Beryl carefully snipped the small stitches and added a panel of almost identical material at both sides.

A part-time position for a landscape designer becomes vacant in an architect's office ten miles from Mountview on the Dale side. The person doing the job is taking a three-year break to accompany her husband on a work assignment to Geneva. The architect is a member of the same golf club as Mark and he mentioned to Mark that the position was available.

"You might find it easier to blend into life in Mountview if you've a job you're interested in, for a while anyhow," Mark encourages.

"It sounds a good idea, Mark, but I don't feel ready to leave Glasgow."

"It'd be a pity to let it pass. Jobs like yours are scarce."

"I appreciate that, Mark. In logic it's good. I just don't feel ready to leave Scotland yet. I think I want to stay longer. Sorry."

"You'd be leaving in a few months anyway," Mark reasons.

"Ummh. I suppose you're right."

"I'm sorry I couldn't leave here with the shop."

For Mark, the only son of a shopkeeper, his destiny was mapped out by tradition. There was no spare male heir. He was destined to carry on the family business, established over a hundred years ago.

"No, I suppose not. Colin couldn't have left home, for good anyway. And I couldn't imagine you leaving here anyhow. Leaving the golf club and the fundraising days and everything?"

"Are you annoyed that I fitted in our wedding day between fundraising days," Mark probes.

"No, I don't think so."

"Or maybe you wanted to put it on the long finger?"

"July felt too soon."

"Now that everything's organised we'd best stick with July," he encourages.

"Yeah, it'd mess things up to change it. Mam has everything arranged."

"Maybe you'll give the job a bit of thought over the next day or two."

"I didn't know leaving Scotland would be so hard for you. I thought you'd look at it like coming home."

"I feel free in Scotland. It's been my home, for all my adult life so far."

She accepts the job even though she feels prematurely ripped from Scotland. With heavy heart she packs her belongings and clears her flat. Colin travels over to Glasgow to help her manage the luggage. As the boat faces towards the coast of Antrim, leaving the Scottish coastline behind, tears fill her eyes. Colin is worried about the unexpected sadness in the eyes of a bride-to-be.

"Are you alright, sis? It's a big change closing a chapter of your life."

She leans across the small circular table her lips close to her only sibling's left ear.

"This is a big secret between you and me, bro. I think I love someone else more than I love Mark."

"That's wedding nerves. Everything will be okay, sis."

"I don't think so. Were you sure when you married Jennifer?"

"I was. We were younger and hadn't met many others. Jennifer was only eighteen when we met."

Cathy is wiping the tears and trying to distract herself by talking about Jennifer.

"Where did you meet her?"

"I met her in the Parish Hall after her grandfather's funeral. You were in College then."

"You made a great choice. She's the best sister-in-law anyone could have."

"Mark seems a very good man too. Mam's so pleased you'll be near, well fairly near anyhow. And she's very happy you met a nice Protestant businessman."

"I know about the latter, bro. It's been mam's mantra. When I told her that I'd doubts about getting engaged, and staying engaged, she was very disappointed. She was really frustrated and annoyed with me at times."

"That might've been overstepping the line of concern," Colin says disappointedly.

"And I think Mark's mother and grandmother wanted a good Protestant wife for him. I'd be wayward in that regard."

"There's no need to worry, sis. Nobody will ask you about your beliefs."

"North of the bay there are fewer grey areas. I reckon I'll be the broken link in the line of good Wright wives."

"You're a good woman too, sis. Don't underestimate yourself."

Cathy gazes across at her brother, ginger-haired like herself and with the same narrow gap between his front teeth. He always appears even-tempered and at ease. Perhaps he does not complicate life. Although he has the same latent concern as everyone else in the community about the threat that lurks across the narrow stretch of the Irish Sea, the ominous nuclear plant, he does not seem to allow fear into his daily life.

He started co-managing of the farm with their father when he was a teenager. At thirty-three he seems contented with life on the farm, with his wife Jennifer and their small son Edwin. Jennifer completed her studies in voice and in piano in the time between meeting Colin and getting married three years later. Now she teaches singing and piano in the loft studio she created above their home and directs the opera each year in Dale Community School.

Colin's copy of *The Scottish Farmer* and the Cathy's *BBC Wildlife Magazine* lie unopened on the circular table while the siblings remain present for one another.

The boat docks on time. They make their way downstairs to the car deck. Soon they are driving across the gangway and Colin notices the sadness on his sister's face. When they are about thirty minutes into their journey he drives in beside a welcoming inn where they have tea and scones together.

"Let's chat about this uneasy feeling, sis, before we get home." Colin's sapphire blue eyes are laden with concern for his sister who might be overwhelmed by all the preparations that Beryl has made for the wedding.

"It was something I just wanted to share with you, bro. I hadn't considered jilting Mark and running away."

"I was hoping for happiness for you, sis."

"In time I could grow to love Mark. He's charming and handsome and generous and someone mam will be happy with," Cathy admits.

"I wouldn't rank the charming first. The generosity might be more enduring."

Cathy realises that Mark and charming have always been synonymous in her mind. Although she did not doubt his generosity it was his charm and his powers of persuasion that brought her this far.

"When I think of Mark, I think of charm, an affable charm," Cathy muses.

"I don't think you should've let yourself get so entangled with what mam wants. The fact that mam will have you near shouldn't be a reason for your marriage."

"I suppose only for mam's insistence I mightn't be engaged."

"I think you'll need to build on what you think are Mark's attractive points for you, even if they include charm."

Cathy listens to her brother's depth of thought and discernment. Although he ferried her to and from the train station on her visits back to the Dale they had never chatted intimately before. Perhaps he never knew there might be a worry hidden beneath her bundle of ginger curls.

Chapter Seven - The Trousseau

"Now that you're back we'll organise your trousseau." Beryl bubbles with the excitement of everything.

"Trousseau what's that?"

"It's the clothes and things a woman gets together for her marriage."

"I've enough clothes?"

"Only a short while ago you were heading off with Mark in a tracksuit from a charity shop."

"He'd no complaints. He likes turquoise on me."

"It's a tradition to have a trousseau."

"I've my trousseau already. Can I show you all I got in three charity shops?"

"Okay, show me."

"Look at this long black dress. It can be made elegant or simple with scarves or chains."

"It's a good quality dress, I have to admit, and in good condition. It just amazes me that a bride would go to a charity shop for her trousseau?"

"These are the other things. And I've scarves and chains for the dress." Cathy spreads out everything over her bed. "I got the whole lot for less than sixty pounds."

"What about my 'mother of the bride' outfit?"

"I'm not discouraging you from buying an outfit. I just don't need to go shopping."

"I was expecting a day out shopping. I thought you'd come along."

"Sorry mam, it's not my scene at all."

"Cathy won't come to Madam Belles for clothes for the wedding? She bought her clothes in charity shops."

"You've led her along quite a bit. I'd pass on Madam Belles if I were you," Andy advises.

"Who'll come with me to pick my outfit?"

"Vera would enjoy a day out shopping."

Vera McKeever, who has been active in the ICA and in the Country Markets over the years, is the public health nurse in the area. As a young nurse in the County Hospital she met Joe McKeever, a native of the Dale, while he was a patient. Less than ten years after their wedding day Vera, was widowed. Hers has been a life of service in the community since. Though love did not come her way a second time she is always ready to rejoice in the celebrations of those around her.

"Pastel green, Beryl, there's a colour that'd complement your red hair. What size do you take?"

"Size twelve's very comfortable. A ten might be a bit tight."

"Go for the twelve. You want to be comfortable on the day."

The sales girl is walking towards the mannequin carrying the outfit.

"Excuse me." Vera halts the girl in her tracks. "We love this colour. Do you have it in size twelve?"

"This is a twelve."

"That's perfect on you, Beryl."

"Would you like something for yourself, Vera?"

"I've the outfit for the wedding sorted. But I suppose I couldn't leave Madam Belles empty-handed."

"That's the spirit."

"I won't be fitting into a size twelve. I usually get a sixteen for a bit of comfort."

Vera never worries about size labels, claiming that if a woman wears what fits she will look good anyway.

"Now we're both sorted," Vera says in a satisfied tone.

"There's just something else," Beryl whispers, "lingerie for Cathy. She says she's happy with t-shirts for nightwear."

"Look at those beautiful French chemises," Vera swoons.

"Mark likes turquoise, I believe, and there's a nice turquoise one."

"I got my outfit, pastel green," Beryl tells Cathy when she returns from work.

"That colour will look great on you, mam."

"And I got some French chemises for you, including a turquoise one. You said Mark liked turquoise."

"Where would I be going with French chemises, mam?"

"On your honeymoon, where do you think?"

"There was no need for that. But thanks for thinking of me?"

"We can make an appointment with the florist next."

"There'll be plenty of flowers around the fields in July."

"Around the fields, that's not where brides get their flowers."

"Meadowsweet would be beautiful. The creamy flowers and red stems will tone in with the dress and with the bridesmaids' pastel pinks."

"I know what they're like, but they're very common."

"That's probably why people don't give them much attention," Cathy quips.

Cathy drives around the bay three days each week to her job in the architect's office. The road is familiar and the job interesting, if more office based than her work in Glasgow. Her uneasy thoughts are familiar too. Little by little they just become part of her psyche and she accepts that in a matter of weeks she will be Mrs. Wright, the third. Mark is a good man she reminds herself constantly. And the days and weeks go by while Beryl ticks off wedding preparation tasks from her long list. The dress, the veil, the lingerie, Beryl's pastel green outfit and a myriad of other items are carefully stored in Colin's boyhood bedroom. Vera has made the cake. As the guest replies come in Beryl inscribes place cards in beautiful calligraphy. Cathy's wedding has been arranged with the minimum of input from herself. How could she call a halt to such activity and shatter everyone's expectations? How could she dwell on the last words of her old flame? 'If you change your mind ye know what to do.'

"Maybe you'd give me advice about who'll sit together," Beryl suggests.

Cathy sees the familiar names from Saint Matthew's. Mark had mentioned all the weddings he attended and now these couples will join them to celebrate their union. Among them are Daisy and Cecil and Patience and Stephen. Stephen Prior, the shy diligent boy from her class, who had found love in the arms of a vicar. Secretly she fancied him herself when she was a teenager but the logistics of romancing north of the bay did not permit such a liaison.

"Are you having a hen party?"

"No, I don't feel like one, mam."

"Everyone has one."

"I don't know who'd be interested. And my energy levels are low."

"What ails you, Cathy? You're too young for talk about low energy levels. In a couple weeks you'll be a business man's wife."

"Ummh."

"We should arrange for Mark's family to visit again."

"No worries. You'll see them soon. Sarah and Hannah will be down the day or so before to do go through the bits and pieces."

"And a rehearsal," Beryl adds.

"I hadn't thought of that. Sure we can follow the lead."

"Who'll be the leader?"

"The vicar, I suppose."

"You must be the most lackadaisical bride imaginable. I've done everything for this wedding."

"You wanted a formal wedding, mam. I wouldn't have gone for anything like this. My head's in a turmoil just hearing you fuss about it."

"Anything else would be out of the question," Beryl says incredulously.

"Patience would be delighted to officiate if it's alright with your vicar," Mark suggests to Cathy one evening.

"You could hardly call any vicar 'my vicar'. I'd say it'd be no problem."

Chapter Eight - The Wedding

Marilyn looks elegant in cobalt blue while Grandma Rosetta is decidedly regal in purple. They sit on either side of Benny in the front pew. Cathy carries a bunch of meadowsweet as Andy links her up the aisle. Mark beams an approving smile. His identical twin sisters, Sarah and Hannah, arrange the champagne-pink dress and lace veil. Beryl can relax now. It is thirty-five years since she wore that wedding dress. For a while she wondered if her daughter would wear it at all or if she had other life journeys mapped out. And she had. Her idea would have been a wedding in the woods and her guests, like nymphs, celebrating around a campfire. That was how her friends performed their nuptials. Mark was accustomed to conventional weddings, plenty of conventional weddings. The only conventional wedding Cathy attended was that of Colin and Jennifer where she was a bridesmaid. Now she is here the central character on this elaborate stage with splendid costumes all around. Above the solid oak altar saints depicted in stain glass are rendered translucent by the afternoon sunshine.

Patience, who is the officiating vicar, asks Mark Bernard Wright does he take Catherine Jane Campbell as his wife. Looking straight into Cathy's eyes he firmly responds, "I do."

She asks Catherine Jane Campbell does she take Mark Bernard Wright as her husband. Haltingly, very haltingly, after a pause, she pronounces "I do."

"Wedding nerves I'd say," Vera whispers to one of the guests beside her. Vera is wearing a cerise pink dress and jacket and a simple string of pearls. A matching hat is balanced stylishly on her highlighted hair.

Cathy's hesitant words of "I do" are witnessed by all, except perhaps by Grandma Rosetta, who is partially deaf. The vicar does not appear to have any problem. Mark and Cathy are married. Beryl's wish has been fulfilled. For Colin, who is best man, there is concern for his little sister. Only he knows that she cried for a lost love.

Mark links Cathy back down the aisle to the mellow strains of Jennifer's voice, and the good wishes which emanate from the pews. The newlyweds emerge into the July sunshine. Photographs are taken with precision. Then the bride and groom's car lead the wedding party to the Bayview Hotel, which overlooks the northern curve of the bay. Cathy is centre stage at the top table and then in the middle of the dance floor for the first dance. She begins to feel lost in the dazzling trance of jubilant guests. Dancing, prancing, swaying, swinging, the movement goes on. Mark seems completely at home. His regular interaction with former classmates at several weddings means he can swirl on to the dance floor as seamlessly as if the last wedding was only a few weeks ago. Everyone wants to dance with him. He appears to be the Adonis of the class still. For Cathy the elapse of more than a dozen years has created a wide chasm between her and her classmates. The only exception is when she has the second dance with Stephen. She feels so at ease that the passage of time seems inconsequential.

Back again in the apparently eternal whirligig of movement and colour, there is no chance to take refuge on the wings. A splash of purple and she sees Grandma Rosetta at the side of the dance floor. Grandma Rosetta appears so stern that Cathy refrains from occupying the empty chair beside her. Marilyn and Jennifer are chatting companionably, perhaps about things choral. She sees an exit.

"I wonder if Cathy's alright. I haven't seen her for a wee while," Vera whispers to Beryl.

Beryl scans the floor and the seats.

"And now we'll have a set of Scottish songs for the bride," the bandleader announces. A pause follows.

"The bride's out of the room so we'll continue with a few more quicksteps."

The guests swarm on to the floor again. Except for Vera and Beryl and Daisy, the guests seem unperturbed by the absence of the bride. Daisy Armstrong, dressed elegantly in a cream halter-necked dress, has taken notice of the bandleader's announcement. Her sharp blue eyes skim the whole room with the precision of one accustomed to supervising an exam hall.

"She could've run away?" She probes at Cecil's arm. "She didn't sound too convinced at the vows."

"I doubt it. I'd say she's about somewhere."

"Mark doesn't deserve this," Daisy reckons.

"Nothing has happened, Daisy. Are you hoping for a drama?"

Mark, who has been constantly swiped off his feet by his friends and his former admirers, glances around. His light grey suit and pastel pink crevette add to his dapper appearance. As if to distract him from his momentary pause, Patience, also dressed in grey and wearing her collar, invites him to dance.

"I hope Cathy's alright," he says apprehensively.

"Maybe she's gone up to the bride's room."

"She wasn't looking forward to all the razzmatazz, as she'd call it."

"What would Cathy have liked?"

"A ceremony in a forest, or at an ancient monument," Mark divulges. "Between me and you, she's a real pagan, and an anarchist at heart. I didn't share this with anyone else."

"Thanks for trusting me, Mark."

He observes her warm sincere expression, framed by soft brown hair cut in a simple bob-style.

"I know I can trust you," he says with conviction.

"I think it'd be good to accept Cathy the way she is, and be proud of her as she is."

"I don't know, Patience. What'd my mother think?

"You don't know what your mother thinks, Mark. You didn't allow her to know the real Cathy."

"I don't think I can risk it for the moment anyway."

Patience surveys his troubled face.

"Give it some thought, Mark. I won't mention it again. You won't need to avoid me."

Outside Cathy scans the seascape. She has ventured out on to a veranda leaving the undulating colours behind her. A ship moves quietly into the bay and over towards the harbour. She breathes in a gulp of fresh sea air. Removing her lace veil and the clips, which tamed her hair into a sophisticated bun, she allows her long red curls to fall free. Before her the gulls swirl and squawk. Behind her, in the banqueting hall, her guests swirl to the music. Blissful solitude, she thinks to herself, as she admires a full silver moon glazed over in a milky sky. The soft colours of the sky at the horizon alter almost imperceptibly. It is a balmy July evening. She takes in long deep breaths, mindful that she is taking in oxygen given by trees and returning carbon dioxide.

"Have you forgotten your guests and your husband?" A scolding voice disturbs her.

"I wanted a break, mam."

"A break, you're the bride. And your bridesmaids are passing no heed on you. They're dancing away with their husbands."

"I'm not under hotel arrest. They don't have to chaperon me."

"You should've had Jennifer as bridesmaid."

"I wanted Jennifer to be the singer."

"Your mother-in-law could've sung."

Beryl escorts her daughter along the veranda and around the corner to the side entrance of the ballroom, scolding as she goes.

"And you've taken off your veil and let your hair down after all the trouble Vera went to this morning. And all the months of work that went into embroidering the veil. Now it's just bundled up like a curtain going into the wash. Give it to me and I'll fold it up if you're not going to wear it."

Beryl discretely stops scolding as mother and daughter enter the hall.

"Cathy's back," Cecil Brown assures Daisy. "She probably left to let her hair down. It's nicer that way."

"I see Cathy," Patience remarks thankfully. "We'll look out for her for the rest of the evening." She squeezes Mark's hand and returns to the empty seat beside Stephen.

The band starts to play *I belong to Glasgow*, especially for the bride. Mark and Cathy take to the floor again. And the guests leave them to do a few whirls alone as if it was the first dance again.

"You look more like yourself with your hair flying free. I never knew Cathy Campbell with a Victorian bun."

She appreciates this complement. The other dancers move on to the floor, couple by couple, until the reunited pair is surrounded again.

"I'm so happy this day has come. Thanks for giving up Glasgow for me," he whispers.

Cathy feels moved by his statement which she feels is laden with sincerity rather than charm.

The band slows the tempo for the *Mull of Kintyre* and Mark holds her closer as they dance. A little while later Stephen invites her to dance again and they move around the floor once more with companionable ease. The moving carousel of colours slowed somewhat as more guests chat at tables around the edge of the dance floor. Colin invites his sister to dance.

"You're looking beautiful sis. Your hair is beautiful that way, the way you always had it."

"I just wanted to let my hair down, bro, to flow freely."

A wave of warmth and understanding passed between the siblings.

"I feel such a great sense of relief now that Cathy's finally married to Mark," Beryl sighs as she and Andy climb the stairs to their own bedroom back in the Dale.

"Ummh," Andy mumbles.

"That's not a great reaction after a long rocky road."

"You couldn't say long. It's only a little over a year since they met."

"I thought she'd never get to the altar with all their disagreements."

"It was a near miss today," Andy reckons. "She wobbled a bit at the vows."

"Anyhow the vicar was happy and I'm happy too," Beryl stresses as she places the pastel green suit under tissue in the wardrobe.

"She's a lovely vicar. Patience, the name suits her," Andy muses. He feels a relief that the wedding is over and Beryl's fretfulness about her daughter's uncertainty are at an end.

Chapter Nine – Beginnings

Cathy and Mark start married life in the stone dormer-type cottage beside Wright's shop. The cottage, with its green trimmed windows and doors, its solid slate roof and high chimney pots, is set in front of a grove of trees which extend up a gentle slope. The grove of trees was planted by Mark's grandfather, Bernard and Grandma Rosetta. Over the years it has evolved into a mature forest-like grove that keeps evolving and regenerating. It provides a natural ever-changing backdrop to the cottage and the shop.

A rocky outcrop at the northern side of the cottage is swathed with colourful flowers. Swifts swirl to and fro catching insects. Their nests are made in small spaces between the stones at the top of the castle. Flying continuously the swifts sleep on the wing. Their high-pitched calls are a familiar ambient sound during the summer. A pair of bullfinches often feed on birch catkins near the edge of the grove. Soon their diet will have changed to blackberries and other autumn fruit.

Mark's mother, Marilyn, an energetic woman in her late fifties, is involved in the Mother's Union, the church choir and the church floral society. Grandma Rosetta, the matriarch of the family, was for many years a steadfast member of the Mother's Union. As if by tradition Marilyn stepped into her shoes. Marilyn also finds time to be treasurer of the Best Kept Villages committee and secretary of the grocers' benevolent fund, a cause also championed by Mark, initially through fundraising golf days.

"Remember I promised I'd go with you for a climb on Mount Nevis?" They are having breakfast together a short while after their wedding, when Mark springs this surprise on her.

"I remember. It was at the summit of our first big mountain climb."

She is pleased that he remembers. The promise, or aspiration she would have called it, was made on that awkward day of the first marriage proposal. Her heart is rattling about inside her, wondering if her feelings for her lost love might be re-ignited if she went to Scotland. It is thoughtful of Mark to remember.

"I know I've been remiss in the past weeks with all the irons I've in the fire," he explains apologetically. "The fundraising days are a great benefit to the charities, especially to the Grocer's Fund."

"I suppose they are," Cathy responds in a deadpan way.

"You don't sound very enthusiastic, love."

"I think I've learned to suppress enthusiasm since you warned me not to speak of my interests."

"Warned? I didn't mean it to sound like a warning, love. It was advice."

"It felt like a warning. And it'd the same result."

"We'll have time to chat over things when we go to Scotland."

"When would you like to go?" Cathy asks as she tries to cover up the annoyance that is permeating her mind.

"If we went before the end of the month we could take in your birthday," Mark speculates encouragingly.

"There are plenty of nice hostels in the area."

"I'd prefer a hotel, Cathy. I never stayed in a hostel."

"They're good for the comradery. You feel everyone's on the one journey," Cathy muses. "I don't associate hotels with climbing and muddy boots and everything."

"We can leave the climbing gear in the car."

They chose a hotel on the banks of Loch Linnhe. To add to the sense of occasion Mark reserves a superior room with a balcony overlooking the loch.

At the base of Ben Nevis they read the warnings and recommendations for climbers and are satisfied that they have all the basics needed. Cathy knows she is quite near the guest house owned by her old flame's parents. She is feeling jittery and wants to keep moving.

"All we need now is stamina," she resolves as she moves towards the bridge over the River Nevis. They cross the bridge and start up the incline, their footsteps falling into a rhythm for the early part of the climb. It gets more difficult as they ascend. They pause for a short while and enjoy the breath-taking view from Halfway Lake. It takes about two hours to reach the summit from this point. They forge ahead along the zig-zag path and reach the scree, a challenging lunar-like landscape near the summit. The ascent is eventually accomplished.

"Nevis is not for the fainthearted. I'm really pleased with myself, pleased with us."

"I'm proud of you, Mark. Here we are on the summit of Ben Nevis."

The mist stays at bay for the duration of their descent.

"We could've a wee rummage in a few charity shops before we go back to the hotel," Cathy suggests.

"I've never been in a charity shop. There are probably other shops I could go into."

"Plenty, you're at the gateway to the Highlands."

Mark finds a pair of golf shoes in a sports shop. Cathy finds a pair of jeans in a charity shop and a tartan shirt of the Campbell Clan in a tartan shop since she couldn't find one of them in the charity shop. By the time they start their short journey back to the hotel they notice that the mountain top is shrouded in mist.

Relaxing on the balcony of their room they look out over the loch. Mark's gaze is passive while Cathy scans the sky and the loch for migratory birds. She sees an arctic skua. This bird is considered a sea-pirate because it attacks other seabirds in mid-air forcing them to drop their food. As she focuses and re-focuses her binoculars, moving the lenses over the heads of a group of guests, she notices goldfinches feeding on teasel seeds. When she starts panning the binoculars again to get a broader loch view a sighting near the corner of the garden causes her to gasp.

"You saw something interesting, love?"

"Think so." Cathy occupies herself hurriedly with the focusing wheel of the binoculars.

Then she slips quietly in through the French door to the bedroom. Her heart is thumping. Imagine she saw him again, his long dark brown curls moving lightly in the breeze. She thought the meeting in Hope Street last March would be the last sighting of him forever. She would love to race out and tell him that they have found each other again, that life is one continuous circle and that souls once connected never totally disconnect. She steadies herself and lets reason prevail. It might only cause him pain. And in fairness to Mark she resolves to keep her feelings in check.

"Would you like some tea?" She calls out to Mark.

"No thanks, love. I'll wait till I go down to the lounge for a drink before dinner. You have some."

"I'll make a cup of coffee."

Sitting back on the loch-facing couch she mulls over her most significant sighting of the day. The old feelings rush into her mind. She sips the coffee slowly and ponders on how she will introduce her old flame to Mark if they do happen to meet face to face.

"Are you alright, Cathy? Have you given up on the bird-watching?"

"I'm sitting on the couch. I can see the loch from here."

Eventually she dislodges herself from the couch and takes out a long black dress, the one she bought in a charity shop before her wedding. Wearing a simple chain with the dress she feels she will not stand out from the crowd downstairs. She applies moisturiser to her skin after its exposure to the winds on the Nevis climb and is ready to descend to the lounge when Mark is ready. She hopes he will not be ready for a while. She is in a quandary now, weighed down with a struggle between her heart and her head.

"That dress always looks elegant, love."

"Thank you, Mark. It's my favourite." She welcomes praise for the dress after Beryl's doubts about its humble origin in a charity shop.

"You're taking the lift?"

"We've to be easy on ourselves after that climb." Deep down she is anxious to be as invisible as possible.

"There's a nice quiet corner," Mark indicates. "We've more than an hour till dinner."

"Just time for a good game of Scrabble," Cathy enthuses, after spying the stack of board games.

"Okay," Mark replies. "You can set up the board while I get the drinks."

The game commences with Cathy giving it an earnest effort and Mark making up his words in a more half-hearted manner. There are highlights of golf on the big thirty-six-inch television set.

"The Dunhill Cup's on in Edinburgh," Mark confirms.

"Would you rather watch it than play Scrabble?"

"I can do my moves as well."

Between moves he peers in the direction of the television while Cathy seriously works out strategies.

Chapter Ten - Compassion

A bell summons guests through the lounge to a room set up for a birthday party. The gaze of a passing guest is drawn to the corner where a handsome man is distracted by the television while his companion is thinking deeply. The fingers of her right hand are knitted into her ginger curls. Her left hand is holding up her chin. It is her. He stops as if stuck to the carpet. The stream of guests flows by him. Then he un-attaches himself from the carpet, blends into the stream of birthday guests and takes his place at the long table.

"It was right not to disturb her, not to cause her trouble or pain", he convinces himself. Her husband is very handsome, he thinks. His attentiveness appeared lax during the short glimpse he caught of him. He hopes he is not usually so lax in his care and attention for Cathy. She always enjoyed a good game of Scrabble. She was not having one of those riveting games this evening.

"What would you like for starter and main course?" The helpful waitress is standing at his shoulder.

"Oh, I forgot."

"Would you like a few more minutes to study the menu?"

"No, it's okay." And he picks up the menu and is initially reading it upside down.

"Butternut squash soup, egg mayonnaise, garlic mushrooms," the waitress prompts him.

"Garlic mushrooms, I love mushrooms," he enthuses.

"We've mushroom stroganoff as a main too."

"Perfect."

"Mushrooms for starter and mushrooms for main," the waitress confirms.

He shakes himself back to reality and becomes aware of the guests at his grandmother's party.

Soon Cathy declares that the game of Scrabble is suspended.

"It's like playing the game on my own."

"Sorry, love. This is very exciting." Mark apologises, with his eyes still fixed firmly on the screen.

They proceed to the Loch View dining room at the allotted time.

"Will we go for the four courses?"

"Two courses will be perfect for me, Mark. But you have a dessert. You always enjoy one."

"What would you like?"

"Definitely garlic mushrooms for starters. I love mushrooms," Cathy licks her lips. "There's mushroom on the mains as well but I think I'll have chickpea curry."

"I'll just have two courses too and I can check if there's anything else good on telly."

"That's a good idea. You could watch it in the bedroom."

"The telly in the lounge is bigger. You don't mind Cathy?"

"Not at all," Cathy replies.

"Are you sure?"

They return to their quiet corner in the lounge. After a short while Cathy excuses herself.

"I'll just head into the cloakroom. Then I'll nip upstairs and make a coffee."

"That'll be your second coffee this evening. You'll never get to sleep."

"Maybe I'll make hot chocolate."

She is fixing her hair in the cloakroom when suddenly a familiar face is reflected in the mirror beside her.

"Cathy," the woman exclaims sincerely, "our hearts were broken. We missed you so much."

"I've missed you all too, Mhairi."

"I know, hen."

"Is Hamish well again?" Cathy asks with concern.

"He's much better. Fond of you he was."

Tears flow down Cathy's cheeks. The kindly woman, who might have been her mother-in-law, tries to console her.

"He's handsome, your new husband. I saw you earlier. I didn't want to hurt anyone, didn't say a word, hen."

"Thank you so much." Cathy squeezes the woman's hand.

"I saw him from the balcony of my bedroom when he was in the garden. I didn't want to cause him pain. So I went back into my room."

"You saw him, poor hen, I'm so sorry you feel sad."

"I should've forgiven him," Cathy laments. "What he did wasn't that bad."

"Life can twist about. Maybe 'twas meant to be."

"Maybe I was meant to see you tonight to have a shoulder to cry on."

"We're at my mother's ninetieth party."

"I'm sorry for spoiling it crying like this."

"Nae worry about that. Happy I am to see you."

"Me too," Cathy lays her hand on the woman's wrist.

"When your folk are older it'll be good for them to have you back in Ireland."

"My mother was very keen I'd come home. I didn't realise it until I met Mark. She never let me waver again."

The older woman views Cathy's tear-stained face.

"Good you're not wearing mascara. Your lovely face would be in a mess."

Lovely face, Cathy thinks to herself. So generous of her to say so after how she hurt her son.

Mhairi starts to dry Cathy's tears with a tiny embroidered hanky. Then she dampens the corner of it and washes the salty bit away.

"Have you any make-up, hen?"

"No, I didn't wear any."

"You might need a bit. Your new husband will think something awful happened to you."

Taking a small jar of make-up from her handbag, Mhairi rubs it around Cathy's eyes and cheekbones.

"You look pretty as ever now."

"I won't forget you, Mhairi," Cathy says sincerely.

The two women embrace warmly.

"Did you get your hot chocolate?" Mark enquires when he notices she has sat down beside him.

"I forgot to go up."

"Where were you?"

"I was chatting with a lovely lady in the cloakroom."

"That was nice." Then an exciting moment on the television whips his attention away.

"I'll head up for the hot chocolate now."

"Don't forget where you're going," Mark teases.

"I might stay up there and do a bit of stargazing."

"You're not disappointed I'm watching this."

"Not at all," Cathy states emphatically.

She turns out the light and leaves the blinds open to watch the stars. Her old sweetheart had an innate knowledge of astronomy. He would point out Cassiopeia, like a W and Ursa Major, also called the plough, and Polaris just at the end of Ursa Minor and all the other celestial wonders. She never became an expert. Now he is downstairs at his grandmother's birthday, while she tries to identify some of the stars on this small section of the star-studded dome. Then she relaxes and allows herself to just be part of the stars and ponders on the miracle that we are made of stardust.

She can still feel the warmth of the embrace she received in the cloakroom. It was laden with love and understanding. The gentle touch of the Mhairi's fingers, as she applied make-up, is real to her. She does not remove the make-up. She wants to keep a connection to the woman who applied it. Eventually exhaustion dictates that she retires to bed. She puts on the turquoise chemise which Beryl bought for her in Madam Belles and rolls into the king-sized bed.

Sometime later Mark creeps quietly into the bedroom. He takes off his shoes and silently moves towards the window and closes out the stars with the dark blinds. Cathy is lying there, half propped up against the pillows, dazed, motionless, listening to Mark's silent movements, appreciating his efforts not to disturb her.

"Are you still awake, love?" he whispers.

"Just dozing off," she whispers back. "Was the telly good?"

"It was great. Then the guests from a ninetieth birthday party came out to the lounge. If you'd still been up, I'd have brought you back down. They're lovely people."

Cathy stops a gasp. Imagine Mark sitting beside her old sweetheart's family and maybe beside him.

"The grandson, a real hippy, was playing a guitar and singing in Scottish Gaelic. One song was Lambs in Springtime but sang in Gaelic."

"Na h-uanin a's t-earrach," Cathy adds.

"You know it?"

"It's a popular Runrig song. I've the record at home."

Cathy tries to sound matter of fact as she imagines every note being poured out by her old flame.

"Would you like to get dressed and we could go down again."

"Not all at all I'll play it when I get home."

"You look a bit sad."

"It's just part of an era," Cathy almost laments.

"An era that's still close to your heart," Mark says sympathetically.

"I suppose it was a way of life for so long."

"Thanks for giving it all up. I hope you eventually feel Mountview is home."

"I hope you weren't lonely up here on your own," he continues.

She hesitates. She was lonely, but for someone else. She feels guilty about that. Despite all his distractions and his activities Mark is a generous man.

"I was fine," Cathy insists.

"Did you have your hot chocolate?"

"I forgot."

"I'll make you a wee cup now."

"That'd be lovely, Mark."

"These china cups remind me of the ones Beryl gave me when I visited."

"Not like the mug I gave you once, remember."

"I remember. Your mother knew you fell below par."

As he beat up the milk and chocolate he continues "See anything good on telly?"

"I didn't turn it on."

"Are you sure you're alright? What were you doing all the time on your own?"

"Of course, I was alright, Mark. I used to live on my own."

"Were you doing meditation, or sky worship?"

"Sky worship, I suppose."

"Sorry I closed the blinds, love."

"No worries, I was beginning to fall asleep." She sips the chocolate from the dainty china cup.

Mark turns on the bedside lamp at his side of the bed.

"You're wearing your beautiful turquoise thingy."

"This is one of the satin chemises mam got me in Madam Belles. I'm more the sloppy t-shirt type myself."

Mark does not admit that he often moves the rebel t-shirts into the centre of the rotary line in case his mother or his grandmother might notice them.

"We'll be up bright and early for our trip down to Loch Lomond," Mark promises.

And the low light is switched off and Cathy notices that he has opened the blinds and she can see the stars again. Sadness engulfs her. She just keeps watching that part of the celestial dome visible between the curtains that Mark has kindly pulled back.

Chapter Eleven - Happy Ending

Cathy sits alone on the balcony before Mark wakes up. It has been raining and the trees and flowers have a well-washed appearance. The berries of the rowan tree are shiny and scarlet. Starlings probe for food in wet grass. There is not a sound about. In the silence she begins to wonder has she woken from a dream. Perhaps her lost love was never standing in the garden. But the encounter with his mother, Mhairi, is real and unforgettable.

She is feeling queasy. Not having the energy or inclination to scan the sky or the loch she lays her binoculars on the balcony table. A sea eagle flies by, she thinks. She hears the piping of oystercatchers from among the small shore-side rocks. A robin trips along on the top of the railing, and stops, and trips along again. It is said that robins bring messages to people to let them know all is well.

"If you've come here with a message for me little robin could you take one back from me?" Cathy whispers.

"Happy Birthday," Mark calls cheerily from the king-sized bed in the room behind her.

"I'd almost forgotten it's the 28th of September."

"You're looking very earthy today in the jeans and the tartan. They're the clothes you got yesterday."

Cathy is walking in from the balcony, wearing a blue and green tartan shirt over faded blue jeans.

"This is one of the Campbell tartans. There are different ones. But I like this one."

"And the jeans you got in the charity shop look great on you too."

"You'd never get a new pair of jeans with character like these in an ordinary shop. You need someone else to fade them."

At breakfast she has a bowl of porridge with flax seed sprinkled over it along with a piece of toast.

"You're still maintaining your beautiful figure," Mark's jokes.

"I'd need to after the wedding dress episode."

"There was nothing wrong with the wedding dress. You looked magnificent."

"Mam had to insert a wedge of material at each side. And three brides had already fitted into it."

"Perhaps they were tied in with corsets," Mark reckons.

"That's how the film stars always looked so skinny," Cathy recalls.

"You're looking pale," Marks says with concern.

"I was awake a bit during the night. I think the rain woke me."

"I hope you're okay."

"No worries. We got to the top of Nevis yesterday and that was our goal," Cathy says encouragingly.

"You could be tired even though you're like a mountain goat."

Before they leave their hotel room she walks out onto the balcony and gazes at the loch-view garden where her old sweetheart stood oblivious to her presence. They make their way down towards Loch Lomond and continue along its western shores. Then they drive eastwards and arrive at a delightful guesthouse with blue window boxes and an amazing view over Loch Lomond.

This charming guesthouse began its life as a toll house in the eighteenth century. Cathy saw it in 1981 when she completed the West Highland Way. It is an ideal resting point on the West Highland Way for walkers who crave additional comfort. She believes it will afford Mark the comfort he aspires to.

"You look a lot perkier now, love," Mark encourages as the boat sails across the short stretch of water and Cathy's eyes light up at the sight of the wooded island. They are on a boat trip to an island on Loch Lomond where a nunnery was established in the thirteenth century by an Irish saint, the mother of Saint Fillan.

Keeping with things ancient they have reserved a table for dinner in an inn which dates from the eighteenth century. It once distilled and sold its own whisky. Mark is giving Cathy his full attention.

"That's a remarkable dress, love. You've changed the whole look of it tonight with the scarf and the necklaces."

"It's just my creative streak," she jokes. "I bought it with that in mind. It saves a lot of packing and can look elegant or low-key."

"You had it low-key last night and it looked great as well. Where did you buy it?"

"Where would you think?" she quips. "I got it in a charity shop earlier in the year, as well as the chains and the scarves."

"That's unbelievable."

When they drive back to their guesthouse they linger by the loch admiring the waning crescent moon reflected in the water.

"Happy birthday again, love."

"It's still my birthday for another hour and a bit."

He pinches her nose affectionately. They are at ease in the moment, far from the distractions of golf and Mountview and even a bit removed from Cathy's own romantic dilemma. She feels it is reminiscent of the early carefree days of their courtship before marriage proposals and disputes about her campaigns changed things.

"I'll go for a walk in the morning if I'm awake early."

"That's grand, love. I'll know you're not lost when I don't see you."

Walking in the northbound direction along the West Highland Way towards Milarrochy and Sallochy Woods, she notices a tree-creeper spiraling up the rugged bark of a tree while it probes for insects. Feeling a little queasy she leans against a pine tree, re-focuses her binoculars and is rewarded with the sighting of a jay.

She hasn't the energy to go as far as Milarrochy. All the walkers are passing her by. She goes back and relaxes in the loch-side garden in front of her guesthouse. Wearing her turquoise tracksuit and a matching scarf, she is already in her travelling clothes. This afternoon they will sail back home.

Leaving her boots in the porch and her binoculars on the bed she rubs a small amount of make-up around her cheekbones to conceal her ashen appearance. When she enters the loch view lounge Mark lifts his head from the road map and smiles.

"I saw you sitting in the garden. Did you see anything interesting?

"I saw a red-breasted merganser. Earlier at the forest I saw a tree-creeper and a jay and a crossbill. It's a long time since I saw a crossbill."

"That sounds a good morning's birdwatching."

"To see both a jay and a crossbill was good. Off course I should appreciate them all."

"Did you walk far?" he enquires as they sit down together for breakfast.

"I didn't get very far. I felt a bit tired."

"The mountain walk must have wiped you out and you such a good climber."

"Maybe I'm pregnant."

72

"Pregnant, that'd be great. Our mountain baby," he marvels.

He then smiles towards their friendly host who is coming towards them, carrying a bowl of porridge in one hand and a pot of tea in the other. She stops in her tracks as she hears the speculations about their happy news and advances again with a beaming smile.

When the car is packed Cathy goes back into the loch-side garden. A goldeneye glides on the calm loch. The red-breasted merganser appears again. This ends the birdwatching in this area for this time. Maybe one day when her heart is at ease she will return to Scotland. Despite his distraction on the evening of the Dunhill Cup, Mark is a very agreeable and pleasant travel companion.

They check the road map and chose the cable-stayed Erskine Bridge which spans the River Clyde. Their journey continues along the A77, so familiar to Cathy for years. The signs for Royal Troon Golf Club distract Mark for a minute.

"Would you like to take a look at it," Cathy suggests.

"I think we're both too casually dressed to visit such an eminent establishment."

"Eminent, what makes it so important?" Cathy teases.

"Its history maybe, founded as it was back in 1878," Mark answers musingly.

"The guesthouse and the Inn where we'd dinner began in the previous century," Cathy reasons.

"I'll think we'll keep going anyway," Mark decides. "It's a bit early in the day. They mightn't have the same casual arrangements for morning coffee as the Bay Club."

"It's easy-going and welcoming at the Bay alright," Cathy agrees. "You wouldn't be conscious you were in a golf club at all."

"That's where we started our first date," Mark says encouragingly.

Cathy is thinking about the first time they met at the Bay. It is only sixteen months ago. She was enjoying a carefree date with the Adonis of her school and at the same time trying to get over a broken romance. Later in the afternoon they returned to the Bay Golf Club and she tasted the most delicious stuffed mushrooms ever.

Mark glances towards her. She has not reacted with romantic enthusiasm at the mention of their first date.

"And I think we'd our biggest row there," he adds mischievously.

"We had. Don't remind me of that though. I think you and Beryl teamed up to get things back on track."

"I've a lot to thank Beryl for. And do you remember almost jilting me at the altar? You just stumbled through the words."

"I do."

"That's clearer than the 'I do' muttered on our Wedding Day."

"Muttered?"

"Yeah muttered and I felt relieved you muttered them at all. Thankfully Patience was happy. Another vicar might've thrown you out."

She feels a fondness for him, thinking about his vulnerability in front of that dazzling sea of guests, including the past pupils of St Matthew's, the members of Mountview Golf Club and all the family.

"I didn't mean to upset you, Mark." Cathy says instinctively.

"I know you didn't intend to upset me. I just wasn't sure if you wanted to marry me. You sort of mumbled "I will" when I asked you to get engaged as well."

They lapse into silence, not a sulky silence, rather the silence needed to absorb the words that have passed between them. The green Volvo moves smoothly along, leaving the Scottish miles behind and soon they realise that they have plenty of time to spare. They go into the town of Ayr and visit the birthplace of the famous Scottish poet Robert Burns and reminisce a bit about Miss Harrison's English classes, though the seamless harmony that goes with poetry is ruffled and an uncertainty lingers. They sit together on a bench. Mark moves his left hand towards Cathy's right hand and they interlink their little fingers and sit silently. Nearby a chaffinch pokes its beak into the gravel to retrieve crumbs from a picnic table.

Chapter Twelve - Feeling Lost

Cathy and Mark arrive back to their cottage, now brightly swathed in nasturtiums. Five giant sunflowers still stand like sentries. Cathy appreciates the beauty of her surroundings and the quaintness of the cottage which has stood solid as a rock for a couple of centuries. The unbroken succession of flowers has been nurtured by Marilyn over the years. The whole village has been maintained by Marilyn and by all the other hardworking volunteers who work to enhance its beauty. But the grove, which Cathy constantly explores, was Grandma Rosetta's creation.

It is nearing nightfall as they carry their belongings from the car.

"Welcome home." Marilyn greets them from the shop door. "Come in when you're ready and I'll prepare you something to eat here."

Marilyn, Benny and Grandma Rosetta live in the accommodation above the shop.

Cathy came to the cottage as a new bride in July. Little by little it might dawn on her that it is home. The first of the next generation may be developing within her. This might help to anchor her and give her a sense of place.

'You'd never see a hippy or a rebel in Mountview. They'd be like an alien species,' Mark pronounced on the day of their biggest disagreement. She often feels like an alien now. She wishes she could follow some of her own interests and not feel tethered in a straight-jacket of pretense and pleasing.

Marilyn, Benny and Grandma Rosetta are in the upstairs sitting-room waiting to greet them.

"Tell me all about the mountain climb," Grandma Rosetta urges. "I used to ski in the mountains in Switzerland when I was in finishing school."

"Switzerland, I'd say that was magical," Cathy enthuses.

"It was indeed. The Institute trained young ladies in social graces and good manners," Rosetta elaborates.

Cathy glances at her father-in-law, Benny, and thinks he is not at all like the son of one with such airs and graces. She wonders if Grandma Rosetta is a sort of alien in her own regal way.

"Our mountain baby," Mark muses, when the tests are confirmed positive.

"Well almost our mountain baby," Cathy agrees.

Mark seems very happy about the prospects of fatherhood. She thinks about his misgivings a few days ago, when he admitted that he just wasn't sure if she wanted to marry him. Maybe giving birth to Baby Wright will be some recompense.

The days shorten. October gives way to November. She always feels that November days end too soon. By December she has usually come to terms with short days. This December she will be busy in the shop for the Christmas rush.

"How are you getting on? You never say," Beryl probes one afternoon when Cathy arrives.

"To tell you the truth I feel a bit lost, and lonely."

"How would you be lonely with four other adults around you, not to mention the customers?"

"I get along very well with Benny. I just feel lost, that's all."

"You didn't marry your father-in-law," her mother answers swiftly. "You never bring Mark down."

"He's usually very busy, going to meetings and here and there."

"He's a businessman. You've to understand he'll be busy. You've all a woman could ask for, and still you're not happy."

"I want to be myself."

"Why can't you find something like the ICA?"

"It's not that I've anything against the ICA. You and Vera do great things in it. It's just not my thing."

"What's your thing? You're a married woman. You'll have to settle yourself."

"Maybe I'm homesick for the farm and the sheep."

"You hadn't got them when you were in Glasgow."

"Maybe I miss Scotland. I don't know. I'll just head up the fields for a walk."

"Where's Cathy?" Colin asks. "I see her car outside."

"She went for a walk up the fields, said she feels lost and lonely, and all she's got going for her."

"Ummh."

"Don't you agree with me?"

"She must feel lonely or she wouldn't have said it."

"It's no way to start a marriage. What'd Mark think if she said the same to him?"

Colin makes no response to this remark.

"I'll head out to meet her."

He finds her sitting on a white rock and sits down on the one beside her. From the house these small rocks look like extra sheep. When they were children they were their special seats.

"Mam said you're feeling lonely, sis."

"I shouldn't have told her. She asked me how I was getting on and it came out."

"I'm so sorry. Maybe you wanted someone to tell you to postpone things when you shared your secret on the boat."

"Don't blame yourself, bro. At that stage I'd decided not to cause pain to mam and Mark and everyone."

"Mark's a good man," she muses. "I just don't think we'd enough time to work out things."

"I think mam put too much pressure on you."

"I'll have to practice forgiveness towards mam. It was the way of things for her. She wanted me back. It'd be ironic if we weren't speaking to one another."

"That's generous of you."

The siblings sit silently for a few minutes on the white stones that resemble sheep.

"I'll give you a happy secret. Only Mark knows."

"I think I know what it has to be."

"I'm going to keep the news quiet for another while."

"That's great, sis. Things might change for you then."

"Thanks so much, bro."

"I'll bring up the pram and cot and the Moses basket before then."

"The big Silver Cross pram," Cathy reminisces.

"I saw Colin and Cathy sitting on the rocks they used to sit on when they were children," their father remarks when he comes into the kitchen.

"Cathy still behaves like a child. She said she feels lost." Beryl sighs. "I ask you, a newly married woman feeling lost."

"She must be when she said she was," Andy reckons.

"She should pull herself together."

"I worried about you pressuring her before the wedding. Maybe give her some space now."

"Good you're back, dad. I was hoping I'd see you," Cathy says cheerily when she comes back in.

"Glad I didn't miss you, Cathy."

"I'm away now, sorry for rushing."

"That was a short visit," Beryl remarks.

"Mark's going to a meeting at the club. And Marilyn's going to choir practice. I'll make dinner early for Mark and then do the shop."

"You'd want to dress up before you go into the shop." Beryl eyes her tartan shirt and her faded denim jeans.

"Mark likes these, thinks I look earthy in them. Got the jeans in a charity shop in Scotland when I was over," Cathy says proudly. "And this is a Campbell tartan."

"Earthy, it's elegant you should be. You'll make a show of Mark."

"I just want to be myself."

"What'll the customers think of you?"

"They won't all think the same anyway." She tries to sound upbeat.

"Next time I'm up your way I'll ring in case we could meet for lunch," Andy suggests.

"That'll be great." Cathy's face lights up. "If it's one of my days off we could've lunch in the cottage.

"You love the cottage," her father affirms.

"I do, and the grove behind it is my special place. You'll love the grove, dad."

"I might get up next week."

"If you meet her will you talk some sense into her," Beryl requests as Cathy's car disappears out on to the road. "Insisting she wants to be herself, I ask you a newly married woman wanting to be herself."

"I won't bring anything like that up unless she mentions it. In time it might work out for her."

Chapter Thirteen - Finding Common Ground

The shop is a hive of activity for the month of December, with everyone in Mountview and its environs procuring their needs and their luxuries. She enjoys the increased activity. New Year arrives, and she shares her news about the expected arrival date of the baby. It is received with jubilation and 1987 begins on a happy note.

"Now that she's carrying Mark's baby it might settle her." Beryl speculates as she knits a lemon coloured jacket for the expected baby.

Cathy's landscape design skills are welcomed when plans are drawn up for the enhancement of the village for the new season. It is thirty years since Marilyn and an eager team worked tirelessly for one of the first Best Kept contests back in the fifties. There have been no gaps in the enthusiasm since. New ideas for the season are shared at a meeting in the hall beside the church. Then the team beavers about to ensure that they bring their plans to fruition before the adjudicators arrive during the summer. Cathy appreciates the local assets such as the grove, the castle and the village pump. The village pump would have been a meeting place in olden times, before running water and taps were installed in houses.

The village is reaching the pinnacle of its floral magnificence as May gives way to June. Each evening the villagers can enjoy the sights and sounds of swifts as they dash around their nest sites in the castle walls. Other significant events around the world are happening as a result of citizen action. On the eighth of June 1987, on the other side of the world, the New Zealand Nuclear Free Zone, Disarmament, and Arms Control Act is passed. The seeds for this success were sown in the 1950s, with the formation of the local Campaign for Nuclear Disarmament.

Another special event takes place on the same date as the New Zealand achievement. Baby Ben Wright arrives into the world.

Here he is a miracle in a Moses' basket. She lifts the tiny bundle and holds him closely. She lays him down again and gets a better look at his scrunched up little face, his tiny waving fists and his perfect little feet. She thinks of all the miles those tiny feet might carry him. Mark gazes at him with great tenderness and he too is enamoured by the tiny toes. They sit quietly, each holding a tiny foot between forefingers.

"Imagine all the places those wee feet will carry him," Mark marvels.

"And to think of all the little bones and muscles that make them up," Cathy muses.

"The scientist within you speaking," Mark jokes and pinches her nose.

Ben is the name chosen for their firstborn son, primarily after his grandfather Benny Wright. They both agree that it is also a suitable name for a baby whose existence was known just a couple of days after they climbed Ben Nevis. Their mountain baby is here.

Sitting at the back of the cottage, she admires her baby as he sleeps in the big pram beside her. Bees busily buzz from flower to flower. Hypericum, now in full yellow blossom, seems to be a favourite this afternoon. Hidcote Hypericum, of the St. John's Wort family, bursts in bloom around the feast of Saint John on twenty-fourth of June.

It is during these summer months that Cathy gets to know Grandma Rosetta, now Great-grandma, a bit better. They often walk together in the grove, the grove Rosetta herself planted all those years ago, Rosetta wearing a floppy straw hat and Cathy carrying Ben in a sling. The biggest impediment to them getting to know one another is Rosetta's deafness.

"Planting native woodland was a generous gift to posterity," Cathy remarks to Rosetta one afternoon. Rosetta cannot hear and an encouraging compliment such as this is difficult to convey sincerely if you have to shout.

"What did you say?" Rosetta cups her hand around her ear.

"I said this grove is like a gift to your grandchildren and great-grandchildren," Cathy repeats, raising her tone by a few decibels.

"Thank you, dear," Rosetta replies.

They have come a long way since the times when Rosetta seemed obsessed with the disappointment that Mark had not married a practicing Church of Ireland girl.

"The Wright wives always had a tradition of duty and responsibility towards the church," Rosetta explained shortly after Cathy came as a bride to Mountview. "That's why the church still stands beautiful, a credit to the parish, and to the workers in the parish."

"It is a beautiful building." Cathy spoke in a very clear tone to enable Rosetta to hear her.

"It's more than a building, dear. It's a church."

This afternoon they are at ease together.

"I once thought Mark would marry a vicar," Rosetta muses.

"His friend, Stephen, did," remarks Cathy simply.

"I don't think Mark made a bad choice. I'm beginning to think he made a very good choice, dear."

"Thank you, Grandma Rosetta."

It has probably taken the whole year for Rosetta to come to terms with Mark's choice of wife. Now they are finding common ground in their mutual love for the grove.

Cathy clears out some of the lower branches of the trees to allow light to filter through. She is mindful that too much disturbance would change the eco-system of the forest floor and interfere with the rich herb layer.

By early autumn acorns are falling to the ground with a gentle thud. One or two might survive to become an oak tree and the grove will go on regenerating itself as it has done since Rosetta watched over it in its infancy. The acorns which do not become oak trees have not lived in vain. More than a hundred birds and animals have acorns as part of their diet.

As Rosetta becomes feebler she usually sits and gazes through her upstairs window and watches Cathy tending the grove like a dedicated steward.

"She's a mystery girl," she remarks to Benny one day. "She has no interest in taking responsibility for the church. On the other hand, nobody else ever took such an interest in the grove. 'A natural temple' that's how she described it."

"Marilyn will look after the church for another while anyhow. Nobody else paid so much attention to the grove since you kept a watchful eye on it," Benny says encouragingly to his mother.

"What's she doing now?" Rosetta is peering curiously through the window.

"She's building a new bench for you around your favourite tree."

The oldest tree in the grove, the grand old oak," Rosetta muses. "That's very kind of her."

On fine sunny days Cathy helps Rosetta down the stairs and links her into the grove until they reach the new bench, where she sits admiring the sylvan wonders. The light filters through and occasionally a breeze blows up through the clearing where Rosetta sits beneath the oak, clutching a rug around her.

An idea occurs to Cathy one afternoon as she links her grandmother-in-law from the grove to her room above the shop. She would empty and refurbish the store room just off the shop sitting room and transform it into a self-contained unit for Rosetta.

"This shows great belief in Grandma Rosetta's future," Marks encourages as he sees Cathy making room for the grocery products in another part of the shop.

"I'm hoping to have the whole project finished for her ninety-third birthday."

Chapter Fourteen - Baby Boys

Ben's soft ginger curls bob about as he wobbles up and down the floor trying out his first pair of boots. He is the only baby among five adults until one brisk April morning in 1989 when his baby brother Jack arrives. Endowed with a head of dark brown hair the new baby looks like the Wright's. Before long Jack seems to be taking over some of Ben's possessions and lies in the pram while Ben sits on a seat at the end.

The former landscape designer has returned from Geneva. Cathy leaves the job, with a mutual agreement that if short term assistance is needed she will fill in. She soon becomes immersed in the responsibilities of motherhood, the shop and, in season, the Best Kept Areas project. The latter activity fosters a common link between herself and her mother-in-law, Marilyn. Care of the baby boys further fastens links between the two women.

By the time Ben is ready to enter kindergarten Andrew, the third-born son of Cathy and Mark, has arrived. The well-sprung pram bounces along towards the church gate and up the slope to the kindergarten, which is in the side room of the church. Baby Andrew lies in the Silver Cross pram while Jack occupies the seat and four-year-old Ben trips along as fast as his little feet can carry him.

The little Wright brothers come first in their grandmother's list of priorities. She ceases her involvement in the grocers' benevolent fund. Another commitment she relinquishes is the Mothers' Union, feeling it might be better to do some hands-on nurturing, and leave the Mothers' Union to younger women.

Mark takes a macro-view of life, immersing himself in wider community activities, including Mountview Golf Club and the grocers' benevolent fund. His charisma makes a success of everything he gets involved in and the success kindles his enthusiasm to do more. It is not that he does not have great fondness for his small sons. He is warm and kindly when he around them.

One by one the boys go to kindergarten and then to Mountview Primary School until they are all in Primary School. After school and during the holidays they play in tree-houses and on swings in the grove, which is carpeted with bluebells in spring and strewn with acorns and fallen leaves in autumn. Hazel nuts, gathered in autumn, are broken open with a hammer on the strong kitchen table. And when there is a winter fall of snow a bakery bread tray suffices as a toboggan to swish them down the slope on a narrow path between the trees.

Like the grove, Cathy's life falls into a rhythm, albeit a fast rhythm of school, homemaking, shop-keeping and village tidying. Every now and then in the early morning before the rhythm of the day speeds up she goes out to the back of the cottage and into what she considers a sacred grove. There she finds solitude. Nemus, the Latin word for a grove, also means sanctuary and Nemetona is believed to be the Goddess of Sacred Groves.

Great-grandma Rosetta has left this world before Finn arrives. She left shortly before her one hundredth birthday, no fuss, just a quiet slipping away after a short phase of removal from reality when her mind was no longer tuned into matters such as the church or the grove. Instead she drifted back into life at the finishing school over eighty years before, when her companions were often the daughters of baronesses. Cathy helped to care for her in her last years and Rosetta had her wish to stay in her new room. She is convinced that Rosetta's spirit lives on in the grove, and especially on the bench which surrounds the oak tree.

Regularly the memories of Cathy's lost love in Scotland rise to the surface as she stands quietly among the trees on a crisp early morning or gazes up through the filigree of branches and leaves to the skyscape above. She often cherishes the precious moments of her encounter with Mhairi in the hotel by the loch on the eve of her thirty-first birthday.

As the years move on, and life's responsibilities increase, she pushes these thoughts to the back of her mind. At those times she thinks of her young sons, Ben, Jack, Andrew and baby Finn. She reasons with herself that had her life journey taken a different direction she would not have had any of them. Eventually through the sheer business of dealing with life's commitments the memory of her lost love is filed away in the recesses of her mind and the pangs of regret become infrequent.

Chapter Fifteen - The Dale

Cathy visits the Dale weekly. She enjoys watching the lambs frolic in spring and the sheep flocking together as they graze or move from place to place. A verse of Runrig's song Lambs in Springtime, Na h-uanin a's t-earrach, runs through her mind one afternoon and it takes her back more than fifteen years to when she saw her old flame in a Scottish hotel and then heard from Mark that he sang that song in the lounge at his grandmother's party.

You are like the Lambs in springtime

Running around jumping and carefree

But have you ever noticed the older sheep

When one moves they all follow

And when the years start departing from you

The difficult days, the darker days

Keep your candle aloft and lit

Walk this world with a young heart

Only forty-five years have passed for her yet. She tries to keep positive in the moment as she watches the carefree lambs.

She hopes the land will remain uncontaminated. The reprocessing plant, a little over hundred miles away across the Irish Sea, is like an ominous cloud. The Chernobyl disaster of 1986, the year she got married, contaminated sheep grazing land as far west as Scotland, Wales and the Wicklow Hills. Sellafield is much closer. A leak or an accident could happen.

In 1952 three years before she was born radioactive waste from the plant, then known as Windscale, started to be released into the

Irish Sea and she was only two when there was a fire at the plant. The Windscale fire of 10 October 1957 was classed as the worst nuclear accident in Britain's history.

When an unexpected calamity occurs, the day after the vernal equinox in 2001, concern about the nuclear plant and all the other trials and tribulations of life lose their prominence for a while. A stark radio announcement portends a dark period as a case of foot and mouth disease is confirmed. The officials and snipers are merciless, garnering every animal from every farm, from every hill, until the Dale is silent.

"Is your journey absolutely necessary?" Cathy is asked as she is stopped at a checkpoint.

"My family lost all their sheep. Sheep's my father's life since he was born. He's devastated."

The car is disinfected. Cathy drives on, knowing that the precautions are useless for the sheep and the farmers in the Dale.

"We could look after the boys. You could take Finn and stay with your family for a wee while. It's stressful going through checkpoints." Marilyn speaks with concern, as Cathy prepares to go to visit her parents.

"That's so generous, grandma." Cathy hugs her mother-in-law appreciatively. Marilyn responds warmly, even though embracing is not part of her everyday culture.

With her pre-schooler Finn, she sets out on her journey. It is now, more than any time before, that she feels the benefit of living close to the Dale. Marilyn looks after her three grandsons, foregoing choir practice and other church duties, to prepare their favourite meals and help with homework. She finds it difficult to explain some of the science to Jack, who struggles with his homework for hours.

Andrew helps Benny in the shop, putting like with like on the shelves, tidying up the newspapers and magazines and checking that the birthday cards are placed in their right age-group.

"I'm going to be a shopkeeper when I grow up," he announces as he gets childlike fulfilment from his work. Andrew is a loveable child, happy and agreeable, with red hair and the characteristic Campbell space between his front teeth. When the shop is quiet Benny encourages him to scan the barcodes, get the total on the cash register and count out the change. The novice shopkeeper gets plenty of encouragement from the customers. This is special time for Andrew in the interval between his return from primary school and the return of Ben and Jack from Hightown Grammar School.

Marilyn takes advantage of the time while Andrew is in the shop to speak to Mark.

"I was hoping you'd take some time off to help Jack with his homework."

"You know how important it is that I don't let a chance go by to promote the Ball," Mark reasons.

"It's also important that Jack doesn't fall behind in his first year."

"Maybe we should ask Cathy to come home. Beryl and Andy must be alright by now."

"Their whole way of life has been wiped out. It's not something they'll get over instantly."

"It's a big upheaval, not having her here."

"Maybe that's because she takes responsibility for so much," Marilyn stresses.

"I've responsibilities too," Mark says defensively. "The money from the Ball eases the hardship of grocers who fall on hard times."

"I know how great the cause is. But just now Cathy's in the middle of a very distressful situation for her family?"

"I suppose you're right."

"I know I'm right, Mark. Cathy threw herself totally into everything here. It mustn't have been easy for her coming from a different community. And only for her Grandma Rosetta would've had to go into a nursing home."

"I appreciate that."

He thinks back to the time of their engagement when he cajoled Cathy to live up to the image of the daughter-in-law his mother would like. Now his mother is firmly on her side.

"You should show your appreciation by not grudging the time she's spending with her family," Marilyn scolds.

"It's not that I don't appreciate Cathy. It's just that this is a critical time to get momentum going for the Ball."

"Things have to be kept in perspective. You do what you can while you can. When you can't someone else will have to step into your shoes. They stepped into mine when I felt it was time to be here more for Cathy and the children. And the charity's still going well over hundred years after it began."

"You're cutting me down to size," Mark concedes. Yet he keeps his affable front and does not cause a major disagreement.

"I often regretted not spending enough time with you and your sisters. I felt I got a second chance when your children came along."

"I do appreciate how you've cared for them," Mark says thankfully.

"Sharon Henderson put a notice up in the shop about grinds in maths and science. I could sort out a few grinds for Jack. What'd you think about that?"

Sharon was one of the many young students who worked part-time in Wright's. Now that she is graduated her part-time activity is giving grinds.

"That'd be perfect. Thanks for that, mam."

Marilyn thinks how quickly Mark can get out of a tangle.

"We can leave Cathy to stay another wee while," Marilyn encourages.

"I hope Finn's not missing us too much," Mark speculates.

"I'd say Finn will be fine."

When the country is declared free of foot and mouth it is down to commendations for those involved in the successful containment of the disease. For the Dale, the quarantined corner of the country, the pain persists. The silence continues as sheep bleat no more.

"The Dale contained the sacrificial lambs." Andy says sadly, when he hears the success of the eradication programme praised on the radio. He has aged over the past five weeks. The once sprightly man, approaching his seventy-eight birthday, now looks stooped and old. His wavy ginger hair appears more bleached and has more strands of grey. He too has that gap between his front teeth which still gives his face an impish friendly look.

As Cathy prepares to go back to Mountview she gazes forlornly at the fields and hills once dotted with sheep. All she can see are the two white stones where she and Colin often sat when they were young. The stones that once resembled extra sheep on the hill now stand stark and white and alone.

Chapter Sixteen – Beryl

The repercussions of foot and mouth disease continue. In some families it takes a human as well an animal toll. Initially Colin and Cathy believe their father's broken heart will never heal and that he will succumb to illness, and maybe death, as other farmers did. Instead it is Beryl who becomes ill shortly after the terrifying silence descended on the Dale.

Marilyn takes the young Wright brothers under her wing again allowing Cathy to spend time with her mother during her last months on this earth.

"You've a very helpful mother-in-law."

"I have," Cathy says with conviction. "I really appreciated how she took care of the boys when I was here last spring."

"That was a hard time," Beryl says solemnly, "the saddest time in my life. And it still is sad to think about all the lovely sheep killed so heartlessly."

"It was heart-breaking," Cathy agrees.

"It was good having you and little Finn with us then."

"I really appreciated Marilyn's thoughtfulness. It probably created a stronger bond between us."

"That's the way of things," Beryl says quietly.

"And Benny's one of the kindest men you could meet."

"You were always fond of him."

"I was, from the very beginning."

"It's good you're living near us, or fairly near us, anyway."

Wearing a lemon-coloured bed-jacket Beryl is sitting up in bed. From here there is a spectacular view through the large Georgian windows of her bedroom. Today Beryl is drifting in and out of sleep and has little energy to enjoy the view. She is wearing a small amount of lipstick and make-up and even a touch of eye-shadow, which is noticeable when her eye-lids close again. Her wavy red hair is styled neatly and there is not a grey strand to be seen. Vera, her ICA friend, has retired from her post as public health nurse. She visits Beryl regularly and often styles her hair. If there are any secrets about how this rich shade of red is maintained Vera is not divulging them.

Cathy sits in silence. Her father takes her in a cup of tea and one for Beryl in case she wakes up soon. He places a saucer over this one. Cathy observes the sleeping face of the woman who so adamantly kept an eye on her until she walked down the aisle with Mark, and even after. She has forgiven her mother long ago for her unceasing pressure. Less than a year ago this same woman was disconsolate when every sheep was silenced. It was during this tragic period that a strong empathy and a deep love towards her mother welled up in Cathy's heart.

"You might've had other life plans in mind," Beryl whispers when she wakes up again. "I'm very glad you chose the one you did."

"You'd have disowned me if I didn't." Cathy tries to add a bit of levity as she hands her mother the china cup of warm tea.

"Mark's a good man. I don't see him often, him being busy and everything." Beryl excuses the infrequency of his visits to the Dale.

"He's not a bad man," Cathy agrees. "His activities certainly improve the situation of some people, especially his work for grocers who might've fallen on hard times, or unexpected illness."

"You'd never imagine grocers falling on hard times," Beryl muses. "You imagine them sitting on little goldmines."

"If you'd known that you mightn't have urged me to marry a shopkeeper at all."

"Only for my coaxing and scolding you'd have let him slip through your fingers."

"If you say that too loud you might invalidate my marriage. You know the question, *did you come here of your own free will.*"

"I hope you weren't that unwilling. I did get a bit of a shock when you stumbled through the vows."

"Yeah, Mark said shortly after we got married that I muttered them."

"It must've been a shock for the poor man there at the altar not knowing what'd happen."

"I remember how frightening it was being central stage in front all the glamorous guests. It's not what I'd have chosen myself."

"It probably wasn't," Beryl speculates.

Beryl recalls the discussions about a trousseau when Cathy had bought her wedding clothes in a charity shop. Her flowers were from the wet meadow.

"I'd have gotten married at the standing stones in the forest."

"What'd Mark's family have thought?"

"What'd you have thought?" Cathy gently teases her mother.

"Where would people eat?"

"The forest would've been my preference for the ceremony," Cathy says. "I'd have been happy to compromise and have a buffet in the parish hall afterwards."

"Ah no, Cathy, that wouldn't be right for a business man's wedding. And when you said you were lost and lonely, just a short time later, I was worried again," Beryl muses. "But you got through it."

"We're married nearly sixteen years and have four sons to show for it."

"I'm proud of you, Cathy."

"You are?"

"I am."

"Remember mam you said that you were introduced to dad as an ideal match. Did you have other boyfriends before that?"

"From I was fifteen I used to spend all my school holidays sneaking out to meet a boy. His name was Donal," Beryl smiles at the excitement of this furtive teenage romance. "We were madly in love, wrote letters all through school term."

"Did you keep them?"

"They're all together tied in red ribbon in a chocolate box." Beryl points towards the top of the wardrobe.

"And what happened?"

"We were speeding down a hill one evening, me on the cross bar of his bicycle, when we met my mother walking up the hill with her bicycle."

"What did you do?"

"We had to keep going. Had Donal braked I'd have been thrown over the handlebars." Beryl recalls her mother's disapproving face.

"Then of course I'd to come back to pack my case for boarding school the next day. She was waiting, furious 'Let me never see you with that boy again. You're leading him up the garden path.'"

"Were you disappointed?"

"I was. I think her biggest problem was he was a Catholic boy."

"I had to write and tell him what happened. I got back a lovely letter and I cried for several nights under the blankets in the dormitory," Beryl recalls sadly.

"Imagine Grandma Jane who didn't get a chance to choose her own husband being so hard on you."

"It was the way of things then. That was back in the forties."

Cathy's mind strays for a moment thinking that the same sentiments prevailed in the eighties.

"And I was very happy to see you married to Mark, even if I'd to be stern with you,"

"Now I've no daughters to coax into the wedding dress. If anything happens to you I'll place it with you in the grave as an artefact."

"Not if anything happens, Cathy, it's more definitive than that," Beryl says stoically. "And if you're putting the dress in as an artefact you might as well put it on me."

Cathy squeezes her mother's hand to quietly acknowledge her statement.

"There's a flowery chocolate box on the top of the wardrobe, with a bundle of letters in it. You can put them in, as artefacts."

"I will mam."

"And I'd like my family and friends to have a buffet in the parish hall. It'd be homely," Beryl muses.

"And you didn't think it was good enough for a businessman's wedding. Of course it was with so much soul and connection and community spirit within its walls."

"I like to hear that, Cathy."

"I know I'm not an ardent church-goer but I appreciate its part of my building blocks."

Mother and daughter smile companionably.

"Jennifer has the details of music and readings. She'll do solo."

They fall into silence for a while.

"Did you ever see Donal again?" Cathy asks when she has allowed her mother time to rest.

"I didn't see him for years. Then one day Vera was talking about the lovely abbot in the friary, Father Donal."

"Did you get butterflies thinking about him living behind the friary walls?" Cathy is having a playful banter with her mother.

"I didn't make the connection straight away. A while later Vera mentioned the great sermon Father Donal O'Neill gave at the novena. I'd heard years ago that he'd entered a monastery."

"Did you decide to go to the novena to be able to go into the friary?"

"I couldn't tell Vera I wanted to go to a novena in a Catholic friary just to see the abbot. Vera doesn't know about the romance."

"You know now that he's safely behind the walls with all the power in his hands."

"I don't think power would sit well with Donal," Beryl reckons. "I did see him a few times," she adds with almost childlike impishness.

"How did you manage that?"

"A lot of people go for walks in the grounds. I started doing some of my walks there too."

"It was probably time for a change from walking all around the farm," Cathy lightly teases.

"They're beautiful grounds. There's a big Way of the Cross all around the grounds, finishing with a replica of Calvary on a big mound."

"I guess you didn't go to follow the Way of the Cross, mam."

"No."

"Who recognised who first?"

"I recognised him. I was looking out for him."

"And what did he say?"

"He said I hadn't changed at all."

"Now I know why you keep yourself all spruced up. Perhaps I should give you a chance to have your beauty sleep."

Cathy removes one of the pillows and Beryl has a chance to dose off for a while. She sits by her mother's bed thinking about her mother's lost teenage romance, thinking how ironic it was that her mother would later steer her into an ideal match. She understands now that Beryl accepted these carefully chosen unions as 'the way of things'.

Chapter Seventeen - The Abbot

Vera slips in quietly.

"She looks very rested and peaceful," Vera says admiringly.

"Her hair's beautiful. You keep it great for her."

"Your mother always took an interest in her appearance."

"She did. I remember how disappointed she was when I bought my wedding clothes in a charity shop instead of Madam Belles."

"I remember that too. I went with her to Madam Belles and we found that beautiful pastel green outfit. I saw it on an assistant's arm. She was about to display it in the window."

"And it was the right size?"

"A size twelve was what your mother wanted and there it was."

"It was really elegant on her and a perfect colour with her hair," Cathy agrees.

"I was at the Country Market this morning. They all miss her. I brought some of the brown bread your father likes, and a jar of Ellen's raspberry jam and Doreen's potato cakes."

"Mam loved going there. Only an hour ago she was wondering how the market went today."

"It went very well today. The customers love the new venue. It's bright and sunny and shows everything in a good light," Vera enthuses.

"Mam said there's space for the customers to relax and have a cuppa."

"Three of your mother's knitted bed jackets sold today, a lemon and two lilacs and one of her lace christening robes."

"She'll be delighted to hear that."

"Doreen bought the christening robe for her grandson."

"I'll bring her down for a short while next Friday if she's up for it. And we can have a cuppa."

"That'd be great Cathy. She's sleeping soundly now."

"She chatted quite a bit earlier. Just a short while ago I settled down her pillows to let her have a rest."

"I might head off to the friary now that's she sleeping. Father Donal's leading the Way of the Cross each Friday during Lent. This is his first one."

"Did you walk down, Vera?"

"I did."

"I can bring you back on my way home."

"I'll come back to see your mother later." She lays her hand lightly on Beryl's shoulder and leaves the room.

Cathy does the same and leaves the room after Vera. She hugs her father and promises him she'll get down tomorrow.

"Don't be rushing yourself if it's not suitable," her father advises. "We'll all be looking out for mam."

"You can give me a call anytime you want, Andy," Vera assures him.

"Thanks very much Vera and thanks for the goodies from the market."

"I'll go on as far as the friary with you and walk home," Vera suggests to Cathy as she slows down the car. Cathy continues. When she gets to the wide gates of the friary she drives up towards buildings and furtively surveys the grounds where her mother used to walk and be rewarded with a greeting from Father Donal.

"There's Father Donal on the steps. He has been remembering Beryl in his prayers since I told him she was unwell."

"He looks a kindly man," Cathy remarks.

"I'd say he was a handsome man in his young days," Vera reckons. "He probably broke some hearts before he landed in the friary."

Cathy turns the car and slows down to let Vera out. The abbot walks towards them. He is tall and handsome and stands erect, belying his seventy-four years. Partly hidden by his greying beard is an affable face and behind his dark rimmed glasses are twinkling eyes.

"This is Beryl's daughter, Cathy."

"It's lovely to meet you, Cathy. I've been remembering your mother in my prayers."

"I really appreciate that. And I'd say she would too."

"I think you're very like her, Cathy," he says fondly. Vera is intrigued to know how he knows what Beryl looks like. She didn't think they met.

"We're all alike, all redheads, my dad and my brother too."

Cathy continues her journey home. She sees her mother in a new light, as one who loved and lost, through no fault of her own. She had heard the love story, seen the grounds and spoken to the boy, now a seventy-four-year old man, once broken-hearted by a letter written under duress. His reply, together with his other letters, is now treasured in a flowery chocolate box.

On Sunday morning the twenty-fourth of March Beryl's spirit leaves her, just in time for a notice to be brought to the church where Cathy's wedding brought her joy, or at least relief, nearly sixteen years ago.

Cathy is climbing on a rickety chair to find the chocolate box when Colin walks into the bedroom.

"Take care sis, you'll fall and hurt yourself," her brother speaks instinctively. "I'd say there's nothing up there except dust."

"Dust, bro? Mam would be horrified to think there were dusty corners in her house."

She doesn't venture up again until she is sure she is alone. Then she finds a strong stool, climbs up again, retrieves the dust coated chocolate box and places its contents, including a youthful photo of Donal, into an embroidered bag. She keeps one photo of her mother, as a teenager, along with Donal. She sits back on the bed, the antique oak bed that faces out on to the Dale, and she reverently removes one letter from the bundle in the embroidered bag and reads it, and a second one. Then the pain of perusing the evidence of innocent teenage love overcomes her.

She returns to the parlour where her mother is reposing in the champagne-pink wedding dress, first worn one hundred and seven years ago. She places the bundle of love letters, written in the forties, beside her mother under the linen cover. Then she sits quietly beside her mother and reflects on the conversation they had only last month.

Early on the Monday morning, before the stream of mourners arrive, Vera's car drives up near the front door. There is no need to use the antique door knocker. The door is open for people to freely walk into the parlour and pay their respects to Beryl. Cathy and Andy are sitting by Beryl's coffin when Father Donal walks through the door with Vera. A friar has never been to the house before. Andy is moved to witness such a gesture.

"The loss of the sheep and all that pain cut deeply into her," Andy says to the abbot.

"It was a horrendous time for the Dale," the friar agrees sadly.

"It's exactly a year ago. Her health went into decline then and she's never really been well since."

"Vera told me how her health was failing. Foot and mouth robbed even more than our sheep."

"We'd nearly fifty-one lovely years together."

Cathy, who is sitting next to the abbot, is feeling emotional that beneath the linen cover are the abbot's love letters written so lovingly in the nineteen-forties. He gazes at Beryl. She looks serene and peaceful. The pain and devastation of the past year and the general anxiety that was part of her psyche are tamed and concealed in death.

"You're very like her, Cathy," he whispers.

A tray of refreshments is place on the table beside them by Vera who slipped out quietly from the room. They sip the tea while they fall into a respectful silence.

Chapter Eighteen - The Fledglings

Ben starts his study to be a conservation officer. His aspiration is to eventually study entomology and to understand some of the insects, butterflies and bees which fascinated him. A new life away from home begins. The succession of baby boys who came into Cathy and Mark's life will launch out one by one onto the next phase in life.

Jack is the next fledgling. He leaves to study history and anthropology. Young love comes his way. At a song and dance movement camp, to celebrate Imbolc, he meets Poppy, a tall slim girl with shoulder length fair hair and green eyes. His study of the origin, development, and varieties of human beings fascinates Poppy. Her musical Donegal accent beguiles him. For the duration of the chilly February weekend, dances are performed to the sounds of drums and singing. Snowdrops bow in pots within, and in crispy iced grass without. Romance blossoms for Jack and Poppy. Love does not impinge on their study, nor does study hinder romance. By the time Jack and Poppy graduate their bond is sealed.

"I'll try to get a third ticket for my graduation," Jack says to Mark.

"Is it for Poppy?"

"Poppy will have her own grad. She's nearly finished her healing course. It's for Grandma."

"Grandma could've my ticket. I'll still be there for the afters," Mark offers.

"Are you sure, dad?"

"She deserves it. She looked out for your studies when I thought I was too busy."

"No worries about that, dad. Everything turned out grand. Hope you won't be disappointed not to be at the ceremony."

"I think Grandma's a great choice."

A very proud grandmother, looking solemn in a midnight blue suit, sits next to Cathy at the graduation ceremony.

Poppy's grandaunt bequeathed her a cottage, not far from Mount Errigal. This gift provides a space for Poppy's healing work and a future home for the pair of them. The cottage is deep down in a hauntingly beautiful hollow, close to different branches of Poppy's family including the Gildea's and the O'Donnell's. Poppy and Jack are not blow-ins. They are an intrinsic part of the community. Their ancient Celtic paganism is no obstacle. She is still the granddaughter of Malachi Gildea.

Andrew's aspiration to be a shopkeeper nears attainment. His brothers' choices cleared the way for him. Benny is pleased that Andrew's wish is being fulfilled. He always assumed that role would fall to Ben, and that the little boy who talked about becoming a shopkeeper would have to find a different way of life. His grandfather hopes that in the face of large hypermarkets a personal business such as Wright's can survive.

The recent addition of the delicatessen and a small bakery greatly increased their trade. Heather Brown's feasibility study, carried out in catering college, showed encouraging results. Heather, the daughter of Daisy Armstrong, who took all the firsts in the cookery kitchen at Saint Matthew's, is following in her mother's footsteps. She is one of Wright's stalwart staff since the year she was studying for A Levels.

The four brothers were virtually raised by four adults. Each brother gravitated towards an adult and that adult in turn reciprocated a special affection. There is a special bond between Ben and Cathy, Jack and Marilyn, Andrew and Benny, while Finn gets plenty of attention from Mark, despite all his father's activities.

In looks, very good looks, he is exactly like Mark was when he left St. Matthew's Academy. He is the only one of the brothers to take sports seriously and the only one who will probably swing a golf club with the ease of his father.

Ben finds work locally. As a conservation officer and is instrumental in the promotion of wildflower meadows, beneficial for bees, butterflies and all kind of insects. He registers in a distance learning course in entomology.

"Entomology, that sounds impressive." Marilyn exclaims. "I feel there's need to raise awareness of insects, and especially honeybees. I might specialise in apiology."

"You always loved insects and creepy crawlies."

"I'm trying to persuade the Amenity Council to make biodiversity as important as aesthetics for the Best Kept Villages."

"Imagine my grandson changing the goal posts of the contest."

"Some untidy bits, like log piles and wild patches, can be blended in discretely."

"It might be hard to make a tidy old woman untidy," his grandmother jokes.

"Wild patches are good for butterflies. There's an increase in Meadow Browns and several other species where places are let go wild," Ben continues.

"We'll go for the bit of untidiness," his grandmother agrees.

"And you might still get a trophy, grandma."

"Even if we don't the real aim is to encourage a community spirit and pride of place with people working together," Marilyn paraphrases the objectives.

"That's the spirit."

"That doesn't mean I wasn't competitive down through the years. We'd our rivals like Hightown and a few others."

"Without the keenness to come first there'd be no contest. Best Kept Villages might've fizzled out."

"I'm getting past my active days. It's good to know the young generation's ready to carry the can."

"Remember you used to have me water the flowers when I was about three. I carried the can all those years ago."

"It did you no harm. You've made a career of it."

"I love it."

"It's good you've work you enjoy. In the olden days it'd have been a given that you'd be the shopkeeper."

"Andrew will be a good shopkeeper. He's very happy."

"When he was a little boy he'd go straight into the shop after school and stay there till you and Jack came home."

"And back again as soon as he'd have the minimum of homework done," Ben jokes.

"Your granddad was patient, letting him work the cash registrar and count out change."

"It was better than homework, more practical anyway," Ben reckons.

"The fact that he'd a choice made all the difference," Marilyn surmises. "Mark didn't have a choice. He did make sacrifices to do what he believed was his duty. But he hadn't the zeal for it."

"Finn knows what he wants to do already," Marilyn continues. "A PE teacher, he's probably the sportiest among you."

"And Andrew inherited your singing."

"We're delighted to have him in the choir, a young tenor."

"The choir will be winning more firsts at Choral Festivals," Ben encourages.

"I'm not sure how long more I'll be in the choir. I'm getting older, expecting to be a great-grandmother in September."

"It's great. Jack and Poppy, having twins," Ben rejoices.

"Like I had myself."

"Jack's starting a genealogy service from home," Ben enthuses.

"He's in a good place for visitors wanting to trace their ancestors."

"Great Poppy got the cottage from her grandaunt."

"She's a kind girl. I'm sure she was very good to her," Marilyn says sincerely.

"She was good to Aunt Ellenora and she's good for Jack. She encouraged him to do the genealogy course."

"Won't you always keep in touch with him, Ben?"

"I will, grandma."

"With mine the twins were a unit in themselves, with no need for their brother. It was Hannah and Sarah and the rest of the world."

"It's amazing they ended up beside one another in Herefordshire."

"Sarah was there first. She got married and made sure she found a husband for Hannah over there."

"Did dad feel left out?"

"They were very young when he went to boarding school. He was nearly ready to leave when they went in. An independent twosome, they were."

"Dad was probably like an only child."

"I feel he missed out on the ordinary interaction with siblings," Marilyn laments.

"Maybe he was lucky, having nobody to argue with him."

"He paddled his own canoe and did his own thing without reference to anyone."

"Ummh," Ben mumbles passively.

He does not voice his misgivings about his father doing his own thing.

"Your mother was right to send you all on the bus to Hightown."

Boarding school takes children away too soon."

"I don't think I'd have liked boarding school."

"It was the way of things when mine were young. Grandma Rosetta was very keen on an exclusive education for her grandchildren. She'd gone to finishing school in Switzerland."

"I suppose Finn's on the edge in our family," Ben remarks.

"You were all so far ahead of him all along the way."

"We'd the fun and the fights up in the treehouses."

"And on the dangerous sledges," Marilyn remembers.

"The bread trays with ropes attached," Ben recalls. "Remember when Andrew crashed into the wooden paling. You minded us when mam rushed to the hospital to have his lip stitched."

"Then Finn came along, so like his father." Marilyn continues. "I'm not sure if he has his father's charm."

"What you see is what you get with Finn," Ben jokes. "None of us have dad's charm."

"Andrew has a very pleasant manner. The customers love him."

"That's different. Dad's charm's as good as a currency. Yet it's a kindly charm, not calculated."

"That's an apt observation," Marilyn concedes.

"He has a very generous side too," Ben reckons.

"I really appreciated when he gave me his ticket for Jack's graduation."

"Jack did too. Would you like to go to visit Jack and Poppy?"

Marilyn's face lights up.

"I'd love to. I'd mentioned it to Mark a few times but he's always busy."

"I'll take you."

"We'll have our planning meeting for Best Kept next week. Then we'll have a nice trip there whenever it suits you," Marilyn enthuses. "Are you going to join us at the planning meeting?

"I think I will. We'll have three generations of Wright's there," Ben jokes.

Chapter Nineteen - Donegal

Ben joins his mother and grandmother on the Best Kept Villages team. Biodiversity is their buzz word this year. Aesthetic beauty was their concern in the past, especially back in the fifties when Marilyn was at the helm. They start with a brain storming session in the school room at the side of the church.

The edible window box is the first idea written on the flip-chart.

"Wildflower meadows," Marilyn encourages. "I used to be for the neat and tidy look. I'm converted now."

"By your grandson," Cathy teases.

"I'm thinking of the butterflies and all the insects."

Wildflower meadows and butterflies are written on the flip-chart.

"Log piles for wildlife and a bug hotel," suggests Ben.

"A bug hotel, what's that," a volunteer enquires.

"It can be as simple as bundles of hollow stems or bamboo canes where insects can crawl in to survive the cold weather."

"Or elaborate, like five-star bug hotels." Ben explains.

"Nest boxes and cover for nesting birds," calls another.

"The swifts are doing well with nesting places in the castle walls," Cathy encourages.

"We could add new swift boxes. At the Arts Centre in Belfast they fitted them in when they were re-building. And they can be put under eaves. They like to nest beside other swifts," explains the vicar, an avid birder.

"We could keep an eye out for suitable walls or eaves," Cassie Anderson enthuses.

Cassie Anderson, a devoted worker on the team for more than five decades, is chairing the meeting. She is a plump jolly little woman whose fresh features belie her eighty years. Though she lives three miles away from the village she has always taken pride in its appearance.

"Any more suggestions," Cassie probes encouragingly.

"A facelift for the village pump," another volunteer suggests. "It could do with a fresh lick of paint."

"Floral displays and signage on the approaching roads," someone else chimes in.

"Enlist the help of residents along approach roads," is another pragmatic suggestion.

"What about an interpretative sign to explain our wildlife and our special features?" The vicar wonders.

"Our next item on the agenda is to monitor the condition of our local assets, the ones that helped Mountview to outshine over the years," Cassie begins encouragingly.

The participants bubble with enthusiasm for the work ahead. Ben's aspiration is for Marilyn to hold the all-over First Prize Trophy while Marilyn wants the vicar to have an interpretative sign. He has been very helpful since he came to the parish, accommodating the committee in every way and this will be his last year here.

Mark is having breakfast when Ben arrives into the living room ready for the journey to Donegal.

"Are you heading away for the weekend?"

"I'm taking grandma to Jack and Poppy's place."

"It might be a culture shock for her."

"I wouldn't say so."

"They're very unconventional, compared to your grandma."

"Ah no, it won't be any surprise. She knows what they do and she's really anxious to see them."

"Well thanks for doing that, Ben. She mentioned a few times she'd like to go. With the Ball and everything else we didn't get there. And to tell you the truth I didn't know what she'd think about their way of life."

"She'll be fine on that score. She loves them. That's all that matters to her."

Loves them? Mark thinks to himself that his mother is far too practical for such sentimentality.

"And you'll bring her tablets and medicine. She didn't get the best of medical reports lately."

"I suppose it's a bigger reason to bring her in case anything happened."

"You're right. I'd have felt bad if she'd missed going, even though I kept putting it off," Mark admits

"Poppy will do some healing therapies on her."

"Thanks again, Ben. I really appreciate it."

"No bother, dad. I'm looking forward to seeing Jack and Poppy too."

Marilyn and Ben set out on their journey. Marilyn is impeccably dressed in a mustard coloured polo-neck and matching cardigan over a brown pleated skirt and a gold locket around her neck. She lays her brown three-quarter-length coat carefully on the back seat of the car. Ben is wearing wide cotton trousers tied in at his ankles. His bundle of curls is in a ponytail.

The sight of the spire of an old church, built from local white marble about two hundred years ago, signals the proximity of Jack and Poppy's cottage and healing centre.

"This is a fairyland scene," Marilyn exclaims.

"It's magical," Ben agrees.

"I'd say this place is beautiful in all seasons," Marilyn reckons.

Within a few minutes they are snaking their way down the narrow winding road to the cottage. Poppy and Jack have left the big red gate open and they run to welcome them as the wheels crunch the pebbles inside the gate.

"Grandma, you're so welcome." Poppy greets her with a warm embrace.

Jack steps forward and the warm hugs are repeated.

"And you're very welcome too, Ben. You know that. Thanks for bringing grandma."

"It was great chatting to grandma."

"I'm up to date on everything, especially bugs and bees and insects."

"Talking entomology and apiology all the way," Jack teases.

"Grandma brought me into a posh hotel. The porter was looking at me. I think I failed the dress code. Grandma made up for that."

"You definitely failed the dress code," Jack observes.

"He was a nice man really, full of attention," Grandma muses. "Appeared important in the tall hat, but underneath was a kind heart."

"Very discerning, grandma," Jack encourages.

The companionable banter continues, especially between the brothers and their grandmother.

117

Marilyn feels at home among Tibetan Bowls, Buddha statues, Druid symbols and many other icons. A Wreath of Staves, symbol of the Reformed Druids of North America, takes pride of place. Beside it is an Awen, with three vertical rays meeting at the top.

"The Awen symbolises harmony of opposites. In the old Celtic language Awen meant inspiration or essence. In modern times it refers to spiritual illumination."

"It's all enlightening to me, Poppy."

"Here's the Sun Wheel and this is the Tree of Life, with branches and roots entwined."

"Fascinating," Marilyn exclaims, as she admires all the symbols.

Above the mantel piece is a big wooden rosary.

"This is the rosary beads Aunt Ellenora brought from Lourdes. I was her helper there twice. This is her breviary. She was a nun, left to mind her mother. Then she wasn't well herself so she stayed out and still minded many others. She was actually our grandaunt."

"She sounds a very kind lady."

"She was. She left us this special space. We like to include her belongings in a special way."

"After dinner we can show you the well," Jack chimes in

Beneath an old hawthorn tree is an orifice leading into the dark waters of the well. It resembles a womb of the earth and gives the well a mystical appearance.

"Pools of possibility are what they're considered to be in sacred circles," Poppy says with conviction.

Tied along the lichen encrusted branches of the hawthorn are bits of rags, some old and mossy green.

"The strips of cloth are traditionally dipped in the well and tied on the tree in the hope that a blessing or healing happens," Poppy explains. "We called it the raggedy tree when children."

There is a chill in the air as they make their way back to the cottage where Marilyn yields to the gentle power of Poppy's hands and the chimes of the Tibetan Bowls for her healing therapy.

"You made me a very happy woman, Ben," Marilyn says as they drive along on their homeward journey.

"I'm glad you prompted me to visit Poppy and Jack. Things can go on the long finger," Ben muses.

"It was great being in their place. They're so real, so genuine. Just being themselves and not trying to change or impress," Marilyn enthuses.

"And so free," Ben adds.

"Freedom," Marilyn ponders. "It's probably the most valuable gift a person can have. People often slot into what they think is expected."

"Did you miss having freedom, Grandma?"

"I suppose I had it and threw it away. After I got married and moved to Mountview I put myself into a mould. I'd ideas of what was expected of a businessman's wife."

Ben could identify with what Marilyn was saying. He felt that his grandmother, despite her generosity and all her other virtues, was usually striving to keep up appearances.

"We paid too much attention to Saint Paul. We'd an idea that we ought to please men," Marilyn continues.

"Mam's very accommodating to dad."

"Mark probably needs more accommodating than his father. Benny wanted little from life."

"I reckon Saint Paul's not to blame in mam's case, whatever's pulling her strings. It must be dad's charm."

"I think so."

"Did you experience freedom among the Donegal hills?" Ben encourages his grandmother to share her thoughts.

"I did in that amazing place, with every belief under the sun honoured. It's one way of making sure you don't get life wrong," Marilyn jests.

Darkness has fallen by the time they arrive back in Mountview.

Cathy is into her last hour in the shop and Mark is at a meeting in connection with the Ball. Benny welcomes them back and the three of them sit together in the upstairs living-room overlooking the grove. Marilyn relays the news about Poppy and Jack and their healing centre and the icons and emblems. And Benny can see his wife almost evolving into someone new before his eyes.

Chapter Twenty - Midges

Ben helps to assemble the information for the interpretative board. When the board is finished Ben is ready to go to Scotland to walk the West Highland Way.

Marilyn is pleased that the vicar's wish for the interpretative board has been fulfilled.

"That's a great job. You deserve a holiday."

"I'll be with you in spirit, Ben," Cathy adds.

"We can text unless I'm out of range."

"And don't forget to put on plenty of that herbal repellent. The midges will eat you."

Ninety-eight miles, from Milngavie to Fort William, are to be covered in six or seven days. By the end of the second day Ben has walked more than thirty miles without any serious blisters. Fourteen of those miles took him along the track close to the eastern shores of Loch Lomond.

On his third morning he awakes in a bunkhouse, once a church, and is watched over at breakfast by saints looking down from stain-glass windows. This former place of worship has a transient population as travellers stop, sleep, enjoy the ambiance and move on. Dotted all over the place are many old churches converted to new uses as congregations dwindle. Ben thinks of the situation back at home. The adaptation of part of Hightown Church to accommodate a heritage centre ensured its survival. Now the vicar from Mountview looks after both parishes, an onerous task for a man advancing in years. Ben is glad he spent so many hours preparing the information for the interpretative board. It is like a parting gift for the old man.

Facing out into the wilds north of Inversnaid, acclaimed in a Gerald Manly Hopkins' poem entitled *Inversnaid,* Ben continues his trek until he reaches Strathfillan. Here he sleeps in a wooden wigwam, after a sociable evening around a campfire with a young couple who had also slept in the church bunkhouse. He feels at one with the place, which just now is plagued by midges. As a budding entomologist he should be able to tolerate them more than the average walker.

A text sounds. "Thinking about you, where are you now?"

"Just left a wigwam and facing out towards Rannoch Moor," Ben replies as a wilderness awaits him on his fourth day.

"I remember Rannoch Moor. It's magical. You've hit the heart of wilderness now."

His mother sings its praises in her reply text. It was a memorable part of her trek more than three decades ago. "You're reliving every day of the trek, love," Mark observes as he sees Cathy smiling at the incoming accounts of the West Highland Way."

"He's going towards Rannoch Moor now," Cathy says dreamily. Mark realises her heart never left Scotland.

For Ben, Rannoch Moor is fixed in his mind as the last location in Scotland for the *Formica Exsecta*, the narrow-headed ant. There are several species of moth around, including the Rannoch Looper, *Itame brunneata,* rarely seen at this time of year because of the long hours of light and the 'Argent and Sable' moth, *Rheumaptera hastate,* which might be seen in Bog Myrtle. Ben will refrain from searching for rare insects or moths today. It's a time-consuming activity. Instead he will be mindful that he is threading in an entomologically famous area while he treks towards his next destination.

With its bogs, lochs and rivers, Rannoch Moor can be challenging for walkers if the weather is inclement. The weather is kind to Ben. He reaches his goal and hobbles into his hostel in a place graced by the wonderful backdrop of Glencoe. Here he has a stimulating game of Scrabble with Lyndsey, a friendly young woman from Dumfries, who is walking with five companions. They both spy the board game at the same time and within minutes they are playing quietly and seriously. There is a marginal difference in the marks at the end when Lyndsey triumphs.

"That was a great game," Ben complements Lyndsey.

"I'd love another one, but we'll have to get rested for tomorrow's trek," Lyndsey advises.

With sixty-five miles covered in four days they are all optimistic that they will complete the entire ninety-eight miles in another two days.

The worst enemies of West Highland Way walkers are not heavy rucksacks or sore feet, but midges. Swarms of them crawl relentlessly over everyone. Lyndsey, his Scrabble companion, gives him a face net before he sets off. He had not bothered to bring a net, believing nets are just for tutorial fieldtrips. Instead, when the smell of his herbal repellents did not repel, he tried to chase the biters away with fronds of fern. Now better equipped to withstand the swarms, he strides out for a fifth day. He eats a small snack on a high plateau where the vegetation is sparse and the wind crisp enough to disperse the midges. Other walkers take a brief respite here too.

Two young women are performing first aid on their companion's heel blister.

"I saw you in Kinghouse this morning," one of the girls greets him cheerily.

"You couldn't miss me. I look like a beekeeper," jokes Ben.

"The net's a great idea"

"I got it from a girl I played Scrabble with last night. I hadn't thought of bringing one, or buying one here."

"Nor did we. They probably sold them in the Welly shop. It has everything."

"I saw it yesterday morning. I didn't stop, didn't want to break the rhythm too early."

"You're from Ireland."

"I am."

"We're from London. It's great to be near the end of the walk."

"By tomorrow evening we should be there," Ben encourages.

"Was it lonely on your own?" asks one of the girls.

"Ah no, it wasn't lonely. I met some really nice people along the way."

"You're nice and friendly yourself," encourages the girl whose foot has been taken care of.

After this friendly exchange Ben starts his long steep descent towards Kinlochleven. Ravens rasp high overhead. A tall wide waterfall splashes on his left and sends water rushing and tumbling beneath a bridge. He tries to record the scene on his small camera while the midges crawl all over the lens and his hands. From his study he remembers that in Scotland the Highland midge, *Culicoides impunctatus,* is responsible for most of the attacks on humans.

He trudges on. Head down, he notices feathery fronds of fern, tiny tormentil and the papery bark of silver birch. Head raised he sees oak, alder and silver birch on both sides and impressive mountains tops that protrude above tree-tops towards ever-changing skyscapes. A jay flits jerkily across his path into the jungle of trees.

He notices the dark tail, the white rump and a flash of buff-brown. He does not notice the patch of blue but is still sure that it is a jay. This is a rare treat. A wary bird, usually only seen when it is flitting from one group of trees to another.

He is coming to the end of his fifth day of walking. The cooperative spirit which exists between walkers endures the course. They are eager to share bandages, repellents, drinks and information. There is no competition, no time keeping, just plenty of friendly exchanges. Most walkers traverse the Way northwards. Fort William is their destination. Ben ponders on all those who walked before him and will walk after him, not only in this season.

This trail was opened in 1980. His mother walked this way shortly after that. Through texts she has encouraged him along his way. He feels the inter-connectedness of this long string of walkers. He thinks about Lyndsey emptying out her rucksack to find the spare net for him and remarking that he had a cosy nest for midges in his long curls. Her own hair, clipped around her face in a feathery fringe, would not afford them such hospitality.

Helped along by his musings he reaches Kinlochleven, where the River Leven rushes along affording a habitat for dippers and wagtails. Stunning mountain landscapes tower over the village. Arriving in the early afternoon he enjoys the sunshine in the company of other walkers in what might be described as a walkers' communal village. At this stage on the West Highland Way there is a feeling of optimism. Their destination is only sixteen miles away.

Chapter Twenty-One - Reflections

Lyndsey and her five gregarious friends arrive and fill the hostel kitchen with their happiness. Their arrival reassures Ben that this free-flowing interconnectedness of walkers goes on. The small inconvenience of the crowded kitchen is more than compensated for by the comradery.

"We're glamping tonight. We couldn't pass the pods when we saw them," Lyndsey bubbles with happy enthusiasm.

"They're a bit like the wigwams down at Strathfillan."

"Are you staying in one, Ben?"

"I'm sharing a room upstairs. The sun was streaming through the skylight earlier."

"It's great to see you again, Ben. Did it go well for you today?"
"The walking wasn't bad today. I got here just after two."

"We did a lot of preparing of food before we set off. And it was almost impossible to eat with the midges crawling into our lunch boxes. I wasn't strictly vegetarian today," she quips. "I'd a fair few midges to eat." Lyndsey chuckles away happily, while she twirls a vegetarian stir-fry in a frying-pan."

"I'd my lunch, well some crackers and hummus, on a rocky area where the midges were blown away, I think."

"I remember that spot. It's like a walkers' respite."

After dinner Lyndsey invites him to play another game of Scrabble. He enjoys a game where he does not have to try to let the other player catch up. He notices Lyndsey's concentration as she makes each careful move. Letter tiles are juggled. Q-U-A-R-R-Y she places across a treble word score. He had been saving a U since the first move. The game goes on, slowly, solemnly, spiced every few minutes with an impressive score.

Some of Lyndsey's companions amuse themselves at the snooker table. Her sister Amy is outside, sitting in a Buddhist pose on a bench overlooking the river, while Chloe, her friend, is checking her phone. An hour after the start of the game Chloe makes them tea. And the game goes on.

One of the lads leaves the snooker table and sits on edge of the sofa.

"This is my boyfriend, Rick. This is Ben. I forgot to introduce you last night."

"Great you're giving Lyndsey a good game. I get bored with it when it goes on and on".

"It's great, Rick. I'm really enjoying it." Lyndsey beams with delight.
"I see that. Two exciting games in a row, that's a real treat for Lyndsey, Ben."

"She's giving me a good challenge and she hasn't made a show of me, yet anyhow." Ben jokes casually. "She won the game last night. It was still very enjoyable."

The scores are close. Ben is finally four points ahead when he succeeds in using his last tiles and Lyndsey loses eight for her unused J.

"We'll call it a draw," Ben suggests in a co-operative spirit. "Ah no, mate, you gave her a good game. It's alright for you to win. She always wins," Rick teases.

Ben sends a text to Cathy when he goes to his top bunk.

"Had two terrific games of Scrabble with a girl from Dumfries, last night and tonight. You'd have loved it, Mam. I'm looking at the sky through skylight now. The nights are so bright. Ben."

"A good game of Scrabble, that's great. Happy stargazing. Night, Mam."

"We'll have a good game when I get back, mam. Night, Ben."

"Ben had two great games of Scrabble with a girl he met in two different hostels," Cathy tells Mark when he comes in from a meeting. "Now he's watching the sky through the skylight in his room."

"He's walking in your footsteps. When we went to Scotland and you just pregnant with Ben we nearly played Scrabble," Mark teases.

"I'd to give up. You were too distracted by the golf on TV."

"Then you went upstairs to watch the stars."

"And you left the blinds open for me to see them," Cathy recalls.

From time to time Mark feels that Ben and granddad Benny compensate for his own lack of attentiveness to Cathy. At those times he resolves he will lessen his commitments. He just never gets around to figuring out which activities to drop.

When Ben wakes on the top bunk there is neither twinkling stars nor bright sunlight, rather a typical Scottish rainy morning. After breakfast he puts some hummus between rye crackers and places them in his lunch box. There is no point in preparing an al fresco meal and having to compete with the midges. He has promised himself a Zanzibar bean dish for tonight. Yesterday afternoon, when he had spare time, he got the ingredients in the village store. They are in his rucksack, which will be ferried to his next hostel. He is pleased he afforded himself this small luxury of luggage transfer on what turned out to be a rainy day.

He leaves the Dumfries companions as they pursue their culinary endeavours. He notices Lyndsey's sweet smile through her black round-framed glasses and his smile is returned through the protective net she gave to him. He climbs the steep path out of the village, pleased to have been among such relaxed companions.

He did not ask Lyndsey to be a Facebook friend. The conversation did not veer that way. Instead she will be part of the threads which are weaved into the almost unending filament of walkers.

The ground is rough and steep and damp. Rivulets of water flow in gullies across the rugged path. This is his first encounter with rain and dampness since he started the walk. He picks his steps carefully and is glad his heavy rucksack will be delivered to his hostel beside Fort William. Eleven Munro's, mountains with peaks taller than 3,000 feet, tower above this section of the walk. The trek is tiring. His legs are aching. The cumulative exhaustion of walking nearly one hundred miles in six days is taking its toll. The rain mercifully clears. The majestic surroundings are visible again. At last he reaches Fort William near the base of Ben Nevis. Ben Nevis holds some magic for him. His parents learned he was on the way a few days after they climbed the mountain.

In the hostel in Glen Nevis he shares the Zanzibar bean dish with another walker, Pierre, from France. Pierre contributes a can of pinto beans as well as chocolate muffins for dessert. There is a different ambiance here. Some guests are resting after their accomplishment of completing the West Highland Way. Others, endeavouring to climb as many of the Munro peaks as possible, are in a single-minded and competitive frame of mind.

Ben sees a game of Scrabble among the board games. He hesitates, reckoning it would unfair to ask a Frenchman to have a game. They admire the slopes of the mountain in the brightness of the midsummer night while the other hostellers retire to bed early.

Morag, the hostel manager's daughter, washes up pots left by errant residents.

"Are you away home tomorrow?" she enquires in her enchanting Scottish lilt.

"I'm going to climb Ben Nevis," Ben proclaims.

"Isn't that very brave, and you just finished the Way?"

"When did you decide to do it?" enquires Pierre.

"Just tonight," Ben replies simply. "My legs were really aching when I got here. They're much better now."

"Have you seen much of Scotland?" Morag asks.

"Not very much, except for what I've seen along the Way," admits Ben.

"There are some pretty spots further north, and west too around Glenfinnan."

"I'll hardly see any more this time. The climb will take most of the day tomorrow and then I'm back to Ireland the following morning."

"It'll be bright all evening. We could take a spin out after you've had dinner," Morag encourages.

"That'll be great."

"I got a new car today. Well it's new to me, a three-year-old Nissan Micra. It'll be a novelty to take spin in it."

Sleepers grumble and shift in their bunks as Ben stumbles across boots and rucksacks and struggles into his envelope-shaped sleeping sheet. He might have foregone the idea of the Ben Nevis climb were it not for the fact that he had told Morag about his plans.

Chapter Twenty-Two - Ben Nevis

As Ben walks towards the beginning of the slope of Ben Nevis in the late morning the hostel manager warns him of the impending mist.

"It's a fair way to th' top and th' mist will be down by two."

"It's my only chance. I've to go home tomorrow."

"I think ye should come back another time."

"I'd like to try it."

Fueled by the folly of relative youth he continues. He had phoned his mother earlier and told her about his plan.

"You're not leaving any room for mishaps, Ben. You're back in work the day after tomorrow," she had advised.

"I'd like to do it now that I'm at the foot of it," he insisted.

She gave him advice about clothing and drinks and torches.

"If the mist falls don't continue," she counselled emphatically. "You don't want to be wasting rescue resources unnecessarily. Check the forecast before you go up."

"Didn't you do it, Mam? I should be well able to do it."

"I was only a few years older than you are now when I climbed it. I carried you there."

"Well, the beginnings of me!"

"There hasn't been time for mountain-climbing for a long while. The excitement's still there though. You're stoking it up," she chuckles.

"You should be encouraging me, mam. And thanks for all the encouragement while I was walking the Way."

"My concern is that you might misjudge your time or your strength. You've covered nearly one hundred miles in less than a week. Your legs were aching yesterday."

"They're much better today. I put on some *tiger balm.*"

"You've probably just eased the symptoms. It doesn't sound you're ready for a climb. And the scree near the top is very tough. It's like a lunar landscape."

"I'd really like to do it now that I'm here."

"Okay, I'll be thinking about you. I'd be much happier though if you left it till another time."

Ben forges ahead, crossing the bridge over the River Nevis and climbing the steps on the initial steep incline. He feels confident on the well-trodden early section of the climb and falls into a rhythm of a moderate trek. He reaches Lochan Meall an t-Suidhe, also called Halfway Lake. Sheep dot the mountain. They remind him of his grandparents' pain back in 2001 when foot and mouth disease ravished the Dale. The view is spectacular and the zig-zag path ahead of him gives an illusion of proximity to the top. He rummages in his backpack for the remainder of the Zanzibar bean dish. It tastes delicious. Moving on again he meets walkers making their descent.

"How far is it to the top," he asks cautiously.

"Two hours, or so," the walkers reckon. "There's a mist forecast. It mightn't be wise to go on."

"Thanks for telling me. I might try for another wee bit."

"Be careful. You're on your own."

Ben persists. His legs ache. The benefits of the balm applied this morning are wearing off. He takes out the small jar and applies the balm again, rubbing it into his muscles. Then he accidently rubs it into his eyes and they sting. The remainder of the zig-zag path and the scree, which his mother compared to a lunar landscape, are ahead of him. The comfort of the hostel and the promise of a drive out to Glenfinnan are behind him. He reluctantly turns back and faces the hostel. Disappointed, yet confident he made the right decision, he steadies himself with his walking poles.

Without much warning the hostel manager's predictions come true and he is shrouded in mist. It is as if the lining of the sky detaches itself and envelops the great mountain. He accidently veers off the beaten track and becomes disorientated. A few other aspiring mountaineers appear and disappear in the dense fog, their appearance being too brief to discuss fear or strategy. He mooches about in the mist. The mooching develops into trepidation, then into fear and finally into panic. He is annoyed with himself for not paying more attention to the warnings of the hostel manager. He could have climbed Ben Nevis in a planned manner at another time. And he is annoyed with himself for not listening to his mother. He is even more annoyed with himself that he did not decide to forego the climb sooner.

A couple of frantic teenagers are searching for their tent. They disappear again in the fog. Ben searches for the beaten track but to no avail. Alone he sits on a pile of stones. He takes out one of the muffins, given to him by Pierre who returned to Glasgow today, and savours the sweet crumbliness. He will save for later the rest of the muffins and the chocolate. He fears that this could be a long wait. His mooching has ceased. He stays static now. He reckons that there might be better ways to impress Morag than by setting out on a hapless climb. Truthfully it would be difficult to impress her with one successful climb when half of the residents were ticking off Munro's like items off a shopping list.

He can imagine her now patiently washing up the pots and pans left by forgetful hostellers. He can see her long thick black hair tied back in a clasp and her brown eyes twinkling. He wonders if those twinkling eyes are restrained by concern now that he has not returned, now that they have missed their trip out to Glenfinnan. Or is the misadventure of a lone walker a normal occurrence in her life?

Her father is anxious.

"I don't know where that laddie be now. It was too late to start climbin'."

"Is there someone lost?" Two walkers, who have completed the West Highland way, ask.

"A young laddie from Ireland went up too late. He'd just done the Way," the hostel manager explains.

"Had he a big heap of reddish curls," asks one of the walkers.

"That's him."

"Ben, you remember Ben? We met him in Inversnaid." The walker reminds her companion.

"He was admiring the stained-glass windows in the dining-room," her companion recalls.

"And we'd a lovely evening with him at Strathfillan. I hope he'll be alright. He was a lovely friendly lad."

"Aye, but nae much sense," the manager reckons.

"We should contact the police." Morag is anxious.

The blades of the helicopter of the Mountain Rescue Team swirl overhead. Ben gasps a sigh of relief. The helicopter descends a short distance from him. Then it takes off again. Perhaps they found the teenagers. He rummages once more and retrieves the chocolate and the muffins. He eats part of his emergency rations and figures he must resign himself to waiting for the mist to rise, and for the light of what will at this time of year be a mercifully early dawn. Tucking his knees to his chin he breathes warm air under his blanket. The feeble torchlight lies beside him, its battery losing power and his mobile phone which has no service is also losing its charge. The blanket becomes damp and cold as the wait for dawn begins.

Back home in Mountview a more immediate emergency is gripping the family, who are unaware of Ben's plight. Marilyn has had a heart attack and is in the intensive coronary unit in the hospital.

"Ben's home tomorrow," Marilyn whispers. "I hope I live to see him."

Cathy clasps her mother-in-law's hand.

"How's he getting on?" Marilyn whispers again.

"He was well this morning anyhow. He'd finished the walk and was going to climb Ben Nevis." Cathy tries to sound matter of fact despite her rising anxiety.

She had sent him some texts to find out how he was getting on with the climb and received no reply. That was completely uncharacteristic. They had a virtual text conversation going between them for the past week. She had phoned several times from the dining-room in the hospital, still no reply. She hopes that he is just out of range. Perhaps his hostel is off the beaten track, she tries to convince herself.

"It's a big climb, all alone," Marilyn mumbles, adding to Cathy's suppressed misgivings.

"There are usually other climbers, Grandma."

"I hope he's alright," Marks says worriedly when they come out of Marilyn's room. "Ben Nevis is tough. And he'd done a lot already."

He bites his lips. He realises he is adding to Cathy's fear and apprehension.

"More than likely he's out of range up in the Highlands," he reckons, trying to sound positive.

"I hope so," Cathy sighs as she looks at her phone again, willing a message to appear.

"It's midnight now, love. He'll hardly disturb you till morning," Mark encourages.

At around three o'clock in the morning the blades of a helicopter swirl again. But light still has not penetrated this misty shroud. Ben tries to get to his feet. His joints are locked from sitting for hours in the cold. He reaches for the torch to wave in the direction of the helicopter sound. The battery has died. He remains unseen by the rescuers. It is nearly sixteen hours since he headed off resolutely in defiance of his mother's and the hostel manager's better judgments. Shamefully he remembers his mother's words, "You don't want to be wasting rescue resources unnecessarily."

Disorientated, he commences his descent when the mist lifts. He hopes he will reach the base of the mountain in time to collect his belongings and make the train and boat connections.

Eventually he is found by a volunteer mountain rescuer who approaches him with the agility of a mountain goat.

"Are you Ben Wright?" The rescuer asks with a sigh and a lilt of a Scottish brogue.

"Yeah, I am," Ben answers with embarrassment and relief.

"I see ye got yourself well off th' track"

Ben looks sheepish and follows the mountaineer back towards the designated path.

His legs are stiff after having been in a folded state throughout the damp and cold night. When he is about an hour into the descent, closely following his rescuer, Ben slips and twists his ankle. The pain increases with each step.

"I can call for an air ambulance and a stretcher," his rescuer offers.

"No, I think I'll be fine. I've caused enough trouble as it is."

"If you change your mind at any stage tell me. It's not wise to abuse your foot."

Ben insists on limping along. His rescuer carries his rucksack.

Chapter Twenty-Three - Morag

The hostel manager shakes his head with a mixture of frustration and relief.

"At least ye're safe, or are ye? Did ye hurt yer foot?"

"Twisted m'ankle," Ben winces.

"Ye should nae 'ave gone up there."

"Sorry. I should've listened," Ben says contritely.

Morag'll give ye breakfast," he points to the door of his own quarters. Ben hobbles through the door.

The warmth of Morag's welcome lessens the embarrassment.

She is full of sympathy. In a few minutes there are potato scones and beans and toast and tea on the table.

"I'm sorry I missed the trip to Glenfinnan with you," he apologises.

"At least you're safe. That's more important."

"Your dad and my mam warned me. Mam warned me not to waste rescue the services' time."

"Climbers often make mistakes. Lochaber Mountain Rescue brought a few teenagers back to us. They couldn't find their tent and had stayed too long looking for it."

"I saw the teenagers. Then they got lost again. I heard a couple of helicopters. They must've been looking for them."

"They were looking for you."

"I caused an awful lot of trouble."

"It would be worse if anything happened to you," Morag insists. "Will I make you more tea?"

"I hate rushing away. I've to catch a train at Fort William for Glasgow."

"It's a pity ye couldn't stay longer. Ye could've done with a wee rest."

"It'd be really nice to stay another day or two. I've to catch the Ferry this evening. I'm due in work tomorrow afternoon."

"Ye're cutting it fine, laddie." Her father has come back into the kitchen. "There's a train in forty minutes." He wears a kindly face despite his understandable frustration at Ben's determination yesterday morning and his dilemma now.

"I'll ring a taxi," suggests Ben.

"The taxi could take a while. You've nae time for that. I'll drive ye in th' jeep. That ankle'll need bandagin' but ye've nae time now."

"I can drive Ben. I'll have time to have a quick look at your ankle," Morag offers.

"I hope my foot isn't smelly."

"Don't worry. I'm studying to be a podiatrist. I'm used to all kinds of feet."

She places Ben's ankle on a cushion and after massaging it with oil she puts on a compression bandage, starting at his toes and continuing up past his ankle. She completes the treatment with a special boot.

"What made you study podiatry?" Ben asks while the treatment is in progress.

"I became fascinated by the sheer miracle of human feet. Imagine a human foot and ankle has twenty-six bones, thirty-three joints, and more than one hundred muscles, tendons and ligaments. The average person takes more than eight thousand steps a day."

"People who walk the Way do much more than that," she adds jokingly.

"You're in a good location for treating sore feet," Ben reckons.

"Here it's a labour of love in an emergency. I can look after the interim care of any foot injury that happens to a resident," Morag confirms.

"Well it's good you're here to see to the interim care of my ankle."

"And make sure you seek further advice when you go home if it's still swollen or badly bruised."

Morag continues to give instructions as she goes towards the car, Ben limping beside her. The heavy rucksack is put into the Red Nissan Micra and they drive off. He can see the whole of Ben Nevis now, reaching towards the bright blue sky. Climbers spiral their way up like matchstick people. He is disappointed that he did not accomplish his goal and he is disappointed that he is leaving Glen Nevis just when he made the acquaintance of Morag.

"Are you nearly finished your study," Ben asks.

"Next year is my final year. I'll be studying as hard as I can to get my degree, hopefully an honours degree," Morag says with resolve.

"That's the spirit."

"Are you finished studying?"

"Nearly," Ben reckons. "I studied to be a Conservation Officer. That's my job. Now I'm doing an MSc to become an entomologist, hopefully."

"An entomologist, that's very interesting. You'd find plenty of subjects around here with all the midges."

Morag stops the car in front of the station with just a few minutes to spare.

"Thanks for everything, Morag. You're a lifesaver," Ben gasps as he awkwardly yanks his luggage from the back seat.

"Be kind to that ankle."

"I might get back to Glen Nevis soon."

"Do that and we can take the trip to Glenfinnan. We could keep in touch on Facebook. I'm Morag MacGregor."

"I'm Ben Wright. Thanks again Morag," and he hobbles towards the platform where the Glasgow-bound train is ready to depart in a few minutes.

Ben Wright indeed, he thinks to himself as he limps towards the platform. Sometimes even Mr Right can get things wrong and turn an adventure into a fiasco. Morag can sense the pain of his ankle as he limps along. His unkempt bundle of curls is tied in a pony-tail which has not been rearranged for twenty-four hours. The walking boot from his injured ankle is suspended from the rucksack.

He turns to wave back again and she can see his soft smile. Then something shiny falls from the side of his rucksack, his torch. She retrieves it but decides not to distract him. The train is about to depart. Instead she will send him a message. It will be a chance to remind him about Morag MacGregor, lest all the rushing and travelling might cause him to forget. Before he finds a seat on the train he looks out through the window. He can see her squinting anxiously, her hand shading her eyes. He notices her attire, her red tartan shirt, perhaps the tartan of the MacGregor clan, her denim dungarees and her brown boots. Her thick black hair is plaited in a pigtail. Her hair and features are decidedly South American. He is pleased to see her standing there. It was not just a dutiful drop-off. The train begins to move off. She sees him waving at the window and waves the torch like a railway official signaling off a train. Then she places it in the pocket of her dungarees. Maybe the torch which failed to lead the helicopter to him might lead to romance?

"Did ye get the laddie to th' station," her father enquires when she gets back to the hostel and starts her usual chores. She works hard during the summer months and in return her father looks after her college fees and helped her buy her car.

"We got there with less than five minutes to spare."

"There was something very likeable about him. It felt as if I'd known him already."

"It must be the Celtic connection," Morag reckons.

"We don't see many laddies from Ireland comin' by here."

"He said he'll come back again. I promised I'd take him out to Glenfinnan. I was going to bring him over last night if he hadn't got stranded."

"Don't start losin' your heart. Lots of laddies come and go. We might never see them again."

"I do think we'll see him," Morag says hopefully.

Chapter Twenty-Four - Marilyn

The train halts at Corrour station, the highest and most remote railway station in Scotland. It crosses a viaduct north of Rannoch, the area his mother described as the heart of the wilderness. She had stayed in touch with him all through his trip and he reckons she was trying to contact him while he was stranded on the mountain. He plugs his phone into a nearby power point. He wants to reassure his mother that he is safe. Despite the pain in his ankle he distracts himself by finishing his holiday journal. He records his disappointments, his failure to climb Ben Nevis and his missed opportunity to go to Glenfinnan with Morag. He is embarrassed about his climbing misadventure. He should have been contented with the completion of nearly one hundred miles in six days.

He writes a text when the phone is charged. "Hi mam, I'm on the train to Glasgow. Ben."

No indication of pain is included. He places his swollen ankle on the seat. The ticket inspector sees the bandaged foot and excuses the transgression.

A reply comes in. "Good you're on the train. Grandma had a bad turn yesterday. She's asking for you. I'll tell her you're on the way. Mam."

The focus of the rest of his homeward journey alters. The painful ankle falls into the background. He is hoping he will get home in time to see Marilyn even once again. It is three months since they visited Jack and Poppy. He had never seen her so happy, so unexpectedly captivated by the shrines and icons and prayer flags and everything else in and around the cottage. He had promised her that he would take her there again the second weekend of July.

Now Marilyn is ill. And his injured ankle might prevent him from driving, at least for a short while.

Cathy is waiting at the train station to take him to the hospital. He hobbles towards his mother and hugs her.

"How's grandma?" He asks with some trepidation in case the situation is worse than what he was told.

"She's regaining strength. What happened to your foot?"

"I think I sprained my ankle." He plays down the injury and makes no reference to the climbing fiasco.

"Get it checked when you're in the hospital."

"That's a good idea, mam."

Cathy drops him off at the set down area.

"Go ahead up to Intensive Care. Dad's up there. I'll take your rucksack home and I'll be back later."

Marilyn's eyes light up when he appears. He manages to keep the limp to a minimum. Mark lays his hand on his son's shoulder.

"We were worried when your mam couldn't get in touch with you."

Ben feels contrite.

"What happened to you?" Mark enquires with concern when he notices the bandage and the special boot.

"Twisted m'ankle a bit," Ben says calmly, even though he feels like wincing with the pain.

"You got it well bandaged, that's good."

"The hostel manager's daughter is studying podiatry. She fixed it up and drove me to the station."

"Good people were looking out for you. I'll let you have time with grandma."

As he makes his way towards the Balcony Café Mark realises his sense of relief at having his eldest son back safely. He had tried to sound calm for the sake of Cathy who kept peering into her phone every few minutes. Marilyn's illness steered his mind away from his worry some of the time. Just when a cloud of apprehension floated over him another doctor or nurse would float into the room to check monitors or ask questions.

"You could've fractured your ankle or tore a ligament." Marilyn's voice is weak, a barely audible whisper.

"It's a bit sore, but not to worry. You're our priority now, Grandma."

"I'm an old woman," she whispers. "My time to leave has to come sometime. I hope we can go over to Poppy and Jack's before my departure."

"I hope so too." Ben squeezes her hand.

"If I don't maybe I'll come back as a bird and I'll fly over."

"If you're a rock you'll have to stay put," Ben teases.

"Did you have to clip my wings?" Her voice is sounding a bit stronger again.

"You get well. And we'll go to Donegal as soon as we can," he encourages.

"Hope your ankle will be okay."

"It will, Grandma."

From the café on the balcony of the hospital atrium Mark watches hospital life flow by. The late afternoon light shines brightly into the spacious interior of the atrium and softens the clinical setting. His usual charisma shines through on the balcony and soon his friendly smile connects with others around him. He welcomes to his table an elderly man who is moving around with a tray looking for a space. Before long they are comparing the medical conditions of Marilyn and the older man's wife, who are in same unit. Mark tells the old man about his son's safe return, albeit with an injured ankle.

"My wife was peering at her mobile phone all night, getting paler with worry every minute," Mark relates.

"That's the trouble with them auld mobile phones. People expect to know everything all the time."

"Hadn't thought of it that way," Mark admits. "I'd just got used to them."

"When ours went away there were hardly any phones at all. We'd to make do with letters that took a week to get there and another week to get back."

A Facebook message awaits Ben when he returns from the hospital. Morag MacGregor has not forgotten him. She has his torch and will keep it safely till he returns. "My father said you're a likeable laddie despite having not much sense under your heap of hair," she continues. "That's a complement from dad. Haste ye back."

Everyone is so busy visiting grandma and sorting a care package in case she needs one when she leaves hospital, that Ben's ankle falls off the scale of priorities. His fiasco on the Ben Nevis is not disclosed.

The cardiac team ensure that Marilyn's heart gets a further lease of life. Two weeks later than planned Ben and Marilyn set out to Donegal. The same ritual is adhered to, a stop at the hotel where Marilyn has coffee and fruit scones and Ben has tea and a falafel wrap. They are given a cordial welcome by the concierge with the tall hat, and on their departure, a friendly farewell.

"I'm glad we're able to make the journey," Marilyn muses as they continue their journey. "I was surprised they worked so hard to repair an old heart. Such are the powers of modern medicine, I guess."

"I'd have hated to come back from Scotland and find you'd left without saying goodbye. Good my ankle didn't hinder us for too long."

"I hope the driving won't put a strain on it," his grandmother says with concern.

The fairy-tale white church in the valley signals their proximity to the cottage. They stop to photograph the valley below. As they admire the magical scene on this warm July afternoon they hear the crackle of gorse seed pods as they split and disperse their seeds in the area around the parent plant. Then they wind their way down the steep road to be warmly greeted. Poppy, now more than seven months pregnant, is carrying a bowl of freshly picked raspberries from the garden. Her face lights up when she sees them drive through the open gate. They go inside and see all the additions to this peaceful space. Poppy has weaved two wickerwork baskets in preparation for arrival of the babies. This is another incentive to keep Marilyn's refurbished heart beating. Despite her astonishment at the efforts of the doctors to save her she is pleased to be able to strike more things of her wish list.

In late September she sees her first great-grandchildren, Marilyn and Malachi, when they are brought to Mountview. She holds the overall Trophy for the Best Kept Village. Over the years the village achieved first in its category several times, but never the overall trophy. The community rejoices for someone who never failed in her efforts to keep their village beautiful for almost six decades. The old vicar is in the picture too, and Cassie and all the team. In a few months the vicar will be leaving. His requested interpretative board holds pride of place in the village.

Marilyn and Benny reach their diamond wedding anniversary in October. Jack presents them with a family tree. Babies Malachi and Marilyn are at the bottom and on the next set of branches Jack and his three brothers, and Poppy Gildea and her sisters. Out and up it extends. It includes Mark and his twin sisters, Cathy and Colin Campbell and Poppy's parents, Manus and Annabelle and their siblings. Great grandparents come next while on the branch with all the other great-great-grandparents is Rosetta, who planted the grove.

Chapter Twenty-Five - Missing Dimension

Marilyn's heart keeps chugging along. Though she had thought that mending an old heart was a waste of the doctors' time she is glad they saved her. It was an eventful year. She spent happy days under the shadow of Mount Errigal in a setting of druidism, far from her usual meetings at the Manse. In Donegal a different spirit ran through her veins. An atmosphere of freedom prevailed. The mould she fashioned for herself in the nineteen-fifties was peeled away, discarded as sure as skin falls from a chameleon.

She had a near death experience and was given a new lease of life. She is eager to use this bonus time well. The most highlighted moment, in the public realm anyhow, was holding the over-all trophy for Best Kept Villages. That happened just in time. Her days of active work on the committee are over, even though she is still there in an honorary capacity of chairperson emeritus.

From her upstairs window, she sees their loyal customers come in to purchase their Christmas fare. Downstairs in the shop all hands are on deck, Cathy, Mark, Andrew, Heather and Heather's cousin, Janice, who is in since college closed for Christmas. This is a week when Mark traditionally sets all other activities aside to be behind the counter and to bestow greetings on his customers. Benny too has nipped down to the shop several times in the past couple of weeks, the spirit of retail rising in his veins again.

At nine o'clock on Christmas Eve the activity grinds to a halt. Cheery greetings emanate from the final customers and from the tired staff and the door is closed on Wright's for almost a week. In the living room behind the shop the aroma of toasted raisin and cinnamon bagels and steaming mulled wine fills the air. Marilyn always loved the well-earned quiet time following Christmas when their customers had enough provisions to keep them going till New Year. Although she does not take an active part in the running of the shop now it is still the shopkeepers' respite.

The bells ring in a new year. She longs to go back to Donegal. It is her number one wish.

"I'm off work for ten days, Grandma. I'll check with Jack and Poppy and I can take you there."

"I wonder if it'll be too much pressure on Jack and Poppy to have the two of you now that they've the twins," Mark speculates after his mother goes upstairs.

"They're really looking forward to seeing Grandma," Ben assures his father.

"Well you've made her a happy woman over the past year with her visits to Donegal."

"She was always good to us. And it's her wish to go there," Ben enthuses. "Her face lights up when we start making our way down to the cottage."

"I hope you're not snowbound down in the hollow, you mightn't get back home."

"We won't worry once she's happy. We'll get home eventually."

"I'll encourage her to drop into the doctor just to check out her heart and her prescriptions before she goes," Mark suggests cautiously.

It is while in her doctor's surgery that she gets an unexpected revelation. Cassie Anderson arrives into the surgery, accompanied by a woman of about sixty. Cassie had mentioned that her niece was coming to visit in the New Year. The younger woman sits next to Marilyn.

"You must be Cassie's niece," Marilyn volunteers.

"Yeah, I'm here for a few days."

"I'm Marilyn. Cassie and I go back for years. We were on the floral committee in the church, and on the Best Kept Villages Committee."

"You'd a great achievement this year, getting the all-over first prize trophy."

"We were delighted, especially for the vicar. He's retired now."

"The village is a credit to all of you."

"I shouldn't be blocking up the waiting-room. My son wanted me to come for a check-up before I go to Donegal tomorrow," Marilyn reveals.

"That's a long trip. I hope the weather keeps up for you," the woman cautions.

"I hope I get away before it shows any signs of changing," Marilyn quips. "I wouldn't mind being stranded once I get there to see my grandson and his family."

"He must be a very special grandson."

"He is. They all are. But I think I'm particularly close to him. He had me as a guest at his graduation."

"That was really nice."

"I've a photo of him on my phone," Marilyn says proudly as she opens the phone.

The woman is admiring Marilyn's expertise on her mobile phone as she trawls through photographs until she reaches the treasured picture.

"Is that his mother?" The woman sounds surprised.

"It is. That's my daughter-in-law, Cathy."

"That's Cathy Campbell. I knew her years ago. Imagine seeing Cathy again," the younger woman continues. "We protested together for years at Faslane and we were at Greenham Common. We even shared a prison cell."

"A prison cell, how did that happen?" Marilyn is trying to contain her astonishment.

"She was very zealous. The police usually picked the zealous ones off first. But she wasn't deterred. She kept the momentum going."

"Zealous that'd describe Cathy well. She puts her whole self into things," her mother-in-law affirms.

"She always did. She was very active at Faslane. It was much nearer to where she lived. She came to Greenham Common too."

The woman keeps pouring out her words of enthusiastic praise without waiting to observe the growing astonishment registering on Marilyn's face. "She was a brave girl, always fearless, got in over fences and under fences," the woman continues admiringly. "She was often arrested. That's how I kept meeting her."

Marilyn is agog. She doesn't want to say to the woman that she has practically lived under the same roof as Cathy for nearly thirty years and never knew anything about her bravery. A hidden dimension of Cathy Campbell is completely revealed in less than ten minutes in a room just down the street.

"I've a photo of the pair of us at Greenham Common in 1982." After some searching on the phone the picture is located and Marilyn sees Cathy's face among the huge line of women.

"There she is," Marilyn says fondly. "That's how I remember her when I first laid eyes on her after a choral festival. She'd been in class with my son in Saint Matthew's and they met again that night."

Marilyn is uncharacteristically chatty. The freedom one achieves in the company of relative strangers has encouraged her.

"She's still very beautiful in her cute way," the stranger stresses, looking again at Marilyn's photo.

"She still looks youthful despite all her hard work over the years," Marilyn confirms.

"She never spared herself on the protests either. There she is in her dungarees and her bandana." The younger woman brings up the picture on to the screen of the phone again.

"She's not into great style now either," Marilyn reveals. "She's lovely the way she is."

"Marilyn Wright," the doctor calls. Marilyn bids farewell to the narrator of Cathy's tale.

"It was good to talk to you I might see when you visit Cassie again. Happy New Year," Marilyn is smiling back towards Cassie's niece as the doctor is gently closing the door behind her.

Perhaps her heart rhythm will be altered after all these revelations.

Chapter Twenty-Six - Errigal

Cathy is helping Marilyn pack for the trip. Carefully wrapped in tissue paper is a gift for Poppy, a stained glass Awen, the Awen which represents the harmony of opposites. Marilyn attended a course on stained glass when the boys got older and hands-on-nurturing from a grandmother was no longer necessary. With three vertical rays meeting at the top Marilyn found it easier to design the Awen than some of the other symbols she admired in Jack and Poppy's cottage. She worked on it for a few weeks in the room downstairs, once Rosetta's room.

Cathy thinks there is something different about Marilyn's demeanour.

"You're really looking forward to Donegal."

"It'll be great to see Jack and Poppy. Poppy's so genuine and real. She doesn't feel the need to impress anyone."

"She's surely free of convention. It's a great gift to have, freedom."

"We had it and let it slip through our fingers," Marilyn says definitively. "When we became wives and mothers, we fitted into a mould, thought we should live up to expectations."

"I think we should've broken the moulds," Cathy sighs.

She would like to tease out Marilyn's train of thought if there was enough time. Ben and Marilyn need to get on the road to ensure that they arrive before darkness, and temperatures, fall.

"We'll have a good chat about things when I get back. We'll have a girl's night," Marilyn promises, "the first evening Mark's out." Both women jokingly agree, "We won't have to wait long."

Cathy feels an affinity with her mother-in-law now, an affinity that might enable her to finally reveal what her interests really are and share how she feels about life.

Marilyn fixes herself into the passenger seat, her face beaming as she sets out to re-experience non-conformity in the welcoming house in a hollow beneath a mountain.

"When I go, Ben, won't you always keep in touch with Jack?" Marilyn requests as they pull in at the hotel where, on their earlier trips, Marilyn enjoyed her tea and scones and Ben his falafel wraps.

"Of course, I will. But I hope you're not thinking of leaving us yet."

"Nobody knows the day or the hour. In my case I reckon the years are definitely numbered."

"Meanwhile we'll have to enjoy things as much as we can," Ben encourages as he tries to ignore the reality of eventually losing his grandmother.

"When I go you'll still come across to Jack."

"I will, Grandma

"I'd say your mother'd be happy to come along with you," Marilyn continues.

"I'd say she'd enjoy it. She has great time for Poppy."

"Poppy might encourage her to follow her own interests now that you're all grown-up."

"That'd be good. She's always thinking of the rest of us."

"And you might encourage her too, Ben."

"I encouraged her to climb again."

"When they met first most of their dates were to mountains or forests," Marilyn recalls.

"And when they came back from Ben Nevis they were expecting me."

"And she could've other interests that she hadn't a chance to follow."

"Like an eco-warrior or an anarchist," Ben speculates. "Imagine mam lying in front of a truck."

"People often risk their safety for what they believe in," Marilyn says admiringly.

"I'd say mam would definitely morph into an eco-warrior if Rosetta's grove was in danger."

"She'll hardly have to fight for the grove. It's safely tucked away between us and the golf club," Marilyn states confidently.

"They won't be coveting it for a motorway anyway. Mam was with the eco-warriors in spirit when we were young. The motorway went on anyhow."

The dramatic scene of a snow-capped Mount Errigal appears before them. They wind their way down to the cottage and speculate how people manage to get in and out of here in deep snow.

"Dad wondered what'd happen if we got snowbound. I told him you wouldn't mind being snowed in once you were here."

"You're right. How we get back is another day's work."

"We're honoured to be first on your New Year list, Grandma." Poppy welcomes them warmly.

"I didn't want to delay, Poppy, in case there wasn't much mileage left in this refurbished heart." Marilyn points towards her chest.

"I'll do some hand, feet and head massage and a bit of sound healing when Marilyn and Malachi settle," Poppy promises.

The log fire burns brightly. The babies sleep in their wickerwork baskets. As the day draws to an early close, the room is mostly lit by flickering firelight and candlelight. A storm lantern is lighting near the door to guide them to the shed if necessary. The icons and symbols which adorn the house appear through the wavering shadows. The Awen, the Wreath of Staves, the Tree of Life, the Sun Wheel and the giant wooden rosary are just about visible in the cosy dimness. Poppy rubs peppermint lotion into Marilyn's feet and hands. And the treatment progresses gently.

The following day they are marooned in the cottage. Snow piles around the big gate making it impossible to open it. Above the cottage the giant snow-covered mountain reaches snow-laden clouds. Jack leaves deep footprints in the snow as he makes his way to the shed for logs.

"You'll have to wait till the snow melts to go home. No need to rush or worry," Poppy assures Marilyn and Ben.

"You both know you're always very welcome." Jack reiterates the sentiments.

After five days of pampering by Poppy the dreaded event happens and Marilyn's spirit drifts away quietly in her sleep. Her refurbished heart beats no more. Poppy, Jack and Ben encircle her remains with herbs and winter jasmine and candles and incense. The Gildea family and their friends and neighbours wait around Marilyn's remains, giving her a proper Donegal wake. The logistics of taking Marilyn home is a worry. Poppy's father, Manus, who has survived adverse weather conditions over the years, comes up with a solution. He will take Marilyn's coffin down from the main road and back up on his tractor. "How we get back is another day's work" was Marilyn's sentiments when she arrived.

Mark arrives with the undertaker, Albert Malcolmson. Manus takes them down the treacherous hilly road on the tractor. He had already towed up Ben's car. Mark sits by his mother. Tears escape from his grey-blue eyes. He wants to wait awhile with her in the place she loved. It is a quirky little place, homely, aromatic and decidedly unrushed. They wrap her coffin in a colourful hand-weaved coverlet and place it on the trailer, surrounded by the jasmine and herbs. They sit beside the coffin on the trailer until it is placed in the dark-windowed car. Mark and Ben drive behind to escort Marilyn home. They drive in relative silence punctuated only with words of appreciation from Mark for his two sons, and for Poppy, who made Marilyn's last year so happy.

"Albert suggested we stop here," Marks explains as Albert turns into the hotel where Marilyn and Ben always had their breaks.

"I'll sit out here. I wouldn't like to leave grandma alone for too long."

"I'll order something for you and when the food's ready I'll text you."

"Thanks dad. I'll have a falafel wrap and tea." Mark writes this in his phone. "Put my coat around you or you'll get your death."

Ben feels the warmth in his father's gestures.

"A falafel wrap and a pot of tea for my son. He's outside. His grandmother passed away and he wants to stay near her coffin."

"It's not Ben," the waitress is filled with concern. "He ordered falafel when he came in with his grandmother last week."

"It is Ben. Sadly, we're bringing my mother home today."

"I'm so sorry to hear that."

Members of the staff approach Mark and offer sympathy. The concierge removes his tall hat and goes out to speak with Ben. Then he suggests to Albert that he park beside the window when Ben comes in so as he would be still near his grandmother.

As they make their way home in the early darkness, they see cars parked by the roadside waiting to escort Marilyn. They are not alone.

Mark goes to the nearest draper shop, which is in Hightown, for white shirts, black ties and half a dozen proper linen handkerchiefs. His mother once remarked that it was undignified for mourners to be sniffling into bits of toilet roll. He had promised her that if anything happened to her he would afford her the dignity of providing proper handkerchiefs.

"*If* Mark?" she had retorted. "I'm sure you mean *when*. I'm not going to go on forever."

Now she has left, quietly and unexpectedly. Although the doctors had forewarned that she might pass away unexpectedly it was a shock to get the news from Donegal. She was determined to have her visit there and nobody could say that she did not fulfil her wish.

The spire of Saint John's Church, at the top of the steep path, pierces the low-lying clouds on the cold January morning. On each side of the path, among yew trees, are the gravestones of those who departed this life over the past two centuries. Reverend Patience Prior, who officiated at the wedding twenty-eight years before, is the new vicar. She speaks admiringly about Marilyn's contribution to the church and to the community in general. Her tribute is full of warmth and sincerity.

"I'm pleased to see this beautiful floral display arranged by the flower committee. For many years Marilyn provided this faithful service as other families came here to say a final farewell to a loved one. Both within and outside this church her discernment for floral beauty was evident. Last autumn, after sixty years working to enhance the village, she held the over-all First Place Trophy. She was a committed member of the choir, a choir which achieved several accolades at choral festivals. She'd have sung many requiems in this church and today the choir perform a fitting farewell to a dedicated singer."

Marilyn is laid to rest in the churchyard which surrounds the white church on the hill, the church she served for six decades.

"Patience spoke so warmly of your mam. You'd think she knew her all her life."

"Patience always did things earnestly," Mark muses admiringly, as more mourners catch up with them and offer their sympathies. Sheltered from the freezing January afternoon, the praises and the expressions of sympathy continue in the church hall where Marilyn provided years of devoted service.

Chapter Twenty-Seven - The Reunions

Facebook posts, and private Facebook messages, have kept Ben and Morag aware of the happenings in each other's lives since they met in June. In March Morag announces that she is withdrawing from Facebook until she completes her college assignments and work placements. She issues a temporary farewell to her Facebook friends. Ben misses the contact. He looks hopefully into her page every couple days. Morag MacGregor is steadfast in her plans. No more posts. No more private messages. The Easter holidays are approaching. His springtime hope of seeing her is growing dimmer.

On an April Saturday morning Ben walks in a National Demonstration in Glasgow. The demonstrators want Trident scrapped and Faslane closed. There have been continuous campaigns against the military's use of Faslane as a location for nuclear weapons and nuclear-powered submarines. This was a beautiful bay before their intrusion back in 1968. Thousands of activists have protested since. There will be a blockade of the entry to Faslane in eight days which will attract police and publicity. Ben is pleased to be here to take a stance. He would not have known about it if he had not spoken to the Dublin students on the boat.

After the demonstration he makes his way to Buchanan Street and boards a bus to Fort William. He hopes he will meet Morag. He checks into the hostel run by her father, Stewart.

"It might be clear for a climb the morra," Morag's father encourages. "But it's very cold at this time of year once ye go to a height."

"I might keep on the level this time. I won't risk it."

"I remember ye, hobbling back with the hurt foot. I often thought about ye since."

Ben is chuffed to be remembered even if his last visit ended in embarrassment and pain.

A group of students and their teachers queue up to register. Ben goes to the kitchen and prepares a simple meal of pinto beans accompanied by several slices of brown toast. He will purchase food for breakfast from the hostel shop when the office gets quiet. Darkness comes shortly after eight. There is no sign of Morag. Crestfallen he heads to his bunk at about ten.

On Sunday morning he gazes out the train window at the banks of Loch Eil, which stretch for about six miles beside the railway track. He is traveling towards Glenfinnan. It is a pleasant trip and he understands why Morag might have selected it as a destination for visitors to Fort William.

"Ye look a bit lost, laddie," remarks Stewart. "What did ye do today?"

"I went to Glenfinnan on the train. It's a beautiful place"

"Braw place is Glenfinnan," Stewart affirms.

"Morag was going to take me to Glenfinnan last time."

"She said she'd take ye there when ye got back. I wasn't sure ye'd be back at all."

"I was hoping I'd see her."

"Ye looked like a laddie lost. She's nae home this weekend. She's doing college work, took a wee break for the Faslane March."

"The Faslane March, I was there too," Ben gasps with surprise.

"She'll be sad she missed ye."

"So am I."

"Many a love affair began in Faslane," Stewart muses.

"I met a lass from Ireland in Faslane Peace Camp, back in the early eighties, when the camp was first set up. She was my Jo for long time," he continues fondly. "A shopkeeper's son, lured her back to the Mourne Mountains."

"What was her name?"

"Cathy Campbell."

"She's my mother."

"To think after all the years Cathy Campbell's bairn found my daughter," he shakes his head with pleasure and intrigue.

"I haven't done too well with the finding. But I'm hopeful."

"You'll find her alright. I think she's a fondness for you."

"That's good."

"I often thought about Cathy, hoped all went well for her."

"I'm her eldest son. I've three younger brothers. She works very hard in the shop. Over the years she volunteered with the Best Kept Villages and looked after us. Ordinary things, I suppose."

"Cathy was no ordinary lass. Brave lass, she was. She often got arrested for chainin' herself to the gates and for gettin' inside. Fearless she was."

Ben thinks about his hardworking mother. He wonders if she misses the call for bravery as she goes about her day to day living.

Stewart is musing too and pondering on the past, the past of the nineteen-eighties.

"We'd a misunderstanding. Aye. Inez Ferreira was over from Bolivia, stayin' here when it was a guesthouse ran by my folk. I was up for the weekend helpin'. I took Inez out to Mull, got delayed, and nay got back in time to Glasgow to meet Cathy." He shakes his head with disappointment as if it had just happened.

"Did she not forgive you?" Ben enquires incredulously.

"There were nae mobile phones then. She was left standin' in th' rain. And she knew I was takin' Inez to Mull."

"And that was the end of it?" Ben is astonished.

"It was. I nae liked it t'end that way."

"I met her again once, near the corner of Hope Street. We'd still a fondness for one another." He speaks affectionately. "She said she was engaged to a laddie from across the bay from her home."

"Yeah, Granddad and Grandma lived on a sheep farm in the Dale. Grandma Beryl died and Granddad Andy's over ninety. At the time foot and mouth, they lost all their sheep. They were broken-hearted."

"A way of life wiped out," Stewart sympathises. "Dumfries and Galloway bore the pain of it here."

Ben is intrigued to hear his mother's love story.

"Happy I am to meet ye," Stewart continues.

"I'm happy I met you too, and Morag."

"Ye mind me of Cathy, same curls and smile."

"They say I'm like the Campbell's."

"Aye, ye sure are. After ye left last time I said to Morag 'twas like I knew ye before. Say hello to Cathy for me."

"I will," Ben answers simply. "It was a pity it ended that way. She'd forgive you if it was now. What became of Inez from Bolivia?" Ben blurts out wishing to tie up the loose ends of the love saga.

"She's back in Bolivia. I married her cousin Eva Vargas. Inez made a match with me an' Eva two years later but she nae settled. Homesick she was. She's back in Bolivia."

"Sorry to hear that," Ben says feebly.

"She's doin' good work there, helpin' people out o' poverty and defendin' their rights, helpin' with clean water and food and income."

"Were you lonely?" Ben asks cautiously.

"She used to g'over to see her mother. Good to her mother she was. She went to stay there when Morag was twelve. Workin' for the community she is and she gets here every December."

"At least I've Morag," he continues. "I'd nae want a young laddie to take her away to the Mourne Mountains," he jokes.

"I could come here if I was lucky enough for it to work out." he explains simply.

When he boards the bus for Glasgow on Monday morning he ponders on the connections and coincidences. He thinks about the misunderstanding between his mother and Stewart which led to his own existence at the foot of the Mourne Mountains and Morag's at the base of Ben Nevis. He thinks about his mother, feisty and fearless, protesting against the military activities at Faslane, activities that could cause destruction. Cathy was no ordinary lass, Stewart had declared. He thinks about Stewart and wonders if it has been lonely for him. Three hours pass as he gazes out the bus window at the magical Scottish landscape and daydreams about all he heard from Stewart MacGregor. He wonders if he will get to see Morag sometime. Stewart seems to be in favour of such a liaison.

A surprise awaits him as the bus arrives in Buchanan Street Station. Morag is standing there squinting towards the bus windows, a red beret perched sideways over her long black hair, which flows down her back.

"Did you get your torch, Ben?"

"No. I forgot it. I'd a great long chat with your dad. I forgot all about it."

"You can come back for it. Dad said you'd tell me all about your chat. Will you've time for lunch?"

"I will. Imagine the two of us were on the demonstration. Only for I got chatting with your dad I wouldn't have seen you this time."

"He enjoyed chatting with you. You reminded him of your mam. After I left you to the station last time he said he felt as if he'd known you already."

At a cosy window-seat in a small café they talk of the love affair back in the nineteen-eighties, when the activists in the Peace Camp at Faslane were probably optimistic that they could change the world.

"I was sorry mam didn't forgive your dad," Ben laments.

"I could imagine you crying at sad movies," Morag teases.

"It was just that it was a sad way for it to end," Bens tries to justify his bout of sentimentality.

"We wouldn't be here chatting together if it hadn't ended," Morag says simply as she dips her spoon into the dessert, with which the waitress had brought two spoons.

"I'll come back again, as soon as you've your college projects sorted."

"Come back anyhow. I'll squeeze in time for the projects when you're not here."

With a happy heart he relaxes in the bus to the ferry and then in the ferry as it makes its short journey across the Irish Sea.

Chapter Twenty-Eight - Stewie

Finn is helping his mother in the shop when Ben arrives home.

Cathy comes back into the living room.

"Did you've a good time?"

"It worked out great, mam."

"Did you meet the girl you hoped you'd meet?"

"I only met her today."

"Is she the great Scrabble player you met last time?"

"No, that was Lyndsey. This girl's name's Morag. I don't know yet if she's a Scrabble player."

"Well it was good you met her when you went so far."

"I went to a Faslane Demonstration on Saturday."

His mother looks surprised.

"You didn't tell me you were going there."

"I didn't decide till I was on the boat. I was talking to people going there."

"It's good to know people are still interested in what's happening at Faslane."

"I heard you used to be there."

"Did you? Who'd remember me after all the years? That was back in the eighties."

"I met your old boyfriend. He said you were a fearless lass."

"I think I know who it has to be." Cathy looks jittery as a teenager. She awaits her son's confirmation of the source of the information.

"Stewart MacGregor sends his fond wishes. He said you were his Jo until you'd a misunderstanding. What's a Jo?"

"It's a girlfriend," she answers simply. "Stewie," she continues fondly. "Imagine you met Stewie MacGregor. It's a very long time ago since I saw him."

"He said you met him on Hope Street when you were engaged to dad."

"Hope Street. It was just at the corner of Hope Street. Imagine Stewie remembered."

Ben sees his mother now like a starry-eyed lover.

"Morag's his daughter."

"Morag's his daughter. I can't believe you met Stewie's daughter."

"I met her in June. She bandaged my foot and drove me to the station. I didn't know the story then."

"How did Stewie make the connection," Cathy is intrigued.

"When I said I'd been to the demonstration he said Morag was there, and she'd be sorry she missed me. He said love stories begin at Faslane and that he'd met an Irish lass there."

His mother is waiting expectantly for more of the story.

"He said ye'd a misunderstanding and a shopkeeper's son, lured you back to the Mourne Mountains."

"It was a big misunderstanding then. I wish I'd forgiven him," his mother stresses earnestly.

"I couldn't believe you didn't. You're the forgiving type now."

"I think I forgive everyone now to be on the safe side. I often thought I should've forgiven him. Then I'd push it to the back of my mind to get rid of the regret."

"If you'd forgiven him you wouldn't have been with dad," Ben remarks.

"It's good to have all of you, you and your brothers. But it was a mean way to leave Stewie."

Ben can see pain in his mother's eyes.

"I remember that evening in Hope Street. We both kept looking back after we said goodbye. Then I saw him sitting on the steps of a house, looking so sad. I ran back and sat down beside him."

"That was a near miss for dad." Ben tries to keep some levity without knocking his mother's thoughts of track.

"He said even though it was sad for him my folks would have me near."

"That was very thoughtful. And they had you near, especially when they needed you."

Ben just sits by his mother and allows her to speak. There was so much work to be done over the years that she never spoke about her past life, her life in the seventies and eighties full of activism and romance. They are in the cosy living room behind the shop. This is where they relax between shifts, where they are ready to give a hand if there is a queue at the tills. Although Cathy, Mark and the boys live in the cottage this is the common room between the two households. Benny still lives over the shop, now with Andrew.

Finn calls in from the shop.

"Will I close the door now in case anyone else comes in?"

"The people who come in are our customers, Finn. But you can close now. It's just time."

The shop door is closed promptly. The sign changed to CLOSED and the lights switched off.

"I'm heading to play a game of snooker with the lads, Mam."

"That's fine, love."

"We must've absorbed the activism by osmosis," Ben jokes after Finn leaves.

"I started to absorb mine as a toddler," Cathy states with conviction. "With a nuclear reactor across the water the people of the Dale felt that the health of the community was threatened."

"Wasn't there an accident there when you were little?"

"There was a big fire when I was two," Cathy confirms. "When I lived in Glasgow I felt it was important to get involved in the Faslane Peace Camp."

"Stewie said you put your heart and soul into the protests and you often spent time in prison."

"I was happy to be a martyr for the cause then. Where did my spunk go?"

"You were minding us and everyone."

"I should've done more."

"Maybe when Finn goes to University in autumn you'll get a chance." Ben recalls one of Marilyn's last requests, that he would encourage his mother in her interests.

"That'd be a new me."

"A renewed you," Ben reminds her.

"Nuclear was our biggest worry. Then a different enemy sneaked in. Foot and mouth silenced sheep, and broke hearts."

"It was awful seeing Granddad Andy crying for his sheep."

"His whole farm was silent." Tears slip out of the corner of her eyes.

"And Grandma Marilyn minded us to let you stay there."

"I always appreciated that. I'm glad you and Jack and Poppy made her so happy with the trips to Donegal."

"I wish I didn't have to take her home in a coffin," Ben laments. "I'd got to know her much better in the last couple years. We were like friends."

"Always remember she got her New Year wish. You made sure of that."

"She was really happy there, fascinated with the idea of souls having reincarnations, whatever they might be."

"I hope she's happy, wherever she is."

"The world has funny twists," Ben reckons. "When I think how things turned out in Scotland I know anything can happen for a reason."

"And across in Faslane the situation hasn't changed." His mother thinks of Faslane again.

"Protestors still organise the Camp and the protests," Ben confirms. "There's a big protest next week like the ones you'd have done."

"Stewie told you about the protests. I should've forgiven him." She shakes her head sadly.

"You sat beside him on the steps at Hope Street. At least you said a proper good bye."

"We were sad it was too late. Well too late for me and Stewie. But your father's a very good man. And I've the four of you."

"I hope we compensated for the heartbreak on Hope Street." He resists the temptation to refer to it as hopeless street. That might block the flow of her thoughts.

She once envisaged that she would eventually move north with Stewie McGregor and live in the Scottish Highlands. That was before Stewie brought Inez Ferreira on a boat trip, got delayed and left her standing in the rain. Some might accept that this was fate. Cathy thinks that fate is sometimes a string of misadventures, which is called fate to dull the pain or regret. She recalls the night she met Mhairi in the hotel cloakroom a year and a half later. She had cried her eyes out while Mark, watching highlights of golf on television in the lounge, was oblivious to the whole scene.

She begins to sob when she recalls Mhairi, her might-be mother-in-law. Ben realises that she is lamenting the loss of a whole way of life, Stewie, an extended family and activism. He does not stymie the flow of her memories but allows space for her thoughts, a space rarely afforded to her over the busy years. He sees the tears flow. He notices the white linen handkerchiefs on a shelf beside them, the ones bought for Marilyn's funeral. Now Cathy's tears for a bygone love and a bygone way of life flow into the strong linen handkerchief.

"I never went up to say goodnight to granddad," she sniffles in the middle of the flow of tears.

"I'll go up. You're not ready yet, mam. I'd like to see him after being away."

"He'll be delighted to see you."

Ben hands his mother another handkerchief.

"Don't rush back down, love. He'll be pleased to chat with you," she reassures him.

"Do you want to go out to the cottage?"

"I think I'll stay here for a while."

Cathy is pleased Ben has a purposeful errand to take him away for a short while. She does not want him to witness any more tears. She does not want him to feel that nearly thirty years of her life were sorrow-laden when in fact they were spiced with all the happy events that happen in the life of a family.

Chapter Twenty-Nine - Benny

Benny is sitting on his usual armchair beside the wood stove. As soon as his grandson comes in he lifts the remote control and turns off the television.

"Do you not want to leave it on for the news or anything?"

"I saw enough news at six. Sit down and tell me about your trip," Benny encourages, as his grandson settles into the armchair at the other side of the wood-burning stove.

"Well the highlight of the journey, I met a girl I was hoping to meet."

"That's great. I didn't know you were on a mission like that."

"Lucky I didn't miss her. She's in her final year, studying to be a podiatrist. I went to her father's hostel in Glen Nevis, and she below studying in Glasgow. But I met her today."

"I'm delighted for you. If you do as well as your father did when he met your mother you'll be alright."

"Mam's a good one alright," Ben agrees while he thinks about her sobbing into the linen handkerchiefs downstairs.

"She's been a great support to us all. And I'd say it was hard for her at the start," Benny admits.

"I suppose it was hard for her coming up from south in the middle of the Troubles," Ben reckons.

"It was. And your grandma, and Grandma Rosetta, who was still with us then were hard acts to follow then. Your grandma was involved in everything, Mother's Union, church flowers, the choir, you name it she did it."

"Mam probably thought she'd be expected to live up to a role model."

"I don't think anyone should try to follow role models. They should be happy in their own skin," Benny stresses.

"Grandma said she used to think married women should fit into a certain pattern or image." Ben remembers their conversations on the long journeys to Donegal.

"I used to encourage her to be herself. I married her for who she was, not for who my mother, your great-grandmother Rosetta, might like her to be."

"She really admired Poppy for not feeling she'd to live up to certain expectations."

"Poppy is a great girl. Marilyn loved to go to see her," Benny recalls fondly.

"She sure did," Ben affirms.

"I often think it must've been hard for your mother having a mother-in-law and a grandmother-in-law to row in with," Benny muses. "Though Grandma Rosetta and your mam seemed very at ease with one another, especially after you came along. The three of you would be out in the grove together."

"I think mam became close to Grandma Marilyn too when we were young and you and Grandma used to mind us."

"Marilyn felt needed when you were all little. It gave her a new purpose."

"She'd a great interest in what we all did, though I think Jack was a great favourite. I got to know her better when we went on the trips to Donegal."

"Ours went to boarding school. She'd an empty nest too soon," Benny says regretfully. "She always felt the twins didn't need her. They had one another."

"She mentioned that to me," Ben admits. "It must've been a real disappointment for her."

"When they married two friends and lived beside one another in England she felt really outside the picture."

"I think Mam still misses Grandma Marilyn a lot."

"She's a good daughter-in-law, your mother. I don't know what I'd do without her, especially since I lost Marilyn. It's probably lonely for her. Mark's always out and about, President of this, Captain of that, Chairperson of the other."

Ben silently agrees with his grandfather.

"He says he's networking when he's out and about. I think the best place to network is behind the counter where he can greet his customers," Benny continues.

"I know some of his activities are for good causes but he could be overdoing it."

"We'll try to look out for mam and give her some time to herself," Ben promises.

"I could do the odd shift," Benny reckons. "Now tell me about this girl you met in Scotland."

"I stayed in her father's hostel last June. When I hurt my foot she bandaged it up and brought me to the station."

"That's a good start."

"We kept in touch by Facebook, till she stopped Facebooking to study for her exams."

"How does Facebook work?"

"People sign up as friends. You can be in touch with all of them at once in a general message or do a private message," Ben gives a brief description of Facebook to his eighty-six year old grandfather."

"It's a whole new world."

"I'll bring in my laptop tomorrow and show you how it works and I'll show you Morag's picture."

They sit companionably for a while. Ben observes his grandfather's kindly, yet ageing, countenance. He remembers how his grandfather used to take down the big sweet jars and let them choose a few sweets. Sometimes at night when Marilyn and Mark were out at meetings he would come in and play chess and different board games with them.

The second handkerchief is soaked and Cathy is sobbing in her sleep when Ben comes downstairs. He is glad that his father is not due home from the golf tournament till tomorrow afternoon. He wakes his mother and makes her a cup of ginger tea before they go next door to the cottage. There is a nip in the air on this April night but the heat from the wood stove, which Cathy lit earlier, wafts in their direction as they walk in the door. Cathy makes her way upstairs to bed in preparation for the early shift.

Finn comes home and grunts goodnight before going upstairs. A few minutes later he sticks his head though the half-open door.

"Did anything happen to granddad Andy?"

"No. Why?"

"Mam looks like she was crying."

"I think she feels a bit sad, life has changed so much." Ben answers cautiously.

"Isn't that what life does? It changes." The teenager reasons and then disappears again.

Chapter Thirty - The View

Cathy wakes before five o'clock in the morning. Her eyes are still tired from the crying and her exhaustion has not been wiped away during her uneasy sleep. She opens and closes her eyelids slowly as if to lubricate them. A small glimmer of daylight slips in through the curtains although it is still before sunrise. Moving her warm feet from under the duvet she feels the cool on her toes and she wriggles them about on the cold side of the duvet. She breathes in some cool air. The tingling in her ears from her tinnitus is noticeable but soon the sound of bird calls blocks it out. Certain that all her senses are functioning and ready for the day, when it starts, she withdraws her feet into the warmth again and pulls the warm side of the duvet up over her nose.

Life begins as usual with newspapers and magazines to be put on shelves and deliveries to be received. The tear stains have disappeared from Cathy's face. She would like to chat more with Ben and to hear about how life went for Stewie. She knows he has a daughter Morag and that he manages a hostel. She wonders if the hostel is near the guesthouse which Mhairi and Hamish owned in Glen Nevis all those years ago. She did not hear about Morag's mother. It was too late to ask Ben anymore questions when he woke her to give her the ginger tea last night.

Andrew is on duty along with Heather, and granddad Benny has come in for the morning as he had planned.

"Would you like to head off an hour or two? We're all here." Benny encourages.

"Are you sure?"

"Off course I am. You head away."

"I'll ask Ben would he like to come to the View."

Although Ben's ankle causes a certain amount of discomfort, since his fall ten months ago, he is able to accomplish the climb to the View. Sitting beside the big stone and looking over the bay towards her old home in the Dale Cathy ventures to ask Ben more about Stewie.

"Is Stewie married?" She asks tentatively.

"He married Eva from Bolivia, a cousin of Inez. She never settled. She went back home to look after her mother and to work on projects she was involved in."

"What kind of projects?"

"Clean water, food security, income generation," Ben lists. "And defending land rights too, that takes courage."

"She sounds very idealistic, a good partner for Stewie. Pity she left."

"Eva doesn't count herself gone forever. She comes back every December."

"I'm sure they miss her."

"We'd have missed you if you'd followed your heart and left for any reason," Ben assures his mother.

"How did they manage?"

"They must've managed alright. Morag doesn't look deprived or anything," Ben confirms. "She was about twelve when her mother decided to spend most of her time in Bolivia."

"That's still young."

"You're still looking after Finn every weekend when he comes home from college," Ben teases.

"I looked after all of you when you came back from college."

"I've fond memories of her grandparents, Mhairi and Hamish," she muses. "Are they still alive?"

"Mhairi is."

"She was a very kind lady. And Hamish is gone. It's sad what the years do. The day I met Stewie in Hope Street his father had been very ill. He took ill a few days after our parting."

"That probably made you even sadder?"

"Yeah to think I wasn't there to support them." Ben notices the tears beginning to choke his mother again.

"Morag's very fond of her grandmother. She's very old."

"Nearly ninety, I reckon," Cathy calculates.

"I'd hate to think of Stewie sad. I should've forgiven him," she repeats again. "Then I wouldn't have had you all."

"And Stewie wouldn't have had Morag. And I wouldn't have met her. It must have been fate." He teases her and is pleased her emotions are not as raw and vulnerable as they were last night.

"It amazing you met Morag, a part of Stewie McGregor," she marvels again.

"She looks more a part of Eva, with long thick black hair, very Bolivian looking. But she's still part of Stewie."

"And the two of you walked in the Faslane March. It's good to know young people are still doing it. I used to think we'd change the situation back in the eighties. Thought we could change the world then," she continues pensively.

Ben thinks tears are ready to fall again. But his mother stays calm and pensive. This is the spot they call the View. Many places can be seen from here, at least on a clear day. Today the sky is clear and blue and some fluffy clouds relax near the horizon. Cathy gazes southwards to her birth home in Dale where her father's sad eyes are almost closing on this world. The glimmer never really returned to his once twinkling eyes since the foot and mouth tragedy. She gazes north eastwards in the direction of the Scottish Highlands where Stewie is mostly alone since Eva went back to Bolivia and Morag went to college.

"Will we walk back down? It might be busy at lunchtime and I want to relieve Andrew for his break then," Cathy suggests.

Mother and son walk towards ground level. Both of them watch their steps carefully. Ben's ankle is fragile. And though still relatively agile in her sixtieth year his mother does not have the fitness level she had in the past.

Mark is surprised when he arrives home just as Ben and Cathy drive up towards the shop from the other direction.

"We went for a walk up to the View."

"In the daytime," Mark exclaims with some surprise. "And who looked after the shop?"

"Andrew and Heather and granddad were all there."

"The customers might like to see you. My father always says it's good for the owner to be there to acknowledge the customers."

"We're co-owners, Mark."

"I'd to be at a tournament," Mark answers simply, without realising that he is usually away somewhere.

They walk into the living room behind the shop.

"Anyhow, I don't think our customers see our children, or your father, as strangers. The boys have been behind the counter since they were knee high. And Andrew will eventually be taking over."

"Eventually he will, but not yet. We're not even sixty,"

"By the end of the year we'll have both reached that milestone."

Mark looks pensive for a few minutes as if he dreads the onset of this milestone. He is still handsome though. He was handsome when she first knew him in boarding school. His grey blue eyes are still vivacious and his dark brown hair though greying at the temples is wavy and full of volume.

"How did my father end up working?"

"He said to Ben he'd like to do some work again. Then this morning he asked me if I'd like an hour or two off."

"He's eighty-six."

"Doesn't that give us hope? We can be helping in twenty-six years' time."

"That's scary stuff. But if we're as alert as my father we wouldn't complain."

"I'll go down home to see dad tonight." Cathy says to Mark before she leaves the living room to let Andrew come in for his break.

It disconcerts Mark that after all the years of marriage Cathy still refers to the Dale as home. He wonders what she feels about her connection to Mountview, where she raised their sons and slotted well into the community.

"What about the shop? We're having a bit of do at the club. I'll have to be there. And I'll have to go down for a while in the afternoon to prepare."

"No worries at all. Ben said he'll do the last couple hours and close up."

"Remind him to wear a hairnet. He can't be near the deli with that nest of hair."

"Remember when you'd a fine heap of hair and the headmaster kept badgering you to cut it."

"I think I've a fine head of hair still, no receding or balding." Mark rubs his hand across his hair and appears quite pleased with its texture.

Chapter Thirty-One - Into the Western Sun

The sun is setting as Cathy drives around the bay. It is adding a soft orange glow to the shimmering water. She always loves this scene, no matter how often she passes by here. It is ever beautiful, yet ever changing, depending on the time of day, the season and the weather.

Usually as she hugs around the bay, whether driving into the western sun or beneath a grey sky, she is going home to the Dale, going home to visit her father who is more than ninety years old. She sometimes wonders if home will change when her father closes his eyes for the last time on the Dale. She is confident that her only sibling Colin will always welcome her. He understood her pain all those years ago. He never queried her or alluded to the pain since the day they both sat on the white stones back in 1986. Later those white stones kept telling a poignant story when all the sheep were gone, slain, and the inanimate stones remained. She recalls how Beryl had reminded her that it would be good for Colin to have her back in Ireland when he would no longer have them.

She rarely explores ideas with Mark. The biggest obstacle to sharing ideas or feelings with Mark is his hectic schedule. Just as a concern might reach his ear a phone might ring and grab his attention, and often summon him away to the golf club or some other commitment. Maybe she could share thoughts with Ben. A new bond has been fastened between them, fortified by their love of a father and daughter. The idea that Hamish has in fact died fills her with sadness even though he would be ninety-two years old if he was alive and he had a narrow escape with death thirty years ago. She was engaged to Mark when she heard of that incident. Beryl got her back on track with the determination of a pilot bringing a jumbo jet to land in an emergency. Mark was to be the man for her and Beryl would not have it any other way.

Mark is, and always was, a good-looking and charming man. Still he avoided Cupid's arrows of love, or at least any firm commitment, until he was almost thirty by which time most of his admirers had settled in their own love nests. Then some quirk of fate brought the two of them to a choral festival. Mark's easy manner poured balm over her hidden broken heart. And the same easy charm won her back when disagreements arose between them on a number of occasions and threatened their engagement.

Deep down she always had affection for Stewie. She sobbed bitterly in his mother's arms in the hotel cloakroom by the shores Loch Linnhe. She never shed tears over her lost love again until last night. She had simply filed the happy memories of Stewie in the deep recesses of her mind until Ben who was carried, as an embryo, up Ben Nevis in 1986, was instrumental in finding him.

Her reveries fill the journey as she drives around the sparkling bay and then on the short distance further to her father's house. Just before she turns into the driveway of the well-kept farmhouse her distraction causes her to misjudge her position on the narrow road. Swerving to avoid a van, her front wheel leaves the road and becomes embedded in the ditch. With the aid of Colin's tractor her car is freed. Her nephew Edwin beats out the dinge in the panel of the car while Jennifer, her ever hospitable sister-in-law, showers her with care and attention.

Andy had been concerned that the pressure placed upon Cathy back in 1986, when she was having doubts about getting married, might lead to trouble further down the road. Sitting now by the aga cooker in the large kitchen he is unaware that these feelings have darted back into her heart. He sits there, ever present for his daughter, while she appears pale and tired and burned out.

"Don't be too late on the road," he encourages.

Cathy sets back out on the road. The shock of the small accident compels her to shelve her daydreams and regrets for the rest of the night. On her journey northwards around the bay she is rigidly attentive.

Back in Mountview Ben has closed the shop and is chatting to Morag on the phone.

"I can't believe the feelings mam had for your dad," Ben reveals. "She cried her eyes out last night thinking about him."

"Dad's hankering and sad about her too," Morag explains. "I went up to stay with him last night. He was delighted to meet you. He talked about your mam and their break up as if it happened last week."

"Mam's delighted I met you."

"Dad's the same. He said imagine you met Cathy's bairn."

"I just said 'there's no pressure on me, dad. I'm going to have to like Ben loads just for you.'"

Cathy starts feeling tired and numb as she drives along trying to keep her full attention on the dark road. She has passed the curve of the bay where the moonlight on the glistening water was a guide and a comfort to her. She pulls her car to a halt in a lay-by and falls asleep near a house with tall chimneys. The ringing of her phone wakes her with a jolt.

"Are you alright, mam?"

"I think so," Cathy mumbles.

"You only think so, mam. What happened to you?"

"I felt a bit tired and stopped for a while. I must've fallen asleep. I'll be alright now."

"I'll ask granddad to come with me to meet you and I'll drive you back."

"Don't disturb granddad. I'm not far away. I'd a swerve just as I was about to turn into the house. A van came around the corner and I went off the road a bit."

"That was a shock for you."

"It could've been much worse if it'd happened anywhere else. Colin got the car out and Edwin beat out the dinge. It looks fine."

"Don't worry about anything. Just stay where you are and we'll be there very soon."

"I'm near the house with the high chimneys"

Chapter Thirty-Two - The Prevailing Culture

"How's Cathy this morning," Benny asks Mark.

"I think she's alright. She's in the shop."

"She'd a mishap last night. She swerved to avoid a van and her car went off the road. Colin got it out with the tractor."

"At least she wasn't hurt," Mark sighs with relief.

"She went into a bit of shock. She pulled in and fell asleep on the way home. Ben and I went to meet her."

"She just headed into the shop like any other morning and never mentioned it."

He hastens into the shop where his wife is arranging the newspapers on to the shelves.

"Are you alright, Cathy, after all you've been through?"

Cathy notices the concern in his grey-blue eyes.

"I'm fine," she replies with a jolt of surprise.

After all I've been through. She mulls over Mark's sentiments of concern. She wonders what he knows she has been through.

"Dad told me about your car and the shock you had."

"Edwin got the dinge out and he'll do another bit of work to make it like new."

"Don't worry about the car. You go in and rest. I'll finish off this."

Cathy goes back into the living-room. She continues to crochet the olive-green-suits for Malachi and Marilyn's naming ceremony which is happening at Bealtaine.

"What'd my mother have thought of two baby druids if she'd lived to see this ceremony?" Mark speculates as he comes back into the living room mid-morning and sees Cathy beavering away at the suits.

"Maybe we assumed too much about what grandma might think."

"Still it's a bit of a leap from everyday Christianity, the kind my mother practiced."

"She must've been happy enough with druidic ways when she kept going back to Poppy and Jack."

"She mightn't have associated the emblems and images with druidism. There were other faiths included. I saw a big rosary beads above the mantelpiece," Mark recalls.

"She was very taken by everything and mentioned what some of them meant. She made a stain-glass Awen for Poppy to bring at New Year."

"She never knew your position. And she spent nearly thirty years with you."

"More to my shame, I think."

"You let her die happy,"

"I wonder did I, Mark?"

"Why do you doubt it, love?"

"She was so eager to get back to Jack and Poppy at New Year. You'd think she wanted to die there. She said they were genuine and didn't feel the need to impress people."

"No doubt about that. But Poppy is not here in the shop. I think you got it right, love."

"Druids believe in honouring the ancestors. Poppy and Jack believe her spirit's still floating around them."

"That's very airy fairy. I suppose there's more room for different shades of belief now," Mark concedes.

"There is," Cathy says simply, not wanting to delve deeper into her disappointment that Marilyn did not live long enough for them to share some of their inner feelings.

"We were following the prevailing culture of the time."

"Ah no, Mark, I wouldn't have been ashamed to say what I believed in."

"Hope you've not been too disappointed with the past twenty-nine years. We've four great sons to show for our time." Mark continues.

"We have four wonderful sons," Cathy agrees. "It's just I suspected grandma knew something and wanted to share it."

"Why did you think that?"

"When she was leaving for Donegal at New Year she said both of us, her and me, had freedom and let it slip through our fingers. And that we'd chat about it when she got home."

"Wonder what she meant."

"She said when we became wives, we fitted into a mould, thought we should live up to expectations."

"That was amazing coming from my mother who never put a foot out of place."

"She definitely had something on her mind," Cathy muses.

"We'll never know now."

"You'll come over to Donegal for the naming ceremony, won't you Mark?"

"What's the date again?"

"It's the first Saturday in May."

"Oh! That's not a good day. There's an event in the club. And you'd probably need to be here."

"Ah no, Mark, I can't be here."

"It's good for one of us to here, love."

"I'm here every Saturday, and most other days. But I can't be here that one."

"Sorry, love. It's just that there are so many events happening at the moment."

"We'll get cover. We've good staff." Cathy says confidently.

"Will you really go? It's a long drive across."

"Of course, I'll go. Ben's going. He promised grandma he'd always keep in touch with Jack."

"Who'll look after the place if you're gone?"

"Andrew, Heather, possibly Janice, and Benny would keep an eye out in case there's extra help needed."

"My father's a bit old for that?"

"He can give that touch of gravitas you wanted," Cathy teases.

"It sounds a bit disruptive."

"Mark, I hope you're joking. I've been working full days almost every Saturday for the past years and you were able to go anywhere you wanted."

"Sorry, love. I have to be at the club."

"I've no problem with you being at the club. To be expected to miss the babies' ceremony for the sake of club event really disappoints me. I feel taken for granted."

"You know how important club events and things are," Mark tries to reason.

"They're as important as you make them, Mark."

Mark is surprised at Cathy's annoyance.

"Maybe I went a step too far," he says cautiously. "Maybe you're still suffering from shock after the accident."

"Take it you've gone a step too far. And it might be good to get someone to deputise for you at the club in case you'd like to go to the ceremony."

"I couldn't let the club down. The golf days bring in much funds to the charities," Mark reasons. And so the wheels of philanthropy are oiled. The symbiotic union between the sport and the charities run seamlessly with Mark at the helm.

"When we were engaged you warned me not to speak about my activities and ever since I'm like a support system to you to do yours."

"I thought you'd forgotten about that, love."

"You don't know me at all."

Fortunately for Mark a delivery van drives up and stymies the possible conflict.

"McHugh's are here, love. I'd better give Andrew a hand."

He lands a kiss on Cathy cheek.

"We'll chat about this another time, love," he promises.

"Maybe tonight," Cathy suggests.

"It can't be tonight, love. There's a Grocers' meeting. Sorry."

This is the story of their lives.

"You rest for another while," he advises with concern. "Sorry about everything." And for this instant a soft smile from those blue-grey eyes mollifies her unease.

"I think I'll make a start on some Best Kept Village work."

"You certainly do my mother proud in that regard," he assures her as the door between the living room and shop is closing behind him and his smile still lingers.

Cathy folds away the baby suits. She needs some fresh April air. Deep down there is a latent sadness. Following the prevailing culture never sat well with the younger Cathy Campbell. If it did she would not have had so many encounters with police on protest lines or in patrol vans or cells. She has allowed her own ideology to be suppressed. Sometimes she feels soulless.

As she crosses to the greenhouse at the back of the cottage she notices the golden furze throwing splashes of warm colour all around, while primroses brighten the low mossy bank at the edge of the grove. She starts to sort the plants by height and colour and texture. As she falls into the rhythm of sorting, arranging, planning and sketching she cannot believe it is less than forty hours since she poured out every tear she had over a long lost love.

Chapter Thirty-Three - Milestones

"You'll come back a different woman," Mark teases as Cathy and Ben set out to Donegal for the naming ceremony.

"I hope so. It sure changed grandma," Cathy jokes light-heartedly as she hops into the passenger seat of her Renault Clio. Ben is doing the first part of the driving. It is a bright May morning and the countryside unfolds like an enormous canvas around them. Heaps of white fluffy clouds are piled up near the horizon of the bright blue sky. Newly greened hedges surround small fields. Splashes of golden furze and larger expanses of golden rapeseed fields glide by. A golden hillock appears ahead, the whole dome bedecked in furze.

"Grandma introduced me to this hotel. I'd have thought it outside my comfort zone but it's really nice." Ben turns into the hotel where the staff offered their sympathies on Marilyn's passing just four months ago.

"It was good you'd had those trips together."

"On our last trip she said I should take you to Jack and Poppy's place."

"That was very thoughtful. And that was her last trip. Nice she left this world in a place she loved," Cathy continues sadly.

"I hope you enjoy it as much as she did."

"I expect I will. Grandma was really taken by how genuine and free Poppy was. It might be a lesson in freedom for me."

"You're not thinking of eloping or anything like that?"

"No nothing as bold as that," Cathy assures him.

Cathy takes the driver's seat and they continue until they are in the shadow of Mount Errigal. Splashes of blue forget-me-nots and campanula appear behind white painted stones in the simple garden when they drive through the big open gate. Some dandelions have found a home here and are left undisturbed as bee food. The usual warm welcome awaits them. Cathy is soon enchanted by the symbols and surroundings that made Marilyn happy. Among the eclectic mix of icons and symbols is a small shrine in memory of Marilyn. Freedom seeps into Cathy's veins as if by osmosis.

With Poppy's grandfather, Malachi, and her parents, Manus and Annabelle, they cross a field dotted with daisies, buttercup, speedwell and red clover. New foliage has unfurled on the dishevelled branches of the hawthorn which grows above the well, the tree which Poppy and her sisters once called the raggedy tree. Unlike the seasonal foliage some rags appear to have been clinging on for decades. It is beside this pool of possibility that babies Malachi and Marilyn, dressed in their olive-green-suits, are named and welcomed to the world.

"I can take you in a cup of mint tea in the morning," Poppy offers. "Would six be too early? Or would you prefer later?"

"Six would be perfect, Poppy, only if it suits you. I'm not used to tea in bed."

Cathy sleeps in the room where Marilyn slept. A magnificent patchwork quilt covers the big bed. She opens her window to allow the strains of the dawn chorus to pour in and wake her. Then rolling herself into a foetal ball she tries to feel Marilyn's spirit around her. She awakes in the middle of the night and feels warm movement beside her. Although she had wished for the experience of Marilyn's spirit she is too apprehensive to take the quilt from over her face and turn on the bedside lamp. She starts a one-way chat, telling Marilyn's spirit that she appreciates her spirit is nearby. She doses, wakes again, doses again, wakes again and the warm light movement persists.

She wakes to the symphony of the dawn chorus. She does not even place her feet out over the quilt as is her morning habit. Instead she remains still, treasuring the warmth. Before the dawn chorus rises to a full crescendo a sudden jerky movement makes her gasp with shock, then a muffled noise at the window and the warmth is gone. Marilyn has left, she laments in her mind. Now she is disappointed she did not remove the quilt from her face.

"You didn't have a visitor?" Poppy asks as she hands Cathy the cup of mint tea just after six o'clock.

Cathy is ashamed to admit she was afraid to look out from under the quilt. In the next room one of the twins wakes with a whimper. Poppy answers the call. As Cathy sips her mint tea she thinks of Marilyn. Grandma had come to visit her and she did not look out.

"If things work out with Morag I'll look for a job in Glasgow."

Ben is in the driving seat on the way home when he reveals his plans to his mother and jolts her out of reveries about Marilyn.

"It mightn't be wise to rush things, or to feel you've to be together for me or Stewie," Cathy advises, as she takes herself back to reality.

"I've a good feeling about this. Glasgow's a cool place to work."

"I loved my years there. I'd be so happy if everything worked out for you and Morag. But I wouldn't want to influence you."

"I think you've influenced me already, seeing as our paths keep crossing."

Morag achieves her honours degree in podiatry and plans to continue her voluntary work in the shelter. Over her years of volunteering she has become familiar with the kind of foot ailments suffered by homeless people, conditions often caused by poor footwear, dampness and untreated injuries. She is not squeamish about fungal infections or trench foot, an ailment reminiscent of war-time when feet were often soaked in cold water for long periods. She avoids showing signs of shock while sensitively treating whatever ailment is presented.

As a respite after her study, she attends a Lughnasadh festival in south west Scotland. Here she partakes in the traditional aspects of the weekend, dancing like a child in high grass, climbing hills and making bread from the first harvested oat grains.

The facilitator, Amy Powell, and the participants relax after their meal on Saturday evening. Morag relates the story of her father and his former sweetheart, Cathy.

"They'd never have met, nor would I've met Ben, if he hadn't stayed in our hostel the night he finished the Way last year," Morag marvels.

"Ben? Has he a big heap of curls?" Lyndsey holds her two open palms around her head to demonstrate the shape of the curls.

"He has."

"I met him. It has to be him. He's from Ireland." Lyndsey bubbles with delight. "Remember, Amy. We met him two nights in a row."

"Of course I remember him, the lovely Irish lad. You played Scrabble with him."

"I'd never such a good a game before or since."

"You emptied your undies and everything out of your rucksack to find a face net for him," Amy recalls.

Lyndsey blushes at the thought of all that tumbled from her rucksack on to the common room couch.

"We met again in our next hostel and played Scrabble again," Lyndsey continues. "He won that game. I couldn't get a place for the J." The competitive spirit, hidden behind this small angelic face, is surfacing.

"You couldn't keep winning or there'd be no fun," Amy counsels her young sister.

"He was lovely. We saw him before he left next morning. Imagine you met him that evening, Morag." Lyndsey is intrigued at the co-incidence.

"It just goes to show the great interconnectedness of people," Chloe chimes in.

"The best example of interconnection has to be Morag's dad and Ben's mum," Lyndsey concludes.

The Lughnasadh festival continues till late Sunday afternoon and Morag cannot help wondering if Lyndsey was enchanted by Ben too.

"I'm a lucky girl to have found you," Morag teases impishly as they sit together in her Glasgow flat the following weekend.

Ben has incorporated a Friday afternoon job interview into his weekend visit.

"If I hadn't gone to your dad's hostel we'd never have met. The sore ankle was worth it. Your treatment got us on a good footing so to speak."

"I still consider myself very lucky," Morag continues playfully. "Someone else really admired you along the way?"

"It must've been Lyndsey from Dumfries," Ben answers simply.

"It was. You remember her. Did you know she admired you?" Morag teases.

"She was the only girl I was really chatting to for long. We played two great games of Scrabble."

"She said she'd never met such a good Scrabble opponent before or since."

"She's a great Scrabble player, one of the best I ever met."

"We'll have to have game of Scrabble sometime," Morag suggests.

"Sorry I never asked you to play. It's boring for anyone that's not into it"

"I'm into it. I used to play Scrabble with dad. With study and everything we got out of the habit."

"I used to play with mam in the evenings when dad was out at meetings."

"They used to play Scrabble together. Dad told me."

"I can buy a game in the morning," Ben offers.

"I've a game somewhere. I won't be as nifty as Lyndsey Powell though."

"How did you meet Lyndsey?" Ben wonders.

"Her sister was our leader at the Lughnasadh festival."

"Amy?"

"You remember her too?"

"She was with Lyndsey on the walk. When we were playing Scrabble she was meditating on a bench beside the river."

"They're really beautiful girls. I'm not surprised you connected with them," Morag affirms.

"They were a very friendly group, Chloe as well, and the three lads that were with them. Rick was Lyndsey's boyfriend."

"They're not boyfriend and girlfriend at the moment. Rick's doing a round the world trip and Lyndsey wasn't interested in going. They split up for a while."

"The morning I was leaving Kinghouse she gave me a midge net."

"Amy teased her about empting her undies out in the common room to find it."

"She was so guileless. Just pegging things to one side till she found it," Ben recalls.

"Imagine an entomologist not having his own midge net," Morag continues playfully.

"Culicoides impunctatus doesn't feel so painful in the classroom," Ben jokes."

"It's amazing you met," he continues. "When I left Kinlochleven I was thinking that all the lovely people I met on the way are weaved into an unending tapestry of walkers."

"That's a beautiful thought, Ben Wright. You should be a philosopher instead of an entomologist."

"I think I can make a difference as an entomologist. It just seems a good sign when you all connected at the weekend,"

"Look no further than our parents who connected after thirty years," proclaims Morag. "I told them about their story. That's how we got to chat about you."

"They were a lovely friendly bunch," Ben muses.

"Are you sure you want to keep job hunting in Glasgow?"

"Off course I am."

"We wouldn't want someone to be relating the Lyndsey and Ben story in another few decades."

"I'm really happy I've met you. I just thought it was great meeting all the friendly walkers. It's probably more special when you're walking alone."

"I'm only teasing you. I was chuffed to hear the girls praising you."

Ben is offered a job. He is to work with a team to promote the enjoyment of the city's natural resources and ensure their protection. He finds a flat in the same block as Morag. Cathy misses him, but appreciates the link with Stewie. She is back to an empty nest now that Finn has left home to study PE at University and Andrew lives over the shop, since Benny lost Marilyn in January. Mark is busy as ever.

Chapter Thirty-Four - Apparition in a Churchyard

Straw bales dot golden stubble fields as Cathy drives towards the Dale on a September day. Hawthorn leaves are tinged with yellow and the haws a deep red. She drives on passed the russets and brown and yellows and turns into her old home, aware that her father, Andy, will not be on this earth for much longer. His health deteriorated rapidly after his ninety-second birthday. Poppy tried to holistically restore him to relative good health. Finally she accepted that he is about to take his final journey.

Cathy is maintaining an overnight vigil at his bedside. His breathing is frail. Were it not for the slight movement of the striped blanket she would think that his gentle, yet resilient, spirit had flown from him.

"What day is it?" His frail voice whispers.

"Sunday, 27th September," Cathy whispers back.

"Your birthday's tomorrow."

"I'm sixty tomorrow, Dad," Cathy replies sadly. She wonders will she still have him tomorrow. He is getting frailer with each passing minute. "I'm glad we're together for my birthday."

"I mightn't be here much longer."

Cathy squeezes his hand, acknowledging what he has said.

"There's a total eclipse of the full moon expected at around three in the morning. You always knew your moons, Dad."

The Blood Moon shines bright rendering the sky red. By the time this spectacle happens Andy is gone into a deep sleep. Cathy walks over to window and sees the Dale in the red glow. Jennifer slips quietly into the room. Then Colin joins them in silent togetherness.

"We're all together for your birthday, sis." Colin holds his sister's hand.

The almost imperceptible movement of the striped blanket ceases at 6.35 am, shortly before daybreak. Three days later, people gather in Saint James' church to pay respects to a hard-working genuine man, a good family man and a good neighbour. Jennifer, a mezzo-soprano and a member of the choir during all her adult life, sings solo in honour of a father-in-law she has loved and admired for nearly forty years. The rich melodies pour out through the open door and fill the air.

Around the grave stand Colin and Jennifer accompanied by their son Edwin. Mark is one side of Cathy and Ben and Morag, who came directly from the boat to the church, are on her other side. Jack and Poppy hold a baby each. The babies, now starting to walk, wriggle to break free. Finn is next to his father. Andrew and Janice stand arm in arm. Is this a budding romance or caring for a friend? Cathy wonders. Her mind turns back again to the final farewells for her father. As the other mourners circle around the family and around the sandy mound of clay she notices someone standing slightly outside the circle. A tall mountainy man with a soft friendly face that has not altered much in three decades gazes towards her. His wispy hair, now grey and long, is blowing about in the wind. It is Stewie. Cathy's pulse quickens, then races. Her face pales. Mark, holding her hand, notices the perceptible change.

"Are you alright, Cathy?"

"Yeah, I'm doing fine Mark, thanks?

"I felt your heart racing. Are you feeling weak?" Mark whispers. Ben overhears his father's remark and wonders if bringing Stewie along was a mistake.

"I'll be okay, just a bit overwhelmed and tired."

The graveside prayers come to a pause and the vicar invites people to drop some clay onto Andy's coffin. This invitation changes the tempo. Cathy stoops down, gets a trowel and starts to place some of the soil, loved by her father for so long, into his grave. Then she takes handfuls of the fine soil and sifts it through her fingers into the almost filled grave until a gust of wind blows some of the fine clay into her eye.

Cathy, Colin and Jennifer welcome the mourners into the Parish Hall, where Jennifer's friends from the church organise refreshments.

"It's so good to see you again, Stewie. Thanks so much for making the journey."

She can feel her legs becoming jelly-like.

"Glad to be here, I am, Cathy."

"It's great to see our children together. Ben's very fond of Morag."

"And Morag too has a great fondness for him"

"It means so much to me you being here, Stewie. We'll get a chance for a better chat later."

Mark approaches Ben in the Parish Hall.

"I wonder would you take care of your mam. I decided I might as well go on the tour after all."

"Oh!" Ben is initially shocked that his father is heading away to Portugal so soon. Then he tries to hide his dismay, thinking it would be less awkward for his mother to chat with Stewie if Mark was away.

"What does mam think?" He asks tentatively.

"Mam's fine with it."

Mam is forgiving as usual, Ben thinks to himself.

"I'm heading home now. Would you like to come with me or would you rather stay longer," Mark asks his father Benny.

"You're leaving early. I'll stay on."

"That's grand. I'll head so."

"Why are you going so soon? There are a lot of people still about."

"I decided I'll go on the golf tour now that's Andy's funeral is over."

"You're off to Portugal on the day of Cathy's father's funeral. I'm astounded, Mark."

"Astounded? Cathy's alright about it."

"What way did I raise you, Mark?" The older man shakes his head.

"Are you going now dad?" Finn hastens towards his father. "Can I go with you?"

"Why wouldn't you stay on, Finn? You've no excuse to go."

"You haven't a good excuse either, dad."

"Why?"

"I don't think a golf holiday's a good excuse, on the day of granddad's funeral."

"Your mam doesn't mind."

"Mam's very quiet," Finn mumbles.

"Better let your mam know you're coming home or she'll be looking for you later," Mark advises. "There'll be nobody at home with your friends all away at college."

"I don't mind that."

Father and son drive quietly along. Mark reflects on his father's very rare reprimand about his leaving for Portugal so soon. Finn rebuffed him for the same reason. Cathy was very reasonable about it. He does not encourage any further opinions on his decision from Finn who is preoccupied on his phone.

"Are you enjoying the course?" Mark eventually breaks the silence.

"It's grand. I didn't know there'd so much school subjects like physiology and psychology."

"I suppose you'd need to understand all about the body and the mind to teach physical education."

"I suppose."

They fall into silence again with only the click of Finn's fingers on the phone breaking the silence.

"Morag did a protest at a military equipment exhibition." Finn sounds animated. "Fair play to her," he continues admiringly.

"How do you know?"

"Ben's Facebook page," Finn answers as he presses like and share.

Mark is jolted by this. He remembers how he censored Cathy's activities, not wanting Marilyn to hear about them. From now on none of the future Mrs. Wrights can be silenced.

They arrive at Mountview. Mark finishes packing his luggage and his clubs. He is ready to meet his golfing friends at the club and then go to the airport.

"Are you sure you're alright her on your own, Finn?"

"Of course I'm alright on my own, Dad."

And for a few minutes Mark appears reluctant to leave his youngest son.

"I don't like leaving you on your own."

"No, I'm grand, dad, its Mam I'd be worried about."

Chapter Thirty-Five - Revelations

"I saw you once since we met on Hope Street," Cathy reveals.

"Was it at Loch Linnhe? I saw you too, playing Scrabble near the TV."

"I'd seen you from the bedroom balcony. I was looking through my binoculars for some rare sightings."

"And you saw a Scotsman, not a rare sighting at Loch Linnhe."

"I gasped. Mark asked if I'd seen something interesting." She giggles at the thought of Mark's question.

"I was at gran's ninetieth birthday party," Stewie remembers.

"I know. I met your mam in the cloakroom."

"She nae said a word."

"She promised she wouldn't. We didn't want to cause you upset."

"That was thoughtful."

"I can tell you now," Cathy says in a lowered voice. "I cried so hard your mam dried my tears, and put on some make-up for me."

"And came back to the party as if nowt happened," he squeezes her hand affectionately.

"When she had me looking presentable we hugged and said goodbye. It was one of the warmest hugs of my life."

"She often speaks of you. She nae forgot you."

Sitting around the fire back at the cottage in Mountview they all chat together.

"Only for ye got lost in the mist, Ben, we might nae be here at all."

"I'm interested in this," Cathy probes further.

"It was my own fault. I didn't listen to Stewie, or to you. When I turned back it was too late."

"We were fretting, Morag and me. The helicopter came with the young ones, but could nae find you."

"I can't believe you'd the rescue services looking for you," Cathy says aghast.

"Poor laddie came back next mornin' with a bad ankle," Stewie recalls.

"Irresponsible laddie, more like it," Cathy chides him.

"Morag looked after the ankle. I didn't want to leave at all."

"You kept your word and came back to Nevis," Morag enthuses.

"I was pleased to hear ye were at the demonstration," Cathy encourages.

"We're second generation Faslaners." Ben moves the limelight back on to his mother.

"Did you miss the campaigning when you left Scotland?"

"I did, and still do, Morag. I do e-campaigning. There are big campaigns to be won, like chemical companies threatening to sue the EU for banning neonicotinoid that destroy bees. Imagine."

"If bees were gone our food systems would be finished," Ben forewarns. "It'd be suicidal."

"TTIP is another worry of 2015. Each successive year brings its own share of concerns." Cathy muses.

"What does TTIP stand for?" Finn, who came downstairs to make a sandwich, enquires.

"Transatlantic Trading and Investment Partnership," Cathy explains. "They don't want restrictions on international trade, regardless of social or environmental consequences. They'd prosecute states if their profits were curbed."

Finn becomes interested in the conversation and joins them.

"You did a protest at a military show, Morag. Fair play to you," he says admiringly.

"How do you know?" Ben asks.

"It's on Facebook."

"Hope you liked it"

"Off course, I did. And shared it and commented on it," Finn confirms.

"Arms companies try to convince people that arms are needed for stability," Morag laments. "The money goes on arms rather than on basic needs."

"With social media at least we know some of what's happening," Ben encourages.

"When I came here in 1986 there was nobody I knew interested in campaigns."

"There was, Cathy," Benny reveals.

She looks towards her father-in-law expectantly.

"Grandma heard about your protests the day before she went to Donegal. She was disappointed she didn't know about them sooner."

"Maybe that's why she wanted to have a girls' night when she'd get back." Cathy says sadly. "Was she involved in campaigns?"

"The women in her family were in the Revolutionary Workers' Group and the Flax and Textiles Workers Union. Millworkers they were, struggling for equal pay and conditions, and communists too."

"Imagine Marilyn a revolutionary. I just thought she was a conventional woman, doing her church work and the choir and all her other community stuff."

"I suppose most people around thought the same. She was always trying to please my mother, Rosetta."

"I wonder if great-grandma Rosetta was trying to please the mother-in-law before her," Ben muses.

"I wouldn't say so. Rosetta knew she up there with the best, with baronesses and ladies."

"If I'd known about Marilyn we could've shared our stories and maybe done things together. We could've protested against fracking or the loss of the dunes or oil pipelines going through people's land. . ."

"Maybe you'd come over to Scotland and join in a Faslane march," Morag suggests.

"I'd love to go to Scotland again."

"Come back with us and you'd have a lift and company all the way," Ben encourages.

"I'd better not go this time. I'm doing the early shifts in the shop."

"That's no excuse, Cathy. I'll cover for you," Benny assures her.

"Are you sure? That'd be great. But I wonder should I leave."

Poppy and Jack, who have settled their babies upstairs, join them.

"Mam's coming to Scotland with us in the morning," Ben says enthusiastically.

"We'll be here for a couple of days and can help too," Poppy offers.

"Fair play to you mam. I'll help when I'm back at the weekend," Finn chimes.

"Hope your dad won't be upset that I'm gone when he's away."

"No. Go ahead, mam. We'll look after stuff."

"Well thanks very much, Finn."

Andrew opens the front door and the hinge makes the usual creaky sound. He had gone up to Hightown to leave Janice home.

"Safe journey and don't worry about anything, mam," he encourages as he and granddad step back out into the darkness to go next door.

"Poppy, you and Jack might like to come over sometime. There's an event you'd enjoy at the end of the month, a Samhain Festival."

"That sounds good, Morag. We might get some of my family to mind the babies."

"Or bring them if you can't. Children are welcome. You just row in with whatever you can."

"Were you there before, Morag?" Poppy asks.

"I was there for the Lughnasadh festival. I met a few people that Ben met on the West Highland Way." She smiles towards Ben. "One of them had such admiration for him I didn't know whether to tell him or not."

"Was that the Scrabble girl?" Cathy asks.

"You heard about the Scrabble girl, Cathy. I think I'm lucky to be sitting here at all."

Chapter Thirty-Six - Back in the Highlands

The phone in the shop rings early in the morning. Benny answers it.

"Is Cathy alright?" Mark remembers her racing heartbeat at the graveside.

"She went back with Ben for a wee break. I'm doing her shifts."

"She went to Scotland? Just like that," Marks exclaims in amazement.

"She'd the chance of a lift and the company. She headed off with Ben and Morag, and Stewie."

"Stewie?"

"Morag's father," Benny explains.

"Oh! And you've to look after the early shifts?"

"I'm glad to help Cathy out. And Heather's here setting up the deli."

"It's a bit of an upheaval."

"The few days away will do her good. And I'm enjoying the shop."

"Are Jack and Poppy still there?"

"They're staying till the day after tomorrow."

"And Cathy left them."

"They encouraged her to go."

"They encouraged her to go, and me gone already?"

"You've to admit, Mark, she never leaves. And she lets you go whenever you wish."

"I've to go with the club," Mark says defensively. "What about Finn?"

"Andrew has just brought him to the train. He'll be down Saturday."

"And his mother won't be there."

"He'll be fine. They were all getting along so well last night. We thought it'd be a good break for Cathy."

"I suppose you're right."

"Are things alright for you out there?"

"They're sort of. When the plane took off I felt I'd left too soon."

"It was a hasty departure alright," Benny concedes.

"Some of the members were surprised to see me. I wasn't sure if they were praising or scolding."

"It's not like to you mind which they did."

"When's Cathy back?"

"She's back the day before you."

Mark mulls over the situation. He left Cathy the afternoon she buried her father. Now she is in Scotland with different shoulders to cry on. Not that he himself stays anchored for long enough to be a shoulder to cry on. He's always busy. He tries to console himself that he has achieved a lot.

The boat docks and the foursome head northwards in Morag's red Nissan Micra. Cathy is seeing Scotland again after nearly three decades. Ailsa Craig, the familiar volcanic island, appears like a domed rock about ten miles out in the sea from Girvan. The island, though appearing tiny, is home to thousands of gannets and puffins. She feels at home seeing the landmark, or the seamark, so familiar on her return journeys to Glasgow all those years ago. By afternoon they arrive at Glen Nevis. Stewie removes the sign from the hostel door which, in his absence, informs travellers about nearby accommodation.

A text comes into Ben's phone. "Thanks for looking after your mother. Take good care of her."

So dad-like, Ben thinks. No reprimands, even if he thought they should not have taken Cathy away while he was in Portugal. Mark Wright could wear annoyance with dignity.

Early next morning Morag takes Cathy to Cow Hill, where the cattle of crofters used to graze along the slopes. Highland cattle graze here now. They are part of a conservation plan to keep the grass to the right level for wildflowers and butterflies. Cathy and Stewie often climbed these slopes, when the hostel was a guest house run by Mhairi and Hamish. It is a steep ascent. From the summit climbers are rewarded with full circle views. She can see Loch Linnhe where she had furtive glimpses of Stewie twenty-nine years ago.

"I was so lucky to meet Ben in the hostel," Morag interjects as the two women admire the spectacular landscape

"He's very happy to have met you too."

"We almost missed one another the next time, and the two of us on the march."

"He said he was hoping to meet a girl when he left home. And you were the girl."

"I'd stopped going into Facebook to study for my finals, and he couldn't let me know."

"Then he'd the chat with your dad and it all worked out."

"It was great you and dad found one another. It means a lot to dad."

"And to me," Cathy answers simply.

By lunchtime they are back at the hostel where Stewie and Ben have prepared the rooms for the small group who are checking in. October sees the hostelling season slow down with a just small trickle of guests passing through.

"Is there anywhere you'd like to go while you're here?" Morag asks as they are having lunch.

"I'd like to visit Mhairi."

They arrive at Sunset Villas where apartments for older people surround a support complex.

"We've brought you a special visitor," Stewie beams.

"I nae forgot you, hen." Tears come to the old woman's eyes.

Stewie, Morag and Ben go to the dining room in the main area to allow Cathy and Mhairi time together.

"Only for Morag met your bairn, we'd nae have met again."

The couch in Stewie's cosy living room is upholstered in moss green corduroy giving it a soft homely appearance. The cushion on the right hand side has a deep hollow. This is the spot where Stewie relaxes after his work around the hostel or in the gardens or his walks, especially across Cow Hill. Books, magazines and newsletters are strewn about randomly. Cathy peruses a newsletter of a Bolivian charity. The charity is instrumental in the provision of clean water, as well as allotments and seed saving banks to ensure food security and micro-finance projects to enable women to weave and sell their garments. Other beneficial projects are at the planning stage.

"This is great work in Bolivia," she enthuses as Stewie returns to the living room with logs for the stove. "And Eva's the director," Cathy sees the name, Eva Vargas MacGregor.

"Plenty o' work, she does for the community."

"And they work for human rights too," Cathy extols as she turns over more pages.

"Aye, marched with the people to stop a road goin' through their land, back in 2011, arrested she was with others."

"She's very brave, an inspiration to us all."

"So were you, Cathy, a brave lass."

"Where's my bravery gone?"

"It's still in your heart."

"Eva was one of the marchers that got the Foreign Minister to walk with them through a cordon," Stewie recalls.

"How did it go?"

"The president supported the native people."

"I remember that. President Morales passed a law that the highway wouldn't be built. It was wonderful,"

"Protectors, they are, not protestors," Stewie reckons, "lookin' after their land. We were protectors too," he adds encouragingly.

The fire crackles in the stove. They sit together on the corduroy couch. Vinyl records spin on an old record-player, the kind her family back home might relegate to a music museum. They hold hands. It is a surreal situation. She had always been in the shop while Mark was away on golf trips. The Portugal trip has been an annual event for years. Now she is here holding hands with Stewie while his wife, Eva, is following her aspirations in Bolivia. Ben and Morag have gone back to Glasgow. Tomorrow Cathy and Stewie plan to climb Ben Nevis as far as the Halfway Lake.

"Am so happy, Cathy, ye came here."

"So am I."

"It's a sad time for you."

"Andy was ready to go. At least I spent lots of time with him in his last months, and over the years."

"Twas one guid thing," Stewie consoles.

"It was very thoughtful of you to come over for dad's funeral."

"It was guid to be there. I nae seen him. But I know he was a guid man."

"You'd have liked him, an earthy man. Like you."

"We can be soul friends," Cathy continues.

"Soul friends," Stewie repeats.

"Anam Cara, " Cathy muses.

She feels at ease as she sails away from the Scottish coast, unlike when as a tearful bride-to-be, she confided her misgivings to her brother. She is happy to have seen Stewie again, to have assured him that she treasured the memories of their times together. It was comforting to have seen him in his surroundings at the base of Ben Nevis, where he lives a life akin to a vocation, welcoming and caring for his residents and behaving like a pseudo father to the lost-looking or the stranded. It was in this role that he met Ben.

In winter, when guests rarely brave the highland weather, he attends to maintenance and improvements and classifies old varieties of Scottish crop seeds in a Seed Kist, his treasure chest full of native seeds. The kist is a symbol of the diversity of the crops that grew and can grow in Scotland. For the past decade Eva has returned from Bolivia for a month each December to coincide with Morag's and Stewie's less busy time and be part of Christmas and the great Hogmanay celebrations. When winter gives way to spring Stewie sows his tatties and his heritage seeds ensuring that there will be vegetables to sell in his hostel shop throughout the busy season. Cathy will think of him from now on moving in a natural rhythm with the seasons.

Chapter Thirty-Seven - Dancing Nymph

Cathy phones Colin to tell him she is going down to their parents' grave and to ask him would he like to meet her there.

They tidy the grave and place a pot of yellow chrysanthemums on the fresh clay before standing together in silence.

Cathy breaks the silence.

"Would you like to come for a wee dander? I've something special to tell you."

"Something special, last time you nibbled at my ear you shared a mighty big secret."

"I've another big secret."

"We could walk in the forest park."

"Perfect."

The siblings are together beside an ancient standing stone within the forest park.

"I'm waiting for the secret."

"Remember I told you then that I loved someone very much."

"I do. And I must commend you on how well you've done since."

"Yeah, well I found him again." Her blue eyes are beaming with delight.

"I didn't think you were looking for him."

"I wasn't. I'd tried to keep the memories of him to the back of my mind."

"How did you find him?"

"Well he found me, sort of, when he met Ben. They made the connection."

"I think I know where this is leading, sis. Are you telling me he's Morag's father?"

"He is," she replies joyfully. And she dances with delight around the standing stone.

"I found Stewie." She continues to dance as if she would never stop. Her ginger curls, now streaked with grey strands, bob about. Her blue eyes sparkle. A beaming smile lights up her lightly freckled face. And the cute little space between her front teeth is even more noticeable.

"Sis, are you sixteen or sixty?"

"I feel sixteen," she enthuses and dances away like a nymph. "I'm wild happy."

"I was concerned when you went to Scotland with Mark when you were only a short while married in case it'd distract you."

"You didn't think I'd run away from Mark when I was there," she teases impishly as she pauses her dancing.

"No sis, I didn't think that at all."

"Mark had said he might climb Nevis with me. That was the first day he asked me to marry him and I said I wasn't ready to get married. I was pleased when he remembered it again."

"And it went grand," Colin assumes.

"This was a chance in a million. I was sitting on the bedroom balcony with Mark, looking out through my binoculars, looking for birds, and guess what happened?"

"What happened?"

"Guess."

"You saw Stewie."

"I did. My heart nearly stopped"

"Maybe it was a mirage."

"No it wasn't. I was in the cloakroom later and in the mirror I saw his mother. I know you're going to say I was having hallucinations."

"Did she see you?"

"She did. I broke down crying. She washed away my tears and put on make-up for me in case Mark might think something happened to me. I never forgot her. I got to see her the day before yesterday."

"I didn't realise when you first told me about him that you were missing him that much. I'm so sorry to hear that." Her brother hugs her as if is trying to squeeze away the pain.

"I'm grand now. I got to see him and I know how he is."

"It must've been meant to be," Colin muses.

"When Ben did the Faslane protest he went up to Stewie's hostel, hoping to meet Morag. They'd actually missed one another on the protest. Stewie told him he once had an Irish girlfriend he'd met at Faslane and the story unfolded."

"How did you feel when Ben told you about him?"

"I was really sad to remember we'd a misunderstanding and I didn't forgive him for what I'd now see as a small mistake."

"Yeah, you're definitely the forgiving type now."

"I cried my eyes out, soaked the linen handkerchiefs got for Grandma's funeral."

"Why didn't you tell me?"

"I was with you and Jennifer and dad the following night. Dad was so frail I wanted those last months to be his time."

"That was thoughtful. You gave him and mam and all of us plenty of time and attention over the years," Colin encourages, perhaps trying to show her how important her proximity meant to them all.

"Thanks, bro. I hope you understand why I didn't confide in you then. I might've ended up crying again."

"I think I could've handled that."

"You did help me that night, when the car went off the road," she admits wryly.

"Being in love could be injurious to your health," he teases. "I'm very happy for you that you've had these moments," her brother continues.

Colin sees her now as a free spirit rather than in the conventional role she has filled for nearly three decades. Even her dress portrays the change. She is wearing a long blue denim dress, bought in the Dog's Trust Charity shop in Glasgow. It is buttoned down the front with brown buttons. And on her feet are brown chunky clogs.

"You've done your family and Mountview proud, raised four great sons, and looked after the shop, and all the grandparents,"

"They're the ordinary things any mother, wife, daughter, and daughter-in-law do," Cathy interjects.

"You did them well," her brother affirms. "You helped Marilyn have her dreams when Mountview received all the awards over the years. She saw the village receive the overall winner's trophy in Best Kept Areas before she died."

"That was something I did mostly for Marilyn," Cathy admits. "Ben helped too. With all the modern technology we could work out colours and heights and bee friendliness and everything."

"It was great she received that trophy. As it turned out it was her last chance," Colin remarks.

"I always appreciated how she looked after the boys and let me stay here at the time of foot and mouth."

"We appreciated having you with us."

"We'll still be around to support one another," she assures him. "You didn't think I was going to leave and head away to Stewie."

"Well I'd never seen you so happy in all your life. I didn't know what'd happen."

"He'll be my soulmate," she says solemnly.

"That sounds very mystical."

"I wouldn't want to spoil what we have by complicating things. And I wouldn't leave Benny. He's the last of the grandparents."

"And a true gentleman," Colin adds.

"And it'd be awkward for Ben and Morag if their parents had a lover's tiff?" Cathy jokes.

"And it's good for Finn to have someone there when he gets home from college. Mark could be busy."

"Well you've some good reasons to stay," Colin concludes. "I'm waiting for another."

"Another?

"Mark," Colin says simply.

"He's so busy he mightn't notice I'd gone. But he's not a bad man," Cathy defends the man she has been married to for twenty-nine years. "It's just he's so single-minded about what he wants to do and achieve. And he does achieve good things for many people."

"He does," Colin agrees pensively.

"It was great chatting with you today, bro. You're like a soulmate too."

"I know dad was the focus of your visits for the past while. But we'd like to see you whenever you can get down. And stay overnight if you wish."

"Thanks, bro. Will Jennifer be home soon?"

"She'll be late today. She's starting the auditions for the principle parts of the school opera. They're doing Princess Ida."

"Maybe we could drop into the Friary Café," Cathy suggests.

"I never was there," Colin admits.

"I brought Vera to the friary just a few weeks before mam died."

"Vera still goes there. I do see her coming and going."

They are back at the cemetery gate now. Cathy gets her own car as the friary is on her way home. Then they drive behind one another into the friary grounds, unchartered space for Colin.

"There is a lovely love story attached to here," Cathy muses as they walk in the direction of the café.

"You're really full of romantic tales today. You're as good as a Mills and Boons Library."

"This story isn't mine. I'd be breaking a confidence if I shared it. It was almost a deathbed story. But I'm just thinking about it now."

"You're really keeping me in suspense. But you did tell me a whopper of a love story today. I feel privileged that you shared that with me."

They find a quiet corner in the café, looking out towards a little bridge which leads to the final stations on the way of the cross. The siblings are sitting together having hot chocolate and coffee when an old friar enters the café. Cathy recognises him and thinks that he has aged a lot in the thirteen years since her mother died. His hair and his beard are whiter and his tall erect posture has given way to hunched shoulders making him appear much smaller. He notices Cathy and Colin and walks slowly towards their table.

"Aren't you Beryl's children? I remember you since your mother's funeral. Cathy, isn't that right?"

"That's right, Father Donal. This is my brother Colin."

"I was sorry to hear about the loss of your father."

"I suppose we were lucky to have him as long as we did. He died on my sixtieth birthday."

She moves out one of the spare chairs beside them and the friar sits down. The girl serving at the counter takes him a pot of tea.

"Your mother's friend, Vera, still helps us in the repository."

"Vera was a great friend of mam's. Mam trusted her judgement in everything and was happy to have her care for her in her last months," Cathy speaks appreciatively. "The Country Markets and the ICA were their first connections and it developed from there."

"I grew up fairly near your mother. We didn't mix very much when we were children. We were in different schools. I suppose this is an amazing thing for an old friar to share but Beryl was my only girlfriend."

The love story is unfolding for Colin. Brother and sister listen encouragingly. The old friar continues. Simply and quietly he relates his love story in the café of his own friary where is still abbot.

"We were of a different faith. That was a very big obstacle back seventy years ago. We wrote weekly love letters and spent as much time together as we could during the school holidays. Her mother met us one evening, the two of us on one bicycle, and that was the end of our romance."

"That was a sad ending. Mam told me the story just a few weeks before she died."

And the friar smiles fondly appreciating that Beryl still remembered him as she was about to leave this world.

Colin looks towards his sister. Another big secret has been hidden within her mind for thirteen years. What an enigma he thinks to himself. Is she full of dormant secrets waiting to burst forth like newly hatched butterflies?

"I'd her bundle of love letters until I was ready to enter the friary. You weren't allowed to bring anything personal from the past with you," Father Donal remembers.

"The evening before I entered I burned all my letters. I kept the ashes."

"That was a nice idea," Cathy commends him.

"It was my only option. Things were severe in the olden days."

"It's amazing to think of the love letters people wrote in the past. Now it'd just be a text or an e-mail," Colin muses.

"Mam had your letters in a flowery chocolate box on top of the wardrobe. The day she told me the story she asked me if I'd place the letters in her coffin. And I did."

"It was good to share my story with Beryl's children," the old friar says solemnly. "It's good to know she'd a good life and raised lovely people."

"We were pleased to meet you too and to hear the story from you."

"Feel free to drop by anytime," the older man says.

As they walk together towards their cars they smile companionably. Colin knows for the first time about his mother's love story. And Cathy was enabled to share with her brother without breaking any confidences.

"That was surely a day of revelations, hearing details of my sister's and my mother's love affairs, and the poor friar having to burn his love letters."

They embrace one another and she hops into her car and heads towards Mountview to start her shift for the busy lunchtime.

Chapter Thirty-Eight - Activism

Benny's mobile phone rings. He walks towards the window to make sure he does not lose the signal. Mark can hear Cathy's voice at the other end of the line. She sounds up-beat as she chats to her father-in-law, explaining where she is and her estimated time of arrival home.

"No need to rush there's enough of us here to keep things going. Mark's just back."

"He must be tired."

"How'd he be tired after a week in the sun?"

"I went to the Friary café with Colin to have a chat. That's how I'm a bit late. We were chatting with the Abbot."

"How did a pair of Protestants end up in a Friary, and talking to the Abbot, no less?"

"Mam's friend Vera helps there. She wasn't there today."

"It was good you and Colin had time out together. I'd say he misses Andy."

"He was always there for dad, just dropping in quietly."

"You take care of yourself. No rushing."

"I'm wondering if Cathy's interested in someone else," Mark says to his father when he comes back to the table where they are having tea and scones.

Benny had come into the living room from his early shift.

"Why do you think that?"

"She sounded different on the phone. And she sounded different when I spoke to her too."

"I think she may've been stifled till now," Benny surmises.

"Stifled? How do you mean?

"She probably paid so much attention to the rest of us she hadn't time to know who she really was."

Mark is uneasy. *'Who she really was'* had been a big bone of contention throughout their engagement all those years ago.

He pours another cup of tea and offers one to his father and cuts in half one of the cherry and coconut scones he had brought in from the deli.

"What brought you to that conclusion?" Mark asks apprehensively.

"We were talking in the cottage after Andy's funeral. I could see her light up when they talked about campaigns she was involved in."

"What started them talking about campaigns?"

"Ben and Morag, and Stewie too, were talking about Faslane. Stewie was praising Cathy for her part in it back in the eighties."

"They knew one another then?" Mark's voice is raised in surprise. "And then she went to Scotland with them."

"When I saw her blossoming out of herself I said I'd do her shifts. Andrew and Heather were here, and Jack and Poppy. And Finn said he'd help on the Saturday."

"It was a real conspiracy to get her away."

"It's not often she'd get the chance."

"She took up your offer very fast."

"She had to decide fast. They were leaving early next morning."

"I wonder if she's interested in him," Mark muses.

"That's really jumping to conclusions."

"He was praising her after all the years. And now he's back on the scene."

"You're being paranoid now. If she's interested in someone else you've only yourself to blame," his father reprimands. "She deserves a bit more attention."

"Do you mean me going to Portugal?"

"I don't think she was upset about Portugal. I'd say it's more deep-rooted."

"You seem to have more insight than me."

"You don't give yourself time to have insight into things, Mark. You're always running."

"I'm beginning to sound like a robot. Do you think things could be improved if they're that deep-rooted?"

"You could make an effort. You owe Cathy that much."

"Maybe it's too late."

"That's very pessimistic."

"Why?"

"In a nutshell you're saying Cathy sounded different, that she might be interested in someone else and it might be too late to change." Benny paraphrases his son's words.

"I won't know where to start," Mark says worriedly.

"Don't start by asking her a question that'd sound irrational if it's not true, or finish things if it is."

Mark rubs his hand around his face anxiously.

"You were away on umpteen golf tours and functions," his father reminds him. "Did Cathy ask you were you in love with someone else when you came home?"

"I don't think I ever came back any different to when I went away."

"This is probably one of the few times Cathy went away. It's a novelty for her."

"I think I'll just leave things as they are."

"Just treat her fair. Find out what interests her rather than always what interests you."

"Ummh," Mark mumbles with trepidation.

"She's always been here to let you do your activities."

"I appreciate that."

"It'd be good to encourage her to do what she'd like to do?"

"Like what?"

"They were talking about anti-nuclear protests, and protests against oil pipelines," Benny recalls, "and dangerous pesticides that kill bees . . ."

"She must've saved millions of bees with all the flowers she sowed, and the wildflower meadows and everything," Mark interjects quickly.

"They were talking about military spending, so much money that could be used for good spent on arms. And fracking and lots of other things," Benny continues.

"They covered an awful lot in one night."

"Did you know about Cathy's protests?"

"I did. I told her not to tell mam. That nearly broke up our engagement."

"I'm not surprised. That was saying you didn't accept her as she was."

"I didn't think mam would understand such a way of life."

"Your mother was nurtured on activism."

"Nurtured on activism?"

"Her aunts and her mother were in the Revolutionary Workers' Group and the Flax and Textiles Workers Union, fighting for fairer conditions for millworkers. Marilyn followed in their footsteps."

"Mam, an activist, after all I said to Cathy about what mam would expect and she a radical revolutionary herself, an anarchist."

"I tried to convince her to be who she was. I'd married her for who she was."

"You did the opposite to me. I badgered Cathy not to tell."

"My mother was a formidable headline for Marilyn." Benny reckons. "She'd airs and graces after doing finishing school in Switzerland. They never left her."

"She'd regal ways alright, our Grandma Rosetta," Mark agrees.

"When Marilyn met her she changed from a feisty young woman to a biddable church worker," Benny recalls sadly. "She never discussed her revolutionary activities again.

"And Rosetta lived to be almost a hundred. There wasn't much chance for mam to let her hair down at that stage," Mark quips.

"I'd have loved her to be more her old self."

"Imagine if she'd reverted to her old self when Grandma Rosetta died we wouldn't have known her," Marks chuckles.

"I think she was about to break the mould when she died."

"At eighty-five," Mark marvels.

"Her trips to Donegal changed her. She was taken by Poppy, and then by the stories of Cathy's protests. I think if she'd got more time the two of them would've changed."

"How did she hear Cathy's story?

"Just before she died she met Cassie Anderson's niece in the surgery. She told your mother she shared prison cells with Cathy, showed her a photo of Cathy at a fence in Greenham Common."

"What did mam think?"

"She was disappointed she didn't know sooner. She folded her arms on the table and sobbed into her sleeves. So cut up she was that Cathy never felt she could tell her."

"If Cathy hears that she'll leave me."

"Imagine if she'd known the story years ago the two of them might've teamed up."

"We'd have had two rebels in Mountview. Funny she never mentioned anything to me about it," Mark muses.

"It was the day before she went to Donegal. She didn't want to say anything in case you didn't know, said she'd wait till she got back."

"I should've let Cathy be who she wanted to be," Mark laments.

"If you shook the branches of the family tree you'd never know what'd fall out," his father jokes.

"There'll be no secrets in the future with Facebook and everything," Mark predicts. "Poppy never hid her way of life. I'd say she helped bring mam's hidden self to the surface."

"And Morag told us about an arms protest she was at."

"I knew about Morag's protest," Mark admits. "Finn was full of praise for her. It was on Ben's Facebook."

"Facebook's a great invention entirely," the older man muses.

"Getting back to where we started I'm still afraid Cathy might leave."

"She wouldn't leave me," Benny says confidently. "She's been a wonderful daughter-in-law. I know she won't leave me now."

"I wish I was so sure. You'd better live to be a hundred so that she'll stay to be with you."

"I can't promise anything. I'm in my eighty-seventh year."

Chapter Thirty-Nine – Evolution

On the camera they see Cathy coming through the shop, greeting customers, some sympathising with her. She flits through the door into the living room wearing her long blue denim dress and her brown chunky clogs, which are carrying clay from the cemetery as well as leaves from the forest. Some of her ginger curls are clipped up in an Adonis blue butterfly clasp. The rest are floating about her. Cheerily she kisses Benny's forehead and thanks him for helping her.

'A definite evolution' Mark thinks to himself. He recalls when they met after the choral festival thirty years ago and they had joked about evolution. He had said it was good, that caterpillars become butterflies. Now this spritely spirit has come through the shop, nymph-like. What will the customers think?

"You're more like sixteen than sixty," Mark exclaims. "You've evolved into a butterfly, an Adonis butterfly no less."

"Remember, you were the Adonis in school, charming and handsome," Cathy recalls.

"Am I not charming and handsome still?"

"I suppose you haven't changed much. The years have been kind to you."

"That's good to hear," he teases. "That's a real retro outfit. You're like a real hippy."

"I got it in the Dog's Trust in Glasgow."

Deftly she twists more of her curls into the Adonis blue clasp and heads towards the shop again.

"I'll give a hand to Andrew and Heather. The deli will be getting busy."

"I'll do that and you have some lunch," Mark protests.

"No, I'll do it and let the two of you have a chat," Benny offers.

They accept.

"Colin must've been pleased to see you. I'd say it's lonely for him."

"I was pleased to see him too. We went for a wee dander to the forest and then to the Friary café," Cathy says lightly even though she had poured out her innermost thoughts to her brother and listened to the friar pouring out his. She thinks of all that what was revealed in that short space of time.

"You always loved that forest. Remember you said you'd have liked to get married there."

"It mightn't have been a culture shock for Grandma Rosetta at all. After all she loved the grove," Cathy remarks with conviction.

"Some of the other guests might've felt out of place standing there in their finery," Mark reasons.

"Or they might've enjoyed the different experience, especially the secret rebels and hippies among them."

"You're transforming into your old self," Mark teases. Without waiting for a comment he continues, "How did you know about the Friary café?"

"It's linked to a special love story."

Mark waits expectantly.

"It was mam's first love story."

"When did you hear about it?"

"A month before mam died. One afternoon the chat came around."

"To old romances," Mark finishes the sentence apprehensively.

They rarely sit together in the shop sitting-room. One of them is usually running in to do a shift, more often Cathy, and Mark is usually dashing to some meeting. So now they are here, their down-time facilitated by Benny who wishes things will run more fairly. It is easier for them to chat about Beryl than to get down to things more pertinent to their own situation, to the nitty-gritty of why Mark went to Portugal under the circumstances, or why Cathy headed off to Scotland with Stewie MacGregor and Ben and Morag.

"It was a lovely story," Cathy continues.

"And you kept it secret for thirteen years."

"I wouldn't have divulged it while dad was alive," she says pensively. "And I didn't reveal it today until Father Donal, the Abbot, told the story."

"You mean the Abbot and Beryl in love?"

"Yeah, back in forties. Grandma Jane didn't approve because Donal was Catholic. Mam told me where his letters were and I put them in her coffin as I'd promised."

"All those intriguing moments that romantics treasure," Mark muses.

"The Abbot told us today that he couldn't bring anything from his past into the Friary so he burned the letters and kept the ashes."

"How did you happen to get talking to the Abbot?"

"Vera asked him to pray for mam when she was ill. Vera doesn't know about the romance though. It was a coincidence that she happened to ask Father Donal."

"This is a real Mills and Boons stuff," Mark teases.

"I gave Vera a lift to the friary one day and she introduced me to the Abbot. I'd only heard the story about an hour earlier."

"And he remembered you after all the years. You must've made a good impression."

"He said I reminded him of mam. He came to mam's wake with Vera and had a cup of tea in our parlour, like you had when you came to our house the first time."

"And at any time, Beryl showed me excellent hospitality."

He smiles as he reflects back to their short and stormy courtship when Beryl eagerly mended the cracks which arose in their romance.

"Imagine her there reposing in the wedding dress while Father Donal was in her parlour. Maybe she was watching him from her other world," Cathy muses.

"I often regret I didn't visit her more," Mark says contritely.

"She never held it against you. In her eyes you were always a good man or a busy man."

"No matter how forgiving Beryl was, I feel I should've been more attentive to one who made sure I got a good wife."

"She was relentless in her quest I have to agree," Cathy recalls.

"There'd be nothing wrong with Andy knowing her story. Didn't he get the prize? And the Abbot got his monastery."

"The prize, is that what you call us?"

"I think trophy would sound worse," Mark teases.

"It would," Cathy agrees.

"I'm happy I got you, no matter who else loved you."

Cathy just smiles. This is such a charming remark after all her emotional upheaval since Ben told her about Stewie six months ago. She wonders does he suspect she might have feelings for someone else. Yet there is no hint of cunning in his voice, just a simple statement about his good fortune.

"Most of us had earlier romances. I remember the day we met at the choral festival you said you'd just come out of a relationship," Mark continues.

"I remember that," Cathy agrees.

"I'd my share of romances too," he says impishly. "Heather's mam, Daisy, was my girlfriend for a while."

"She fancied you when we were in Saint Matthew's."

"Would you blame her?"

"No, not at all," Cathy answers lightly. "You're quite at ease with Daisy now."

"I was at her wedding the year before we met, well before we met again."

"I remember you talking about all the matching and hatching."

"The same year I was at Patience's wedding to Stephen, the boy you liked."

"Patience Prior, the vicar, was your girlfriend?" Cathy says with amusement.

"She used to be my girlfriend in the past, like Beryl and the Abbot."

"So you saw two of your girlfriends safely up the aisle in the one year."

"Then I found you and I was lucky to get you to walk up the aisle at all and to say yes when you did."

Cathy now recalls how Patience had spoken so admiringly about Marilyn as if she had known her very well. Patience had stood opposite them at Marilyn's grave. Cathy did not notice Mark's heart racing as her own did when she saw Stewie at her father's grave nine months later. She thinks back to when Patience officiated at their wedding and witnessed her faltering yes.

"Did you feel jittery when you saw her again?" Cathy teases.

"No. I knew she was on her way here for her next appointment. Mam told me. Stephen comes to the golf club now."

"The circle of life's amazing."

"But you've settled with me in our wee nest in the cottage. That's all that matters." Mark says simply.

"I always loved the cottage. I love looking out through the upstairs windows at the mountains. And I love the grove."

"Your pagan place," Mark adds.

"It's an almanac of each season, a haven for bees and butterflies, a larder with food for foraging and honey from the hives."

"You're getting carried away."

"And, it's a bird sanctuary. Several of the nest boxes were used this year. And when our boys were small it was their playground."

"I suppose when all's said and done it's just a cluster of trees," Mark surmises. "The birds would find a home anywhere and the boys don't need it to play in anymore."

"It's more than a cluster of trees. Sacred groves are living spaces. New plant successions evolve and take their places with old ones. Each grove has its own story."

"The one out the back looks ordinary to me."

"It's a sacred grove, a nemeton."

"What's a nemoton?"

"Nemetona is the Goddess of Sacred Groves."

"What makes out the back a sacred grove?" Mark probes.

"Groves represent circles of hospitality, like circles of friends in a community. New saplings are accommodated and all the trees adapt to survive. Poppy sanctified our grove in a special ritual at the summer solstice."

"Poppy sanctified it. You never told me."

"I didn't think you'd be interested. You silenced me in matters like that thirty years ago."

"Silenced? That sounds a bit severe. It was what I thought best then." Mark's voice almost trails off as he ponders on his advices of thirty years ago, advices he now knows were misguided.

"We won't go down that slippery road," Cathy cautions.

"What happens when sacred groves are needed for development? Remember, back in the nineties, when an old forest was being taken for road-widening, all the talk about eco-warriors."

"It was ancient woodland, Mark," Cathy contradicts. "As usual the developers won out in the end."

"No heed paid to Goddess Nemetona," Mark teases.

"That's the way in so many places. I don't think our grove would ever be threatened," Cathy reckons. "But we should be mindful of other groves or woodlands and fight for them."

"It was good to have a chat together while the shop world turned without us. It reminds me of who you truly are," Mark affirms.

Cathy is pensive again. "We'll do this again, have lunch together," Mark vows as Cathy places the last of her olives into her mouth. "I'll go in now and let Andrew and Heather in for lunch," he offers.

"I'll go in too and let Benny come in for a rest."

Chapter Forty - Secrets

After the shop closes Cathy and Mark relax again beside the stove in the cottage. Cathy is surprised that Mark has not gone out to the club or to any meeting. Perhaps he is feeling tired after the travelling and late nights.

"This was a day of secrets. When I got on the plane this morning I didn't realise I'd be so much wiser by nightfall," Mark marvels.

"If you stayed settled you'd hear more," Cathy teases.

"How do you mean?"

"You know the idea that a rolling stone gathers no moss. Usually you're in a big rush. There has to be the right ambiance for secrets."

"I'm settled now. I could get to enjoy this relaxation."

It is such an unusual scenario for Cathy that she is not sure how much togetherness she could enjoy. Accustomed as she is to signing petitions and e-campaigning on the computer, restlessness might set in if she sat by the fire every night with someone she rarely relaxed with over the years. And she is not ready to reveal any more secrets. The experiences of the past week are new and fragile. All the emotional trauma of the year, and particularly the emotional giddiness of seeing Stewie after thirty years, has to be sorted out in her own head.

"You're very pensive," Mark jolts her out of her thoughts.

"Ummh," Cathy mumbles, with the hint of a thoughtful smile spreading across her face. She is looking into the log fire that Mark has set. The flames are dancing about. There is an atmosphere of cosiness about the whole room. A week ago, while Mark was in Portugal, she sat here with her sons and with Poppy and Morag and

Stewie while they set the world aright. Now everyone has dispersed to Scotland, to Donegal, to college. Here they are an empty-nest couple, alone beside their own fireplace. Mark is settled. He is not leaving tonight.

"You told me about the love affair between Beryl and the Abbot at lunchtime. We must've had the perfect setting then."

"I told you about Beryl and Donal, before he became an Abbot. I won't be telling that story widely. It'd be like betraying a trust."

"Well thanks for trusting me with the secret."

A thoughtful smile still lingers on Cathy's face.

"You told me about Daisy and Patience. Thanks for sharing that too."

"For so long we've kept things under wraps. My fault, I know," Mark admits.

"We'd a culture of cover-up alright," Cathy agrees.

"Now we know there were secrets in the previous generations." He tries to take some of the sting out of the veil of secrecy that he had determinedly safeguarded.

"Patience seems to be a very kind person. It was good Stephen met her," Cathy muses.

"It was," Mark agrees. "Stephen's much more at ease with himself as an older man than as a teenager."

"She must've instilled confidence in him," Cathy concludes.

"It was good I left her for him," Mark says in a light-hearted tone.

"Did you? That was very generous."

"No, I'm only joking. I introduced them to one another. I knew they'd be good together."

"How did you know?"

"I knew she'd be sensitive enough for him and that he'd be the flexible kind of man a vicar would need. He wouldn't break her heart."

She would like to ask Mark more about his romance with Patience but that would be unfair if she herself was unwilling to share her own story. There is a pause in the conversation as Mark gets another log and places it on the glowing fire.

"Would you like a mug of hot chocolate?"

"I'd love one."

"Remember when we went to Scotland after we got married and you made several attempts to make hot chocolate and kept forgetting," Mark recalls.

"And you made me some in a dainty china cup. That was nice."

"We'll go Scotland again," Mark announces as he moves around at the sink area. "Now that Ben's there it'll feel more familiar. And you enjoyed it last week, came back a different woman."

"I hope you like the woman that came back."

He thinks of her dancing through the shop like a teenager in blue denim.

"I heard another secret today," he admits as he places the hot chocolate on the small table in front of her.

"Did you?" Cathy is alarmed. Her heart is racing. She wonders if Mark has relinquished his usual evening activities to tell her something very pertinent to their own relationship.

"My mother was an activist too, fought for the rights of textile workers. Dad told me today."

"And you'd me believe I'd be the only activist in Mountview."

"I knew auntie Ada was involved in strikes and in the Communist Party. I thought she was the tearaway. And she lived a bit away."

"We could've been kindred spirits, Marilyn and me. I actually heard her story from Benny too."

"You never said anything."

"I only heard it last week when you were in Portugal."

"She knew about your story just before she died?"

"You didn't tell Marilyn my story behind my back, after all you said about saying nothing."

Cathy is shocked, peeved and angry. Every emotion seems to be bubbling up, each giving way to the other in quick succession.

"I didn't tell," Mark interjects.

"How did she find out?" Cathy is astonished.

"Cassie Anderson's niece told her when she was in the doctor's surgery before she left for Donegal."

"I wish I'd told her myself. I feel I lived a lie. I knew that morning she wanted to share something."

"It wasn't your fault. I stopped you."

"I should've risked it and been open."

"She was proud of you anyway," he encourages. "My mother chose to hide her own past even though my father encouraged her to be herself. She'd have shared with you if she'd the time at the end. So dad said."

Cathy just breaks down sobbing.

"I'm so sorry I lived a lie. And Marilyn thought I was her friend. She did so much to help." And the sobs go on.

"She'd understand, love. She didn't reveal things herself." Mark tries to console. "That's the way of mother-in-law daughter-in-law relationships. They put the best foot forward to please."

"It shouldn't be the way. Putting the best forward in a deceitful way is disgusting." Cathy berates herself.

"Mam did it for Rosetta."

"That was different. By all accounts Rosetta was a snob," Cathy protests. "I found her very nice in the end though."

"You looked after her well and she'd her wish to die at home. And her grove, you looked after it with her."

"And I'm still looking after it for her," Cathy confirms.

"And you softened mam," Mark continues. "She could appear stand-offish enough too. I was surprised you two got on so well."

"We could've got on better if I'd been honest," she laments. "It was Poppy that helped her to be happy with the person she was."

"I have to agree. She was a different woman once she started visiting Poppy and Jack. I thought she'd be shocked when she'd see their pagan place."

Chapter Forty-One - The Grove

October grey skies persist for several days with silhouettes of birds criss-crossing the grey celestial canvas. Contrasting with the greyness is a wealth of warm autumnal colours. Cathy tries to come to terms with the transience of life. She lost her father on her sixtieth birthday. That was when the blood moon set the skies ablaze. She saw Stewie after thirty years at her father's grave. Her heart raced and Mark thought she was ill. He still went to Portugal though.

Mark is spending more time with her in the evenings now. In the beginning she did not know how she would handle all the togetherness. But there have been so many changes since the beginning of the year that she has learned to keep adapting. The composition of the household changed dramatically. She lost Marilyn just after New Year when they were about to become kindred spirits. Now she is the only Mrs Wright. The nest of once baby boys is empty. She floats into the shop each morning, usually dressed in clothes she bought in the Dogs' Trust or in Bernardo's.

"Mark, would you be able to do from about ten until four on Saturday," Cathy's asks as she works through the rota on Monday morning.

"Sorry love. It's a big day at the club. Remember I told you."

"No worries, I'll sort something out."

"Who's off that day?"

"I was going to take off from about ten o'clock until three-thirty or four."

Mark's bites his lip realising he is always able to be away himself whenever he wants.

"What did you want to do then, love?"

"An anti-fracking meeting," Cathy answers simply.

"An anti-fracking meeting," Mark repeats. "It's important to you. Isn't it?"

"It is. Imagine fracturing the earth with chemicals and poisoning water and land."

"I know how you feel about these things."

"Do you?"

"Dad told me. But I couldn't be missing on Saturday, sorry. We'll be finalising details about it tonight."

"I'll ask Benny."

"Dad's a bit old for doing shifts. I know he's done shifts when you needed him."

"I think he enjoys being part of the place still."

"He likes to help you. And I'm glad. It was good to see the two of you getting on so well over all the years."

"I felt at home with him from the start."

"Only for him you mightn't have stayed at all. I owe him that."

She does not react to this remark and Mark does not dig for affirmations in case they are none forthcoming.

"Janice might do a few hours," Cathy continues, tapping her fingers on the sheet of paper.

"That sounds good."

Chairing the meeting at the golf club, John Balfe speaks briskly.

"That sorts out Saturday. We'll move to the next item on the agenda."

"Land for extension, we made progress on that during our Portugal trip. We're looking at the land between here and Wright's."

"Things have changed," Mark interjects. "This grove's not available."

"That's a bit of a jolt," John says with some consternation. "It'll be impossible to find any other adjoining land."

"We might've to be happy with the club as it," Mark says simply. "The grove's important to Cathy."

"You didn't say that before."

"I didn't realise how much it meant to her until we were chatting the day I came home."

"You should've got her to be part of the club long ago and she'd be more amenable to this," John Balfe says glibly.

"Without her I couldn't have given so much time to the club. Maybe I should've chatted more to her sooner."

There is no empathy forthcoming from the thwarted committee members. He feels disappointed. Despite all the time he has given to the club there is nobody to support him.

"I'll talk sense into Cathy," John Balfe offers.

"No, I'm asking you not to speak to Cathy about this. I've given my final decision."

"You're home early," Cathy exclaims.

"I came back when the meeting finished."

"You didn't go into the bar."

"No."

"Was it a good meeting?"

"No."

"Never mind, the next one'll probably be better."

The autumn leaves swirl around the cottage. As Cathy sweeps them up she notices some of the birdlife in the grove. Goldfinches gorge on rosehips. A tree-creeper spirals up along the rugged bark of a tree, busily probing for insects as it moves. To give insects and bugs an optimum chance, she built bug hotels to ensure some overwinter shelter. The profusion of berries in the grove has attracted goldfinch, fieldfare, redwings and many other berry-loving birds. She hopes the abundance of acorns will entice the woodpeckers to stay around. A whirly breeze suddenly whips up the leaves and sends them swirling away again. Gathering them up again she places them in a frame to make leaf mould and then goes to front of the shop to sweep up the leaves there. A shiny dark blue jeep pulls up beside her.

"Maybe there's something we could do to change your mind, Cathy."

"Change my mind, John, about what?"

"About the bit of land behind you," John Balfe says in off-handed way.

"I don't know what you're talking about."

"The ground behind you, I was hoping you'd let us do a feasibility study on it, at least."

"Do you mean the grove?"

"Yeah, whatever you call it."

"It's Rosetta's Grove," Cathy emphasises. "I promised her I'd always look after it."

"From what I remember of Rosetta she'd be a practical woman. If you let us do the feasibility study we could talk more then."

"Why would you want to do a study?"

"To see if it'd be suitable for the extension to the club."

"An extension to the golf club, that's impossible."

"We'd need to check the topography and the gradients and a few other things first," he continues, disregarding what she has said.

"There's no point in wasting money on a study. The grove's definitely not up for grabs." The leaves swirl away again.

"You're busy now. We can speak about this later and you might change your mind."

"I won't be changing my mind, John. It's an important habitat for birds and bees and trees, and an important place in its own right."

"It has very good potential as a site for the club. You know how important the club is to Mark."

"He never spared himself when it came to working for it anyhow," she retorts.

"I can't believe the golf club want the grove for an extension," Cathy says incredulously to Mark when she joins him in the shop sitting-room.

"How did you hear that?" he asks warily.

"John Balfe asked me if there was any way he could change my mind. I didn't know what he was talking about. A site with good potential for an extension, that's how he described the grove. A sacred grove reduced to a site."

"It's not going to happen, Cathy. I know the grove means a lot to you."

"Thank you, Mark."

"I'm annoyed with John. I explained the situation about the grove and asked him not to approach you."

"No worries. I'm used to fighting for things. Anyhow it's ours, he can't take it."

"You won't have to chain yourself to the trees," Mark adds, trying to lighten the situation.

The idea that the club might get the piece of land was first muted in Portugal. If Mark had realised then how important the grove was to Cathy, he would not have allowed his co-travellers to believe there was a possibility of acquiring it for the club.

"I'll head in and give Andrew a hand in the shop," Mark offers. "There might be something you'd like to do instead."

"I could usefully raise awareness of the anti-fracking meeting."

"Did you ask Janice to come in?"

"If she gets her thesis progressed a bit she'll be in. She'll let me know tomorrow."

"I think she has a soft spot for Andrew," Mark muses.

"I think so too, and he for her. She could be the next Mrs. Wright."

"You're probably thinking she won't be inhibited by convention like previous Mrs Wrights," Mark says impishly.

"Touché," she replies wryly.

"Saturday's very busy. We'd be fairly stuck if Janice can't come in," Mark reckons.

She is pleased to hear him referring to 'we'. Up until now it seemed to be her responsibility to ensure that the rotas were complete.

"I couldn't have Benny standing in the shop anyway," Cathy concludes. "His chest was very bad yesterday. I think I'll stay and help out in the shop and look after Benny even if Janice can make it."

"You haven't got a chance to do anything in years. I'll stay."

"What about the tournament?"

"It'd go on without me."

"You never said before that a club event would go on without you. Hope what John Balfe said about the grove isn't troubling you."

"I'm mad at him for approaching you when I'd said it was a non-runner."

"Don't let that stop you. Just make up your own mind whether to go or not."

"In fairness it's your turn."

"This is unprecedented. The club members will be down to see what's the matter."

"You went to Scotland when I was away. That was unprecedented. You'd never done anything like that before."

"No, I never did. I rest my case."

"Nothing is sacred nowadays. John Balfe wanted the grove for a site for the club. About to do a feasibility study, he was," Cathy exclaims when she goes up to check Benny before he settles for the night. "

"You must've got a shock."

"I surely did. I love that place since the first day I saw it. And now we've woodpeckers and beehives and nest boxes and everything."

"It won't happen," Benny assures her.

"Mark said he wouldn't let it happen when I told him."

"If we're all on the one side nobody can take it," Benny concludes.

"I think Mark feels under some pressure."

"Why?"

"He said the tournament could go on without him."

"That's a first for Mark," Benny agrees.

Chapter Forty-Two – Samhain

Morag, Ben, Jack and Poppy arrive at the Scottish venue for the Samhain Festival. Through the mist three people walk towards them. They are silhouetted in a crimson-tinged shroud, against the backdrop of a blazing sunset. Lyndsey hastens her pace to a gallop when she notices them. Her sweet smile is unaltered since Ben met her on the West Highland Way.

"I should've been here meeting and greeting."

"No need to run. We wouldn't go away," Jack says light-heartedly.

"You must be Ben's brother, Jack."

"That's me, and this is Poppy."

"You're very welcome Poppy. I heard you guys met at an event like this."

"We met at an Imbolc festival."

"I'm delighted to see you again, Ben, and you too, Morag."

"Morag told me about the Lughnasadh festival. So I'm hoping to row into this one."

"You will, Ben. You're adaptable. It's great you two met. You'll be lovely together."

"We met the night I finished the West Highland Way," Ben adds.

"He was lucky he stayed in Glen Nevis," Morag teases.

"You never realised what good things might happen when you headed out that morning," Lyndsey continues. "We're all connected in the spiritual web of life."

"It's amazing how we've all reconnected," Morag marvels.

"And how your parents reconnected, that story's amazing." Lyndsey enthuses. "Life is one big tapestry. Even when we cannot see all the threads they're there holding the whole fabric together."

"Very well said," Poppy agrees.

Lyndsey's sister, Amy Powell and her friend Chloe emerge more mindfully from the mist.

"Good to see you again Ben, and Morag, and to meet Jack and Poppy too," Amy warmly welcomes the foursome.

"We're happy to be here," Poppy replies. "We were pleased Morag invited us to come over, just a month ago, after Granddad Andy's funeral."

"We'll remember Andy and all our ancestors this weekend," Chloe says solemnly.

"You're first to arrive apart from ourselves. Most of the participants will arrive early in the morning," Amy explains.

"We're the early birds," Jack chimes.

"You'd a long way to travel. It'll be good to have time to rest tonight," Lyndsey encourages.

"Over the weekend we'll focus on aligning with our ancestors. We've different activities on the programme and people can join as they arrive." Amy clarifies the schedule. "But there's room for consensus, if participants have suggestions," she adds cheerily.

As well as remembering Andy, whose leaving was so recent, they will remember Grandma Marilyn, whose spirit drifted away while she was in the cottage ten months ago. And Ellenora who gave Poppy the cottage will not be forgotten.

This is Ben's first time at an event such as this. He has not been accustomed to active participation in groups. Even on the West Highland Way he was alone, enjoying friendships as they came in the hostels or at resting points. That was where he met four of the women standing here beside him. And his encounter with Morag ended in romance.

Back in Mountview, Cathy is concerned about leaving Benny to go to the anti-fracking meeting. She considers asking Poppy to send him healing but realises that to send such a request to Poppy would alarm the four of them.

Saturday morning dawns and Benny looks perkier. His temperature is nearly back to normal.

"I'll take good care of dad," Mark promises.

"I've done a fair bit of promotion for the fracking meeting. I'd be happy to stay and go to the next meeting if you'd like to go to the club."

"No you go. I've texted John Balfe. Told him Dad wasn't well and that you'd an important meeting to attend."

The idea of Mark saying she had an important meeting raises her self-esteem and she decides she will leave the home and shop responsibilities in his hands for the next five or six hours.

Mark's fellow golfers are astonished.

"Did Mark say why he isn't here?"

"Benny wasn't feeling too well in the past few days," John Balfe explains, "a bad chest infection."

"Cathy usually looks after everything," Elspeth Balfe remarks. "He even got off to Portugal the day of his father-in-law's funeral."

"He said in the text it was Cathy's turn to do what she wishes. She's going to an anti-fracking meeting."

"Imagine Cathy going to an anti-fracking meeting today. There's something amiss." Elspeth stresses. "She was always so amenable."

"I don't think she'll change her mind about the plot of land though," John Balfe reckons. "I spoke to her and nothing'd change her."

"Mark asked you not to contact her," Edward, the secretary, and oldest member of the club, says disapprovingly.

"I decided I'd give it a try."

"That might explain his absence."

"Did you give the club any idea that you might let them have part of the grove?" Benny enquires after Cathy leaves.

"Why?"

"John Balfe asked Cathy if she'd change her mind about the grove. The idea couldn't have jumped out of the blue."

"They were talking about the great idea it'd be when we were in Portugal," Mark says sheepishly. "I didn't realise how much it meant to Cathy until the day I came home."

"What were you thinking of in Portugal. Surely you knew how important it was to Cathy? She has looked after it since she came here."

"My thoughts were all over the place. And Cathy had suddenly gone to Scotland and left you all behind."

"She'd just buried her father. We encouraged her to go. It was her first time to head away anywhere."

"It was so unexpected my head was in a spin. She was always here looking after things while I was away," Mark insists. "And I was feeling guilty I'd gone."

"You should've waited till you came home to discuss any idea about the grove with Cathy, and with me. Your grandmother, Rosetta, would turn in her grave if you let any harm come to it."

"John Balfe came up with the idea that there was wasteland between us and the club."

"I wouldn't call it wasteland and I wouldn't want to see it damaged either."

"I didn't realise you'd be disappointed. I imagined you more pragmatic."

"From the time I was a small child my father and mother were planting it, a tree for this occasion, another for that occasion, all native trees," Benny explains.

"I didn't know much about its beginnings. When I was little it was just there," Mark admits.

"By the time you came along it was about twenty-five years old with mature trees and more regenerating all the time. The oak where your grandmother Rosetta used to sit was one of the oldest."

"Maybe if you'd let the club know things had changed as soon as you came back it might've been easier."

"I let it be till the meeting last Monday when I knew they'd be discussing it."

"Hopefully they'll let it be too."

"You've a rest now. My job's to look after you for Cathy."

"And to look after Cathy too," Benny adds.

"She's pleased the grove won't be sold."

"She believes you're the great saviour, refusing to let it go. Is that why you didn't go today? You never missed a club event before."

A kind of," Mark admits. "I've always been at the ready to do everything that was needed. And when I said I couldn't sell the grove I got such disapproving looks."

"Maybe stand back a bit from the hub of things. It mightn't be wise though to completely give up something you've been involved in for so long."

"I'll see what happens."

"Nothing will happen unless you let it happen."

Mark feels lost as he moves about the shop and into the sitting room and up to Benny's bedroom. Patience drops around to hear how Benny is getting on. Stephen had sent her a text explaining that Mark missed the tournament on account of Benny being unwell.

"The members probably couldn't believe it when you weren't there."

"Cathy's on her first activist project in thirty years, an anti-fracking meeting," Mark tells Patience. "She's always been here, for the past thirty years," he muses.

"It's good she went to the meeting. It's a big step after all the years," Patience reckons.

"It is. To tell you the truth, Patience, I'm embarrassed about the site. I couldn't have faced them. The club thought it was all cut and dried. But the grove means a lot to Cathy."

"I don't think you should cut yourself off from the club. Stephen said you've been a big part of it."

"I don't know, Patience. I'll see what happens."

"You'll need to make an appearance soon, before it feels like a big issue."

"I know I should listen to your advice. I didn't listen before. I never let my mother know about Cathy's activism."

"Did you not?"

"No. And my mother found out from someone else a few days before she died."

"And what did she say?"

"She never got a chance to share with Cathy. She died in Donegal. But Dad said she was proud of Cathy. And sad she didn't know before."

"I want to say thanks to you" he continues. "You never pressured me again."

"Maybe I should've."

"It upset Cathy she didn't tell her herself. Especially when she discovered mam was a revolutionary. Imagine mam a revolutionary. We never knew."

Those presenting the information at the anti-fracking meeting are passionate and well informed. Some of them had stalled the progress of fracking in their own countries. Most of them are young. Many wear their hair in dreadlocks and their fashion statement is decidedly retro and well-worn. Without exception they are zealous about their cause. The facts are disturbing.

Cathy resolves to put her energy into whatever campaigns are deemed necessary to save the water and land of some of the counties in Ireland from such a fate. The young protectors of the land are pleased to have the support of an older woman. Dressed in her Dog Trust denim Cathy feels she blends in somewhat and yet it felt a giant step to attend the meeting today. She drives home, enlightened and frightened. The desecration that fracking would bring in its wake to any country is unimaginable.

"You're home early, Cathy." Mark is pleased to see her.

"Thanks for encouraging me to go. It was a very good meeting. How's Benny?"

"He's much better in himself."

"Would you like to head down to the club to see how things are going?" Cathy encourages.

"I'd rather stay here."

"I hope you're not disappointed you missed it."

"No, I'm grand."

"I'd a text from Ben. They're getting on great at the Samhain Festival," Cathy tells Mark. "Imagine a girl Ben met on the West Highland is there."

"Our two eldest sons gone the pagan way, it's amazing."

"Mountview might be full of activists and pagans yet," she teases.

"It might be different if they lived here. John Balfe was aghast that a fracking meeting came before the club. He phoned after you left."

"Not as aghast as I was when I heard about the grove. He'll need to get his priorities right."

Chapter Forty-Three - The Monologue

"Great to see you again, Ben," was the cheery greeting from the rolled down car window early on Sunday morning. "Lyndsey said you were here."

A new arrival at the Samhain festival sets Morag's mind at ease. The easy rapport which she observed between Ben and Lyndsey was unsettling. Now Rick, Lyndsey's boyfriend, recently returned from his world trip, joins them.

"Good to see you too, Rick. Lyndsey said you might get here."

"Couldn't be missing out on all these New-Age celebrations," Rick continues in his light easy-going manner as he leaves the car.

"This is my girlfriend, Morag."

"Pleased to see you, Morag," Rick says happily. "I heard you met the last night of the walk. For a little while I feared Lyndsey might run away with Ben."

"I feared the same." Morag tries to sound upbeat in her rejoinder.

Lyndsey sees Rick from the common-room window and arrives beside them.

"I was saying to Morag we're both lucky you didn't run away with Ben."

"You're such a tease," Lyndsey brushes off the remark light-heartedly and the four of them head back into the common-room and join Amy, Chloe and some of the other participants.

On and off during the day Morag chides herself for being jealous of Lyndsey. She had been quietly analysing their romance over the past twenty-four hours and wondering if she was living a dream for her father. He was so happy that Cathy's bairn, as he called Ben, was her boyfriend. Was Ben living a dream for his mother? The questions rumbled through her head and disturbed. They were very fond of one another, no doubt about that. But if their romance failed would they break four hearts, rather than two? Her misgivings subside and the final day is eventually filled with the generous comradery she had hoped for.

While the Samhain celebrations are happening in Scotland Cathy also takes time out to pay respects to the grandparents who have left this life. She heads south to the Dale to visit Beryl and Andy's grave. Colin meets her there and then they go to the Friary Café. They want to keep their promise to the old friar who shared his life-long secret with them just over three weeks ago.

"We might even see Vera if she's in the repository this morning," Cathy surmises.

As they arrive at the repository a sombre notice awaits them. 'As a mark of respect to our Abbot, Dom Donal, the repository will remain closed until Tuesday."

They re-read the notice. They are stunned, disappointed.

The café is open. They find a place in the same quiet corner as before. They know there will be no elderly friar to occupy the chair beside them. Sister and brother quietly mourn the man whose only girlfriend was their mother.

As the final celebrations of the Samhain Festival draws to a close the participants part company with optimistic promises that they will meet again. Lyndsey and Rick travel due east the short distance to their home village. Poppy and Jack drive south towards the port. This was a special weekend for them. They felt totally immersed in the rituals, sounds and movements and they plan to have an Imbolc ceremony at their own healing centre in Donegal.

"I was amazed how much in love mum and Stewie were," Jack muses. "We just saw mam as looking after us and the shop and everything."

"I wonder if she thought of Stewie always." Poppy is intrigued.

"Dad was always so busy he probably didn't realise she might be lonely."

"Your dad's lovely too in his own charming way."

"He is. And he's very generous. He has made a great difference to so many people. And Mam gives him lots of freedom."

Benny is settling himself into his armchair by the stove when Cathy drops up to see him after her visit to the Dale.

"You look a bit shaken, Cathy," Benny says with concern.

"I went to the Friary café with Colin. The Abbot died this morning. He'd asked us to call in again. We wanted to keep our promise."

"And you did."

"I suppose we did," Cathy concurs. "It's great to see you in your chair again. Are you sure you're feeling well enough to be up?"

"Ach aye, I feel better than I was. But I'm not up to going up to the grave."

"I'll bring up a pot of chrysanthemums and say hello to Marilyn for you. Will you be alright?"

"I'll be grand."

Sitting on the edge of the granite surround at Marilyn's grave, in the shadow of the beautiful white church, Cathy starts her monologue to the spirit of her mother-in-law.

"I went to a fracking meeting yesterday. I'm an activist again like the two of us once were. Mark missed the club and minded Benny. He's less eager to go to the club now. John Balfe wanted to take the grove for the club. I set him straight on that. Ben's keeping in touch with Jack, like he promised you. They're at a Samhain Festival in Scotland. Oh, I wonder do you still visit your room in Jack and Poppy's."

It is a mild late afternoon on this Samhain day, the first day of November. People in many locations are marvelling at the same pre-sunset apricot mist.

Morag and Ben, driving north towards Glasgow, find a spot to park and admire Ailsa Craig silhouetted in the soft mist.

"I've a confession to make," Morag says suddenly. "I was jealous of Lyndsey."

"That means you like me," Ben answers impishly.

"Off course I like you. I thought Lyndsey liked you too."

"Maybe she does, but not in the same way."

"I just wouldn't want someone telling the Lyndsey and Ben story in years to come, sweet and all as our parents' story is."

"No, it's not like that."

"Now that I've met Rick, I know it's not," Morag admits. "But when I saw Lyndsey galloping out of the mist to meet us when we arrived I thought her smile beamed mostly at you."

"It was probably because we hadn't seen one another for nearly a year and a half and she'd heard all the stories from you."

"I suppose that sounds plausible enough, Ben Wright."

"Maybe we were too enthusiastic about meeting again, and then the game and all. Sorry."

"I've to admit the Scrabble was in a league of its own," Morag encourages.

"Thanks Morag."

"Lyndsey's good. You must feel it very boring playing with me."

"Everyone can't be good at everything. Who else could care for a human foot, with its twenty-six bones and thirty-three joints, like you can? I've first-hand, or first-foot, experience of that."

He can see the glint of a smile on her face as she carefully reverses out of their parking space.

"I suppose I feel I've to be sure. I wouldn't want us just to be a fairy-tale ending to our parents' love story."

"Before there was any inkling of parental love affairs I came all the way from Mountview to Fort William to find you again."

"Like a prince charming on a white horse," Morag teases affectionately, remembering that weekend when she had stayed in Glasgow to study and they almost missed one another.

"I'd no white horse though, just on trains and boats and buses. But it was well worth it," Ben affirms.

As Cathy is about to leave Marilyn's grave, Elspeth Balfe is passing to go her own family grave.

"We're disappointed Mark's activities at the club are set back for the sake of a few trees."

"What do you mean?"

"Mark never missed a golf event before," Elspeth stresses.

"No, he didn't. He missed the babies' naming ceremony in May and many other family occasions so as not to miss club events. He even went to Portugal the evening of dad's funeral."

"That's right," Elspeth admits, taken aback at the list of Mark's sacrifices. "We were surprised he came with us."

"Yesterday he wanted to stay with Benny and let me go to the fracking meeting."

"A fracking meeting, you never went to anything before when Mark was going to a club event.

"No I didn't. Now I'm beginning to think I was foolish."

"Fracking meeting aside, I think the real reason Mark didn't attend was because you didn't let him sell the bit of ground," Elspeth persists.

"The first I heard about the club wanting the grove was when John asked me if he could change my mind."

"Mark was full of the idea when he was in Portugal. Then when he went to the monthly meeting on Monday he said it couldn't go ahead because it meant a lot to you."

"I'm happy he realised that, although, believe it or not, he hadn't asked me directly."

"Oh. That's amazing. Maybe you'd change your mind if it was talked over with you."

"No, Elspeth. You have the final answer."

"It's a pity it changed things for Mark."

"I suspect the committee caused things to change. He's given more than thirty years to the club, sorting matters out, covering where needed to the exclusion of family events."

"I appreciate that," Elspeth mutters more contritely.

"I think it is John's turn, as chairperson, to iron out this problem. Mark never spared himself."

Cathy is perplexed now. Mark had said there would be no sale of the grove because he knew how much it meant to her. Yet Elspeth is implying that the idea of the hoped for acquisition was common knowledge since Portugal and that Mark had been all for it there.

Elspeth moves on briskly. She wants to tidy up her family grave and get back home to prepare to go to the golf club with John.

"The club story's a bit fuzzy." Cathy addresses Marilyn's spirit again. "And Rosetta," she continues to Grandma Rosetta as she reads her name also inscribed there. "We'll definitely have to look out for your grove."

She moves away slowly from the grave and walks towards one of the yew trees. The yew represents eternal life and rebirth and is associated with burial grounds and with the Celtic Festival of Samhain. She tries to be deeply rooted like the yew as she circles the tree clockwise towards the sun.

Chapter Forty-Four - Chapel in Grove

As Cathy is about to leave the yew tree and make her way down the path, Patience calls her.

"I'm delighted to see you, Cathy. I wanted to chat to you about Mark."

Cathy looks puzzled.

"I was talking to him yesterday," Patience says with concern.

"Were you?"

"Stephen texted to say Benny was unwell and Mark couldn't go the club. I called to see how Benny was."

"He'd a high temperature till Friday night. I wanted to stay with him and to go to the next fracking meeting. Mark insisted I go ahead, which I really appreciated."

"Stephen said you're always supportive of him going places."

"It's how things evolved. Mark went to events and I looked after things in the shop or at home."

"Would you've time for a cuppa, Cathy?"

"That'd be lovely, thanks."

"I'm a bit concerned about Mark. He's very embarrassed about the site. The committee members assumed that getting the grove was a given. Then Mark explained that the grove meant a lot to you. Maybe that's why he didn't go yesterday," Patience speculates as they walk into the Manse.

"The grove does mean a lot to me. I never knew it was coveted by the club till John Balfe asked me if he could change my mind. I didn't know what he was talking about."

"Coveted," Patience repeats. "That's sounds a bit menacing. It's one of the deadly sins."

"It'd surely be a transgression to desecrate a sacred grove," Cathy reckons.

"I'm not well versed in sacred places other than church buildings. It takes all my energy to look after the two in my care," Patience admits.

"Sacred places could be hilltops that represent summits on life's journey, or wells or groves. Wells signify pools of possibility and groves circles of hospitality. The grove's my chapel, perhaps as real to me as that beautiful church is for the congregation." Cathy points through the high Georgian window.

"Or perhaps more real," Patience encourages. "You've given it a lot of thought."

As Patience goes into the kitchen she marvels at how Mark and Cathy ever made a couple, and how they remained a couple with their apparent differences. She recalls when she and Mark dated. He was charming and affable, mostly self-assured, very occasionally vulnerable, and at those very occasional vulnerable moments he was so lovable. That was when she was in her first posting at Hightown and destined to move many times. Mountview is her sixth home in thirty-five years. Logistically a vicar and a family businessman would prove to be an incompatible match.

She recalls the wedding day when Cathy faltered at the wedding vows. If ever Mark was vulnerable that incident surpassed all. A man admired by so many standing in front of friends, former classmates, former girlfriends, while his hippy bride hesitated at the vows. She realised how protective she was about him that day. Then as if there had been some break in transmission, Cathy's words were uttered. Mark confided in her later in the day that a ceremony in a forest or at an ancient monument would have been Cathy's preference, that she was a real pagan and anarchist at heart.

Cathy is looking out through the Georgian window of the Manse. From here she can see the church with its high spire and the arched leaded light windows. She can see the yew trees and the gravestones, mostly old grey granite, some leaning to one side. The apricot coloured sun now appears like a big round ball behind the mist. The Manse itself is reminiscent of her home house back in the Dale. The only difference is that while their parlour in the Dale was packed with antique heirlooms this room is functionally furnished with a modern pine computer desk, an antique table and plenty of sturdy chairs. She assumes this is the room where Marilyn attended the many church meetings. Along one wall is a packed bookcase. Along another are family photos. Stephen Prior, the once shy teenager, is smiling down from the wedding photograph and again at the christenings of their daughters Karen and Stephanie. In much later photographs Patience and Stephen are pictured with Karen at her graduation and with Stephanie at her ordination. Covering the intervening years are informal photos of Stephen and Patience and the girls at different stages of their lives.

Her musings cease when Patience returns with a tray laden with cups of coffee and an assortment of biscuits.

"It's interesting to hear other points of view. We vicars don't often get to share the views of New-Age Pagans," Patience speaks with the interest of an anthropologist. "Oh, forgive me, Cathy," she continues, "if that's not what you call yourself."

"No worries at all, Patience. I don't call myself anything."

"Marilyn probably sat in this room many times at her church meetings," Patience muses, mirroring Cathy's thoughts of a few minutes ago.

"She'd just say I'm heading to the Manse. The Manse covered all her church activities, except her choir practice which took place in the church," Cathy recalls.

"Marilyn's was the first funeral I officiated at after I came here. It was a privilege to do that. I'd great admiration for her."

"You paid a very good tribute to Marilyn and made everything so personal to her."

"I knew Marilyn well when I was in Hightown over thirty years ago. The two parishes often came together for different ceremonies and I was a friend of Mark's."

'A friend of Mark's,' Cathy thinks. Very discreetly put. But it might be unbecoming for a vicar to tell someone that she was once her husband's girlfriend. Maybe when she is older, like Father Donal, she will reminisce about past events and romances.

"I was in class with Stephen, and Mark too," Cathy remarks. "Stephen was always so genuine and helpful and diligent. I remember on our wedding day I felt so lost. Stephen asked me dance a couple times and I felt at ease again in the middle of all the razzmatazz."

"I'm glad he was a reassurance to you, Cathy. It's a big day for a bride and it must've been an ordeal when you felt sort of lost in the middle of it all."

"It was outside my comfort zone, almost scary. Something I wouldn't have planned or wanted myself."

"I didn't realise it was such a terrifying experience for you. We just assume we're officiating at the special celebration of a happy bride and groom."

"I didn't mean to mention the wedding day after nearly thirty years. I was more thinking about how Stephen was such a source of comfort when one was needed."

"He's a good kindly man and it's not easy being married to a vicar," Patience muses.

"I'd imagine a vicar's partner has to make many sacrifices," Cathy reckons.

"Stephen often had to change his plans to fit in with my parish commitments, especially when Karen and Stephanie were little. A businessman's partner makes sacrifices too," Patience adds.

Cathy appreciates the acknowledgement of her work over the decades.

"Thanks for the affirmation."

"I was lucky to meet Stephen." Patience continues. "Mark introduced us. I've still a sense of thankfulness towards Mark after more than thirty years, like you have for Stephen."

And the two women chuckle companionably.

"Maybe that contributed to my concern for Mark when I thought he was losing confidence over the incident at the club."

"I see where you're coming from. Experiences of past kindnesses and vulnerabilities of people become part of our life's fabric," Cathy volunteers.

"When I heard the grove story first I've to admit I just felt concern for Mark. But after chatting with you, Cathy, I understand your sadness that a place so precious to you was under threat, and unknowing to you."

"Thanks for understanding, Patience."

Cathy felt it was an encounter full of warmth and concern. It softened the bristles that began to rise after Elspeth's short exchange at Marilyn's grave. She makes her way back towards the cottage with a new slant on the grove story. The sun has now slipped down on this Samhain day.

She had considered that "soul friend" might be a concept too ethereal for Mark. Yet in reality he had his very own soul friend in the Manse on the hill. Maybe they have more common ground that she realised. The smoke is curling from the high chimney of the cottage. Mark is at home still. She hears Ben's text coming in on her phone. He and Morag are nearly back in Glasgow. They had seen the remarkable sunset casting Ailsa Craig in silhouette. Jack and Poppy will be boarding the boat at any moment and will stop off at Mountview for the night and travel across to Donegal in the morning. It will be good to have them. An empty nest is disconcerting now that she is trying to work out the mystery of the grove.

Chapter Forty-Five – Disenchantment

"You didn't go to the club," Cathy exclaims.

"No, I won't bother tonight. I was up with Dad."

"Is Benny alright?"

"He seems in good enough form. He's watching TV with Andrew and Janice."

"Janice is there? That's nice."

"You're being a real romantic," Mark teases.

"I just like to see them happy."

"They're heading up to Hightown soon. He feels very at home with her family."

"He does. I'll pop up to granddad soon."

"Did you have your wee chat with Marilyn?"

"I did."

"What did you tell her?"

"I told her John Balfe was annoying you about the grove."

"Did you get any answers from beyond the grave?"

"I got some this side of it."

"Did you?"

"Elspeth said I caused you to stay away from the club for the sake of a few trees, that you were full of the idea when you were away."

"I told John and Elspeth it couldn't go ahead. I asked them not to annoy you."

"I'll get over the annoyance. I've to be vigilant about saving the grove though."

"Nothing'll happen to it now," Mark assures her.

"You told them you'd save the grove for me. But I never knew they had their eyes on it."

Mark makes no comment.

"Patience was concerned for you, said you were embarrassed about the site," Cathy continues. "Imagine Rosetta's grove, a site. She'd turn in her grave."

"I'm sorry, Cathy."

"What were you thinking about in Portugal?"

"I wasn't really with it. I felt bad I'd left you after your father's funeral. And when I heard you were gone to Scotland I was afraid you might leave altogether."

"Leave? You think I'd leave your dad at nearly eighty-seven years of age."

"You were always fond of him, and he of you. I admit I wasn't here enough for you."

Cathy feels sad to see him sitting dejected at the fireside rather than at the golf club as usual. There are times when, despite his confidence and charm, he looks like a little boy needing a big hug.

"Nor would I leave you after thirty years without doing you the courtesy of an explanation."

"That's a relief."

"How did the idea of the grove start?"

"The idea that it'd give some space for an extension took wings."

"Then everyone expected it'd happen," Cathy prompts him.

"I suppose they did."

"I see."

She takes a pause in the interrogation. They were not a couple who had much experience of dealing with conflict. They had settled into their respective niches decades ago. She carried most of the domestic and business responsibilities, and some big secrets, while he dedicated his time to different charitable organisations as well as to the golf club.

"What do you see, love?" He asks uncertainly. "You just said I see."

"I see where Elspeth and Patience are coming from, albeit with different emphasis."

Cathy sits down on the armchair opposite Mark. A silence fills the room which is softly lit by the fire in the stove and the glow of one small standing lamp. Texts sound on both of their phones, but they remain transfixed on the conflict that appears to be bubbling up between them. Mark hopes it will subside. Over the years conflicts usually subsided like water in a flood plain. A text on Mark's phone disturbs the silence again. Another follows. He places his phone on silent. Cathy does the same.

"The day I came back from Portugal we were chatting at lunchtime, a rare event I must admit. You said the grove was an almanac of the seasons and a bird sanctuary. And to crown it all you called it a sacred grove."

"It was good we'd a chat. John Balfe was planning a feasibility study before anything was said to me."

"I'm sorry."

"Do you know what upsets me, Mark? We're together thirty years and you didn't know the grove was important to me. It makes me feel you don't notice what I'm interested in."

"I was taken up with too many things. I promise that'll change."

"You could've told me the predicament you were in? You're home over three weeks."

"I hoped it'd get sorted at the meeting."

"So looking back you were avoiding the club. And I was thinking you liked us being together."

"I did, Cathy. I found out I did."

She wants to believe that their new-found togetherness is not just an excuse to skulk away from the club.

"I wanted to see how it'd go when I'd tell them at the meeting last Monday."

"You came home with a very sad face Monday. Maybe you should've told them sooner."

"That's what my father said yesterday."

"You must've been worried when you told your dad and Patience about it."

"Not going to the club yesterday made me realise I'd more to face. Thanks to you I hardly ever missed a club event."

"I'd have looked after Benny yesterday too."

"I know you would. It was a wake-up call to realise how things could change."

"No matter how they've changed you keep playing your golf. You gave the club plenty of time and energy over all the years."

"When I saw no supportive faces Monday I thought I've given up so much for this." He shakes his head with disappointment.

This is uncharacteristic. He always carried himself with dignity no matter what a situation might throw up.

"Don't lose your charm and confidence. You've worn them well till now," Cathy urges.

"Thanks, love."

"What about Stephen?"

"Stephen's not on the committee. I'm glad he didn't see what happened Monday. It might've disappointed him."

Cathy goes over and sits on the stool beside him. Mark places his arm tentatively around her shoulder.

"I was pleased Patience was concerned for you. That's what real friends are like. And she was your girlfriend."

"She's a very nice person," Mark muses.

"She's great warmth and understanding. It's good Stephen has someone so lovely."

"Remember you said you'd just come out of a relationship when you met me. Did you think of him over the years?"

"You've been honest with me about past loves so I can say yes."

Mark is twirling her long curls around his fingers.

"What was his name?"

"It was Stewie," she answers anxiously, wondering if her revelation is going to place their marriage on the ash-heap.

"Stewie MacGregor?" Mark's voice is raised in disbelief. Cathy's curls fall from his fingers.

"Yeah."

"I didn't realise he was the one."

"He was."

"Did you never stop loving him?"

"I put him to the back of my mind for a good while. Then Ben told me he met him. It came back again."

"This is history repeating itself. It's only a few weeks ago since you told me Beryl's story."

"Maybe we all have stories," Cathy reckons.

"I was fearful you'd leave with Stewie MacGregor when my father said how well you were all getting on so well. Now I realise I'd reason to be fearful."

"Why would you think I'd leave like a runaway teenager?"

"He came all the way here to be with you at your father's funeral."

"He did."

"And you headed away with him to the Highlands."

"I did."

"Imagine dependable Cathy Campbell leaving all behind to follow a clandestine love affair."

"Imagine." Cathy smiles to herself at the idea of it.

"You never did anything like that before. Or I don't think you did anyhow."

"I didn't. I'm glad I went though. I mightn't have gone had there been planning time. I'd see too many things that needed doing here."

"I couldn't have gone on all my trips without your support. I should've encouraged you to go places of interest to you."

"You didn't want Marilyn to know my interests."

"She found out in the end and was proud of you. I'll have to start encouraging you to go," Mark promises.

"There'd be places I'd like to go, even the odd protest. An oil company got permission to drill in a beautiful forest just up the road. It's beside the source of water for a huge number of people."

"I see the real you again. I hope nothing'd happen to you on the protests."

"I'd be grand. It's dangerous enough for environmental activists in some places, like in South America. Fatalities are rare here. I'd like to go and show solidarity."

"That'd be good, to see the real you. I'd never have encouraged you to seek out Stewie MacGregor." Mark teases.

"I didn't seek him out. Ben and Stewie made the connection when Ben went back the second time."

"You never said anything. I suppose I got my comeuppance. I urged concealment."

"There was never time. I could be in the middle of sharing something when the phone'd ring. Then the hinges of the door would rasp and you'd be on your way."

"That sounds familiar, sorry," he admits contritely.

"You'd usually say the hinges needed oil and that we'd finish what we were chatting about later."

"We'll make more time for one another from now on," Mark vows.

Cathy realises that Mark sees a future for them. She wondered if this evening's revelation might lead to their parting.

"I'd love to go back to Jack and Poppy's place," Cathy muses.

"I'd like to go with you. We could stay in a hotel nearby."

"We'll stay in Marilyn's room. It's lovely."

"It is. I saw it in January when I went to take her home," Mark says sadly.

Cathy feels sad for him. When Marilyn died people mostly sympathised with Benny, who was not with her when she died, and Ben and Jack and Poppy who were. Mark was considered the stoical one who looked after all the details down to buying real linen handkerchiefs, the handkerchiefs she herself used three months later to absorb bitter tears shed for Stewie.

"It was a sad journey for you going all the way knowing you'd lost her."

"At the time I just thought of the boys and Poppy. When I got there I saw the flowers and incense they'd around her. They'd organised a real wake. And Ben wanted to stay outside the hotel to keep her company." Cathy sees tears coming into his eyes. That vulnerable look, always so loveable, is spread across his face.

"We'll have something to eat," she suggests.

Chapter Forty-Six – Togetherness

On the small coffee table Cathy arranges sprouted lentils, home-cooked beetroot, walnut salad, olives and more.

"Heather sure inherited Daisy's cooking talent," she remarks as they sit side by side again.

"She's bringing excellence to our deli," Mark enthuses.

"And providing us with supper," Cathy adds.

"I'm glad I didn't go out. It was good having the chat."

"Sure you don't want to go around to the club?"

"I answered Stephen's text, said I'd see him during the week. He wondered if the two of us would like to drop around to them sometime."

"That'd be nice. Do you want to answer the other texts too?"

"I'll look after them later. Phones should be kept in their place."

Cathy smiles at Mark's absolute transformation.

They sit companionably again until Mark has had the last piece of beetroot and she the last olive.

"Did you sleep with Stewie when you went over?" he asks curiously as he piles the empty dishes on top of one another.

"No I didn't. I wouldn't want to spoil what we had," she answers emphatically.

He wonders who she means when she said 'we'. He recalls his first proposal and Cathy's doubts. "I didn't want to spoil what we had, Mark." He had mulled over that phrase until he got the courage to propose again. And she accepted, not in an over the moon excited way.

"You wouldn't want to spoil what you had with which of us?" Mark enquires apprehensively and sits back on the chair.

"With both of you, I suppose. I've different things with each of you."

"You've different things with each of us. I know I was suspicious that something new had happened in your life but to hear you confirm it is a shock."

"You shared with me about your girlfriends. Why's my sharing with you a shock?"

"They're from my past."

"And Stewie's from mine."

"Are you sure you're not still in love with him?" Mark asks doubtfully and before waiting for an answer he continues. "He was with you on the protests?"

"How did you know?"

"My father said Stewie was praising you the night of your dad's funeral."

"He was often with me at Faslane. That's where we met."

"Were you in touch with him in the meantime?"

"No."

Silence falls, just for few minutes.

"And Ben knows you're in love with Stewie. And Jack and Poppy probably know too."

"It's past tense. I've got closure now."

"It took a long time to gain closure, love. Our thirtieth wedding anniversary is next July."

"You'd seen your girlfriends safely up the aisle to men you were happy with. I didn't know how things turned out for Stewie."

"Was it important to you?"

"It was. When I saw him fitted into his surroundings I felt he was complete in himself."

"It re-echoes the story of the abbot and his monastery."

"It's the same for you and Patience. She said she'd concern for you."

"I think she willed the vows out of you on our wedding day. You probably weren't in love with me at all."

"I think we got married too fast. We were still working through things. I didn't want to cause upset when I realised I wasn't sure."

"You probably were sure you didn't want to get married," Mark says disappointedly.

She does not deny his assumption.

Silence shrouds them again. Mark remains dignified. He tries to absorb what his wife of almost three decades has revealed. She thinks this could be the death-knell of their relationship.

"I could move out," she offers. "But I couldn't go far away and leave granddad."

"You couldn't leave granddad," Mark repeats sadly. "He's like your anchor."

"Maybe I could go next door and share with granddad and Andrew for a while."

"We've got this far, me concealing the real you from everyone, you concealing an old true love from me. But I don't want to throw away whatever we have."

She is speechless now.

"You married me because you didn't want to upset me. That was very noble," he blurts out sadly.

"I'm so sorry."

"Why?"

"When I think of how it was in Saint Matthew's when all the girls liked you. And this was how it ended for you."

"It was worse for you. I'd thirty good years without hearing this so candidly."

"I'm really sorry. I didn't mean to upset you."

"I know. Did you tell anyone then?"

"I just told Colin, on the ship, when he came to bring me home. I said I didn't want to cause upset or trouble. He said it was probably wedding nerves." She nibbles her lips with apprehension.

"It was good you'd a sibling to confide in. I could never confide in the twins. It'd be like confiding in two," he quips. "Colin's a real gent. I don't feel bad he knew."

"Were you ever in love with me?" he asks plaintively.

"I remember us dancing at our wedding and you said 'Thanks for giving up Glasgow for me.' I was feeling lost in the crowd and you said it so . . . sincerely."

"I should've said it often since and not taken it for granted."

"No worries. You said it then. I remember other times too like when Ben was born and we were together holding a wee foot each," she continues pensively. "That was so magical."

"Ben's wee feet," Mark muses. "They surely made an impression. He even found love through his feet and met a podiatrist. But I'm glad his wee feet kindled love in you."

"I remember thinking of him and his little feet as our miracle creation," she continues dreamily.

Mark appears really moved by this incident. Then as if to bring the whole romantic interlude down a notch or two he says "they were the feet that walked a hundred miles and found your fella. And you gained closure, hopefully."

Without waiting for a comment he continues "In the olden days people were matched and no word of love at all, like the Student Prince."

"We're hardly in the same league as royalty. But mam said if I enjoyed your company what more would I want."

"Beryl was always on my side. But I failed you when it came to company. I wasn't here for you."

"No worries," Cathy says simply.

"Well love or no love I've had the best wife anyone could hope for. Everyone said that."

"Until the grove incident," Cathy says wryly. "Then I was an ogre."

"That's why I was so disappointed. You did more for the club indirectly than many who were there."

"We won't let it worry us. The feeling of entitlement only causes resentment. But thanks for standing in my corner, love."

"You called me 'love'. That's nice. You usually call me Mark".

Mark entwines the small finger of his left hand around the small finger of Cathy's right. They sit like they did in Ayr when they spoke about the wobbly wedding vows all those years ago.

"Thanks for staying with me despite what I've just heard, and for caring for four generations of the Wright family. They all loved you, including Grandma Rosetta."

"We'd special times together, after her initial shock of you not having a nice Protestant wife. She said once she thought you'd marry a vicar. She was probably thinking about Patience."

"She used to say to me 'you made a very good choice after all, Mark'."

"She said that to me too. Then I knew I was accepted. It took a year to get that far."

"It took us thirty years to get to know one another," Mark adds.

It has been a long day since she went to her parents' grave and to the Friary where she heard about Father Donal, and to Marilyn's grave, where she met Elspeth and Patience and finally home where she and Mark chatted more in one evening than perhaps in the past decade.

"I learned sad news today. Father Donal died this morning."

"Maybe he'll help us from afar. He knows about love triangles."

Helping us from afar, Cathy thinks, is a new concept for Mark. She remembers him referring to the idea of honouring Marilyn's spirit as airy fairy.

"The grove that nearly tore us apart might bring us closer," he continues encouragingly.

"Good energy will come from it now that it's saved," Cathy says solemnly.

"We could renew our wedding vows there, if you'd like to. You wanted to get married in a forest. It'd be good to hear you saying a resounding I do."

"I think I'd rather celebrate our life as it is, rather than do vows," Cathy concludes.

"Or we go back to the giant sequoia tree where it all began."

She tightens her little finger around Mark's like a lovers knot. And the stillness continues until the creak of the un-oiled hinge crackles into the silence. Jack and Poppy enter. Their surprise is palpable. Mark and Cathy are sitting side by side on a Sunday night. Traditionally Mark was at the club and Cathy was doing whatever she did on her computer. A month ago they discovered it was e-campaigning. The fire is burning out. The older lovers do not notice.

"I'll put a few logs on the fire," Jack offers.

"I'll get a drop of oil for the door. I noticed it rasping when ye came in."

"And disturbed your cosy evening," Jack teases his father. "Had we known you were so cosy together we'd have gone up to granddad."

"How did the twins get on without you," Cathy asks.

"Nana Annabelle stayed with them in the cottage. She got a big fright last night. She woke in the middle of the night and felt something warm beside her. It was the neighbours' cat. Imagine a black cat in the bed on Halloween night," Jack exclaims. "I think Annabelle thought it was Aunt Ellenora's spirit."

"Imagine," Cathy says disappointedly. "Imagine I thought it was Marilyn's."

"I'll go out to granddad now and do some healing on him." Poppy's green eyes are twinkling.

"That's the most important job of all, Poppy. I want my father to live to be a hundred."

Poppy's twinkling eyes become perplexed on hearing Mark's aspiration. She hoists her bag of Tibetan Bowls on to her shoulder so as to do some sound healing.

"He's the anchor in our family," Mark elaborates as Poppy steps back out into the November night to go next door.

Within a few minutes Poppy rushes back through the newly oiled cottage door, pale-faced.

Granddad has a terrible fever and a chest pain.

The four of them run up to Benny.

"So sorry, Benny, I should've been up sooner," Cathy laments. "We were just chatting by the fire, Mark and me."

"Have more chats together," Benny counsels in a very weak tone. "That's what I like to hear."

"I shouldn't have forgotten you."

"Forgot? You didn't forget him." Mark reminds Cathy. "Only a few minutes ago you said you'd never leave granddad."

Poppy continues to work her healing hands on Benny while they wait for the ambulance. The blue swirling lights flashing between the curtains signal its arrival. Poppy relinquishes granddad's care to the paramedics. "Won't you look after Cathy when I'm gone," Benny requests earnestly. "And keep having chats by the fire."

"You're only going in to have this fever checked." Mark tries to sound positive despite his fear that the one who kept Cathy anchored could soon leave this earth.

They make their way downstairs after the paramedics and the stretcher. The paramedics let Poppy travel in the ambulance and Jack waits to be with Andrew when he gets back from Hightown.

"Mind granddad well, Poppy," Cathy beseeches as the door is closing.

"I hope we don't lose him," she says sadly, as Mark places his arm around her to keep out some of the November cold.

"One day it could happen, love."

"Don't say that, Mark. I can't think of granddad gone."

"I hope by then I might be your reason to stay."

And the blue flashing lights disappear around the corner as they make their way to the car to follow along the same road to the hospital.

ABOUT THE AUTHOR

Fran Brady is an environmentalist, social justice activist and writer with a keen interest in sustainable living. Her interest in the environment began in the early eighties when she became a member of Birdwatch Ireland. In the early nineties she studied for a Diploma in Environmental Resource Management and later for a MA in Development Studies. She has two grown-up children and a grandson and she lives with her husband, Tony, in Dublin. Her first novel was Debbie's Dream.